THE
FINAL
SENTENCE

CORY GILLAN

The Book Guild

First published in Great Britain in 2025 by
The Book Guild Ltd
Unit E2 Airfield Business Park,
Harrison Road, Market Harborough,
Leicestershire. LE16 7UL
Tel: 0116 2792299
www.bookguild.co.uk
Email: info@bookguild.co.uk
X: @bookguild

Copyright © 2025 Cory Gillan

The right of Cory Gillan to be identified as the author of this
work has been asserted by them in accordance with the
Copyright, Design and Patents Act 1988.

All rights reserved. No part of this publication may be
reproduced, transmitted, or stored in a retrieval system, in any form or by any means,
without permission in writing from the publisher, nor be otherwise circulated in
any form of binding or cover other than that in which it is published and without
a similar condition being imposed on the subsequent purchaser.

The manufacturer's authorised representative in the
EU for product safety is Authorised Rep Compliance Ltd,
71 Lower Baggot Street, Dublin D02 P593 Ireland (www.arccompliance.com)

This work is entirely fictitious and bears no resemblance to any persons living or dead.

Typeset in 12pt Adobe Jenson Pro

Printed and bound in Great Britain by 4edge Limited

ISBN 978 1835741 405

British Library Cataloguing in Publication Data.
A catalogue record for this book is available from the British Library.

For Nigel for his inspiration

PART I

CHAPTER 1

JUNE 2017

Her small Sobranie between her lips, V. J. Wheeler leant towards the bar; Lloyd obliged with the lighter, turning a blind eye to the rules. As she drew on the Russian cigarette, she placed her hands face down on the polished surface of the bar. Standing back again, she noticed how her fingerprints had left no whorls. She looked around, but no-one had noticed the blank smudges.

"Must be lonely being a writer?"

This was a question that Viv, or V. J. as she was known, had heard a lot, sometimes in interviews and sometimes from people she hardly knew. It sounded innocent enough, but if she answered at all she generally parried the question with a non-committal answer. Today, though, it was Lloyd, lovely Lloyd the barman at her club, who was asking, and her defences were softened by being in this safest of all places. It was eleven o'clock as he poured her the first drink of the day and she heard herself admit, "Yeah, sometimes." And then, "It depends what you mean by lonely!"

Loneliness was one of the reasons for her coming almost daily to this retreat of a club. It was down near the ungentrified part of Tobacco Dock, an old building with low ceilings and doorways, built from slabs of stone painted with cream paint; the wood of the doors and window frames was so old it could tell its own story. She had, she reassured herself, walking over to her favourite wing chair and picking up the paper, made a very good life for herself as a successful author. With each passing day of being V. J. Wheeler, she felt herself moving away from her past, away from being the teenage runaway Evie Riley.

She had hoped Arun would be there this afternoon; he was always good company. Arun was witty and quick, and Viv liked that, but she couldn't see him. It was unlikely he'd be there; she knew he'd been working on an important case. She'd wait for a bit, then take her walk. Part of her envied Arun having parents who cared so much. He came from the second generation of an immigrant family from Delhi, the Seths, and they had valued him and pushed him to succeed in one of the professions. He'd chosen well though with the bar, she reflected, an occupation which allowed him to use his natural charm and precision with words. Viv had a quick wit of her own, borne of experience, and her most treasured compliment one boozy night was that she must have been Dorothy Parker's love child. That's what people saw, and it suited her. Not for her, the trap of love, marriage and children, that had been anathema to her even before she had left home. No, she sought out companions as she came across them. Most were women, some were men, but men of an unthreatening kind. She did not allow any of them, men or women, to get close enough to hurt her.

She checked her oversized watch. It was already after three and she was due to meet Amanda Rosberg, the filmmaker, at five. She was about to pick up her heavy coat when she saw Arun coming in.

"Good day, V. J.!"

"Good day, yourself, or is it?"

Viv checked her watch, showily this time. "Time for a drink?"

Arun gestured towards Viv's coat.

"Why not?" said Viv. "Always time for you, Arun."

Turning round to the high-backed chairs, which afforded a sense of privacy, Arun began to offload his morning in court. Viv took stock.

"Pretty pleased with yourself, aren't you?"

"Well, not a bad morning. This case was stacked against me, and I had Saunders prosecuting."

"Oh."

"Yes, indeed, so to get an acquittal with the quick jury return was, as they say, beyond my wildest dreams!"

"Cheers to that!"

Viv raised her glass to Arun Seth, a barrister not only with an exciting future ahead of him, but one who had forsaken the safety of prosecuting for the valour of defending.

"Time for my walk!"

Arun had affected the courtesy of chambers and the habit of half rising in his seat as Viv left did not escape her notice.

"Stop that at once or next time I see you, I shall pass you in the street without a nod!"

Amanda Rosberg had contacted Viv directly, which in itself was unusual. Her proposal was to make a film of Viv's first book *Riots Inc.* and while her initial response was that it was thrilling, that changed quickly into fear. The proposal, as Viv well knew, could change her life and catapult her into a new realm of success. As a writer, she had managed anonymity well. No-one recognised her and she had been careful to avoid any photographs. But here, with this offer, the risk of exposing herself to publicity was too high and she decided without further thought that her answer would be no. She was, however, intrigued to meet Amanda and she had agreed to meet and hear more of the proposal.

Heading to the door, Viv collected her coat from where she had thrown it over the back of the chair. Just as she was emerging into the old alleyway, she heard Maurice the doorman call after her. She turned, a question on her face. He was holding an envelope and even from a distance she could see that it had her name on it: *V. J. Wheeler*.

Her hand was out, a 'thank you' on her lips as she took it from his outstretched hand. *How odd*, she thought, *that mail should be delivered here*. Who knew that she was even a member, apart from the other members? She glanced down, turned the envelope over and, as there was no further clue and her curiosity got the better of her, she ran her finger under the flap and took out the note. Just a simple note. She checked, but there was nothing else inside. It read, *I know who you really are, and I know exactly what you did. Clock's ticking.*

The blood drained from Viv's face. She couldn't move. She was still staring at the words, trying to make sense of them, when she heard, as though from far away, "Are you alright, Miss Wheeler?"

That was Maurice, who always stayed to see more than he should.

"Miss Wheeler? You are very pale."

Viv looked up and at Maurice, but he seemed far away. She was trying to process the shock caused by what she had just read.

I know who you really are, and I know exactly what you did. Clock's ticking.

"Fine, Maurice. Fine. Nothing to see."

And with that, she shoved the note back into the envelope and the envelope into her pocket and left the club. A couple of seconds later, she doubled back.

"Maurice, did you see who left that note?" Her heart was beating so fast.

"No, Miss Wheeler."

It was too civilised a club to have anything as crass as CCTV, so what was she to do? She could not think clearly. A fine film of sweat broke out on her forehead. She tried to brush it away.

I know who you really are, and I know exactly what you did. Clock's ticking.

It rang in her ears, bounced around her brain. Oh God. She had always wondered if someone would discover who she really was and bring her world crashing down. But what did the second part mean? Viv knew that the real issue was that although she knew she could not remember possibly the most significant days of her life, someone else did. She had tried, but there was a stubborn gap where her memory should have been. It was terrifying, but there was nothing she could do about it.

She needed to breathe fresh air. She looked at every face in the small alleyway. Was this person or that person the one who had left the note? Was it a member of the club? Were they watching her now? What had the note meant? She was talking to herself now as though by doing so she could come up with the answer. Panic rose, choking her. She knew, of course, that her name was now Viv, but that once she had been Evie, and that her surname had not been Wheeler, it had been Riley. Evie Riley. She shivered. She had never revealed this to anyone at all, she knew that she hadn't, she would have known if she had been off guard, but she had never allowed herself that luxury. What had Evie Riley done to deserve that note being delivered to her? Where had she tripped up? She cut down a narrow lane out of sight of anyone, and leant against the wall. *How unfair! How bloody unfair! I've worked so hard to make this life. Why would anyone want to bring it all down around my ears?*

"You alright?"

At the question, she realised she had been talking out loud.

"Of course."

Pulling her fedora further down over her face, she kept her head down. She turned and continued on her walk. It wasn't long before the shock turned to anger; she would find this person before they could hurt her more. She would not be exposed to the world, not again. It could not happen. She had to find out who it was. She remembered Amanda's offer; now it would be really impossible to do, after this note. It was just too dangerous for her. She began to call Amanda's number to cancel, but something stopped her.

She headed down a cobbled side street, away from the main street with its traffic and honking and pollution and people. She felt pulled by an invisible thread towards the estuary beyond the city, where the tourist river becomes the working river with the sea beyond. She wasn't proud of having taken her name from a gravestone, with weeds already beginning to obscure the untended legend 'Vivienne Jasmine Wheeler', but in that moment, it had seemed the right, the only, thing to do. How had anyone found out? How long had she got before she was shamed?

She had lived a brutal two years on the streets, cold and hungry, in squats and with handouts until she had started working for the *Big Issue*. That had changed her life. That was when she had begun to feel she could write. And then the long slog, the slow climb.

She walked on past Canary Wharf on the north bank towards that part of the river where it becomes more of a working, somewhat industrial area. That was the bit she liked. It was honest, rough and had a purpose beyond tourism. Pausing for a few moments, she rested on the stone wall. She loved the way the birds knew their path, wheeling around the banks at low tide, settling on the worms. They knew what they had to do and were consumed by their focus on staying alive. Her thoughts were broken into by the half-mumbled question.

"What's the point, then?"

Was the man speaking to her or himself? Viv turned her head sideways. Even for Viv, this remark was a bit challenging. It had the implication of depression or worse, of presenting an obligation to respond, and her instinct was to walk away. But just as she was about to turn to walk back to where she had come, pretending not to hear, there was a hand on her shoulder. In an instant, she reacted with violence, spinning around and holding the man's wrist in hers, high in the air. Her face was contorted with rage and fear.

"Never, never, never do that!" she screamed at him.

She was shaking. Her words hung in the air. In that split second, the incongruity between her response and the man's demeanour shocked her. Relinquishing the wrist, noticing now the frayed cuffs, she stepped back. Her heartbeat was calming. The wrist had fallen limply. He had no fight in him. He had given up long ago.

"I'm so sorry, I didn't mean… Are you OK?" She moved towards him, her hands out, but by now the man had turned away and was walking further downriver.

Hearing the distant chime of four o'clock, she checked her watch. She had to hurry now and began to walk back the way she had come.

What had happened upriver on the towpath would probably have been neither here nor there to most people. She was surprised, though, that it had happened to her, and the unclear memory that it had brought back was one she could not shake off. She retained an image of something that had really happened; she felt certain that there had been another man on another night who had threatened her. She prayed that one day it would be clear what that image had been, what she had run away from and was no longer able to recall.

In the meantime, she now had mud on her walking boots.

CHAPTER 2

"Nice walk?"

Viv had an odd relationship with Maurice. Sometimes he overstepped the mark, and sometimes his mindless remarks could be comforting. She chose to ignore him and strode through to the bar. She was in time for her meeting with Amanda but queried why she was going ahead with it when her fears and events of today underscored that it would be madness to be involved.

She knew that Amanda Rosberg was a film-maker who had read all her books. That was flattering, Viv conceded. Since the publication thirteen years earlier of *24 Hours*, the reluctant acceptance that she might write things that people might want to read had grown. There had been three novels. She recalled with a smile the first time she had visited the house of another writer. In the time he had taken to settle himself and come back in with some coffee, Viv had scoured his bookshelves and, unseen by anyone, had blushed with shock and pleasure at seeing *Three Steps Left* by V. J. Wheeler.

From her chair, she had the perfect view of anyone who came in or went out. Five minutes later, Maurice appeared in the doorway half raising his hand to indicate that Amanda had arrived. She followed him out and there was Amanda Rosberg. The sight of her made Viv catch her breath. She covered her hesitation with a brief handshake and a half-smile and invited Amanda to follow her. Viv's head was spinning. Amanda was so much more vital than her photo. She looked as though she was straight off a Viking ship, her hair white-blonde, her features aggressively regular, her smile uncompromising and brilliant.

Viv broke the ice, ordering drinks and drawing another chair closer to hers.

"I'm flattered that you like my book." Viv fidgeted, straightened her chair.

Setting out to create trust, Amanda asked Viv, "Where do you feel this book came from? When did it start?" And, leaning forward, "What is *its* story?"

Viv sensed it was a gambit she had used before, creating a sort of third party where the book had a life of its own, enabling confidences that wouldn't have come if she had used the more direct 'you'. In *Riots Inc.*, Viv had depicted an England where democracy had broken down, fear had taken hold, a civil war of thoughts and ideas was emerging, and violence on the streets had become commonplace.

Viv shrugged, parrying.

"Well, how did *1984* come about? It's in the air."

Amanda's legs were slender, elegant and the height of her heeled shoes only emphasised this. Viv pulled her jacket tight around her.

"Well?" urged Amanda, gently this time.

"I… I'm sorry. Yes. How did it happen? Well, why would it not happen? You feel something all around you, you can't escape, that's what happened, and it's happening again. Don't you feel that all that is just under the skin, even now, like a blister waiting to burst? Everyone with a grievance in a club of one?"

Amanda leant forward slightly and smiled.

"I would love to make the film of your book. Would you be interested? I have admired all your work, but this one is incredibly filmic."

Every now and then, there was no more than a catch in the odd word, but Viv could hear it. English had not been Amanda's first language.

She knew Amanda was trying to disarm her.

"You've seen my films?"

"Of course..."

Viv knew that Amanda, despite the Nordic princess of an exterior, had grit and was not about to blink first. Amanda had brought a copy of *Riots Inc.* with her and began to leaf through the bookmarked sections and to read out the best of the hero Farrell's moments. Viv's demeanour gave nothing away, but she felt she needed to cut this short; she could never agree to this proposal, and she shouldn't encourage it any longer.

As Viv listened to her text being read aloud, the memory of five laughing children that first term at the convent throwing her diary around between them, high above heads and hands, beyond Viv's reach, surged back into her. She burned with the feeling of exposure and shame but all the while she could not take her eyes away from this compelling woman.

Amanda continued, unaware for now of all this. Farrell carried the story; he was the brave protagonist who exceeded his own strength to break down barricades. She mentioned two names, settling for her favoured one. He wasn't a well-known actor, but he would, in her view, be completely right for the part. She had seen his work at the BFI the week before.

As they continued talking, Viv knew that she needed to say no.

"Amanda, I have had a shock, well, a couple of shocks, today, so perhaps today is not the best time to be going forward. My world is that of a writer, and I don't think…"

She met Amanda's clear gaze. Her ice-blue eyes seemed to burn right into Viv's soul. She had never before felt such a magnetic pull to another person. That was how she would describe it later. She knew that it was a cliché, but a true one this time; it was not a moment she would ever undo, or want to undo. It was as though she had met Amanda before and today was just a recognition, not an introduction. She heard Rumi's words, "Lovers don't meet somewhere, they are in each other all along."

She remembered the note she had been handed earlier that day: *Clock's ticking*. She was terrified. The note could expose her. But if she said no to the film, how could she see Amanda again?

She spoke quickly before things went too far.

"Amanda, I can't do this. I'm sorry you've had a wasted journey, I—"

"Are you alright?" And for the second time that day, Viv heard, "You are very pale suddenly."

Amanda was wrong-footed. She had only just met Viv. What had gone so wrong that the opportunity was already lost?

"I apologise if I have taken things too fast, I am a little too direct sometimes. Perhaps we could talk another time? You must tell me your concerns then. I promise I will take care of them… and you."

Viv stood up, held out her hand.

"I'll walk with you…" She motioned towards the door.

"Please think it over. Let me know if you change your mind."

Amanda passed her card to Viv. Then, as Amanda left the

club through the low doorway, Viv turned and saw Maurice, Maurice who would always be standing by the door. Then one day he would be gone, and people would say, "Do you remember Maurice?" And Maurice would be gone, under the sod with nothing to show for it. Was she about to miss the opportunity she had yearned for?

"Amanda," she called, and Amanda turned and walked back towards Viv. "I… you must think me crazy…"

"Yes?"

All Viv wanted to do was kiss this beautiful woman. Instead, she continued as calmly as she could.

"I'm not thinking straight today. I do want to… see you again."

"I'll be in touch!" And the gentle perfume that was Amanda disappeared.

Viv could feel the envelope still in her pocket. *I know what you did…*

She was at a crossroads; had she taken the wrong turn?

CHAPTER 3

NOVEMBER 2003

It was Paula's sixteenth birthday the following week and she and Evie had decided an early cinema treat was in order. It had been a great film. They were on a high as they came out that night. Paula, still jigging to the music, waggled her arms like a plane dive-bombing a crowd. Paula had smuggled out the brandy flask her father kept for football matches and, between them, passing it back and forth with a lot of tutting from the row behind, they had polished it off. Paula still had her phone on. More tutting, but she had wanted to show Evie a viral email that was going round. Someone tapped her on the shoulder.

"Turn your phone off. The film is starting."

"Here, look at it later," she whispered. And Paula passed her phone to Evie, both of them completely forgetting that she had until it was too late. Outside, near the front of the cinema, they scanned the pavement for Paula's dad's blue Maxi but there was no sign of it. So, even with it raining so hard, they agreed on taking the bus home, each in their separate directions.

"Here, take these." And Paula had given Evie her green leather gloves. "You're going to get wetter than me!"

Two hours earlier, when they had gone into the Odeon, it had been a dry, clear night with no hint of the rain that now hit Evie's face like a smack, or of the wind that whipped her coat round her legs. Outside, turning to her friend Paula, she tried to speak, but the noise and wet were too much to contend with. Both shouted, "See you at school tomorrow!" to each other.

Evie glanced at her watch. She'd have to hurry to catch the last bus; it was half past ten. Pulling up the hood of her raincoat, she walked with her head down, shielding herself from the worst of the rain. The cinema was in the middle of the town. The last stretch of the walk to the only bus stop that would go to the next village was about three hundred yards along on a deserted part of the road. Here there were no houses, no streetlights and no people as far as Evie could tell. The last bus was at ten-fifty and she hoped that it had not gone early. She looked at her watch again, but the rain had got into it, and it had stopped. She shook it. How could she get home if she had missed the last bus? Her parents would be furious. There was at least a shelter here, and she perched on the red plastic ledge seat. The streetlamp next to the bus stop wasn't working. Around the shelter, the trees and bushes were overgrown, and this provided another buffer against the driving rain.

*

Her father, a magistrate, had also been out that night on the other side of town, delivering notes for the next day to his clerk, Jeanine, or so he had told his wife Rosemary. He was in a hurry to get home. He was tired and it was cold and dark. So, he had taken the back roads and that meant that he was in the unlit lane opposite the bus stop just as Evie was walking towards it. She had angered him by going to the cinema like that without permission and, in that single instant, he had chosen to punish her. He would keep in the shadows of the trees and not give her a lift home. She would have to learn.

*

Few cars were passing. Evie heard a noise in the bushes behind her, and imagined it was a fox. But before she could make out what it was, the man was already out of the shadows and up close to her. She smelled his breath: spirits, beer, filth. She recoiled, stepped back over the kerb, searched for the lights of an oncoming bus. He grabbed her by the shoulder, pulled her towards the shadows, slammed her head down on the hard pavement. She saw his face. She was about to scream when he put his large, hardened hand around the back of her neck and dragged her into the complete darkness of the bushes behind. She yelled at him, she screamed, she pleaded until he put one hand so firmly across her mouth that she could not even move her head. He was panting now, muttering, "Bitch," under his breath. He pushed her down, ripping open her coat, pulling up her skirt, tearing her pants. He was on her, yanking himself inside her, ready, violent. Her arms were out wide as though she could steady herself. Under her right hand, her fingers curled around a rough, stony lump of concrete. She held it tight. She could feel herself tearing inside as he did all this. It was as though all her emotions had frozen and each detail was a separate act, minutes apart. She noticed, as though she was not connected to her body, that the rain had stopped. It felt like hours, although it was probably less than a minute, and his power slumped for just a second as he fell forward. Evie did not miss a beat. Her hand, moving wildly over the ground, felt the shape of a large concrete stone. She grabbed it and, with force, smashed it against the back of his head. What power had been in him went in that moment. She paused for a moment, held her breath. Was it over? Her hand was sticky with the spattered blood. Still holding the stone, she pushed his shoulders with the palms of her hands until she rolled his bulk over her and to the ground. His dead weight made a soft sound in the darkness as it landed. She slowly stood up and stared at his unmoving form. Then, raising her hands high above her head, she brought the stone down on his head twice more, quickly, bang, bang. Silence.

*

Douglas, waiting opposite, had turned off his lights but left the electric engine running. What he did not realise was that the video camera on the dashboard that he had installed for insurance purposes was unwittingly recording his daughter being attacked and raped at the bus stop. When he glanced up and saw what was happening, he panicked and turned off the engine. Despite his previous harsh thoughts, he was halfway out of the car to go to Evie's aid. But in that split second, Douglas saw who the attacker was. It was Reg Dawson. Douglas should never have become so involved with Reg. He was afraid of Reg and the hold he had over him. Reg was never up to any good, he knew that, but now it was too late. Douglas turned and got back in the car, hoping he had not been seen.

*

Evie glanced down at the body and stood up carefully, wincing with the pain. She was shaking, shivering uncontrollably, her teeth chattering. She tore off the remainder of her underwear and shoved it in her raincoat. All she knew now was that she had no way home other than to walk the three miles in the dark and that she could never tell anybody what had just happened.

*

It was nearly midnight when she reached her semi-detached home in the heart of the small village of Reston; she had to knock and wake up her parents. The lights flew on. She straightened her wet hair and checked that her coat was completely wrapped around her. It was her father who came to the door. She noticed that his own jacket was still wet.

"What time do you call this? Did you want to wake your mother?" Both rhetorical questions. She took a step back. Evie stood mute waiting for permission to come in. She hoped her face gave nothing away. She was shivering. Her father didn't move. Was he about to say something more? Evie waited.

"You look like a tramp!"

And, before she could move, he slapped her across the face. Evie reeled, but it wasn't the first time she had told herself, "I can take it."

*

Alone in her room, Evie looked down at her clothes, her blood-spattered hands. She asked herself over and over how this could have happened.

"You can apologise in the morning!" she heard her father call up the stairs.

The lights were clicked off and her parents' murmurs across the landing ceased. Her hand held the side of her face; it was burning. Her teeth chattered. She had never felt so cold right through to her bones. She took off her wet coat, but otherwise fully clothed, got under the duvet. She couldn't think, she couldn't recall what had just happened, already it was a blur. There was no chance of sleep. She turned over and lay with her eyes shut. She woke with a nightmare and sat bolt upright. She wanted to bathe, but she could not do so, the noise of the taps and the toing and froing on the landing would be sure to wake her parents. You could hear every sound in this house.

It was only as the day's thin light began that she eased herself up in the bed, hugging her knees. What had happened between getting to the bus stop and getting home? Her shoulders slumped. Evie knew with every fibre of her being that something bad had happened, but it was all a blank, a blur. What should she do now? Turning on the bedside light, she could see that her hands still had blood on them. She rubbed them frantically on the duvet, trying to remove the mess. Her breath was coming in short gasps. Paula would know that she had been at that bus stop even if no-one else did and her parents would soon work that out too. The staff at the cinema would know what time they had left too. Had she dropped anything that would identify her? And *what had happened?* She could not remember. But with clarity, she knew for different reasons that she could not talk to her mother, or to her father, who would never be her champion.

Pushing back the bedclothes and retching at her own smell, she packed a small backpack and waited until seven o'clock when she could wash, dress in her school clothes and leave home and Reston behind her. She knew she couldn't stay. She found her phone and, remembering that she had both of their phones, emailed, *I'm leaving. Something happened last night. Meet me at that hotel after school, please. I need money. Can you bring some?*

Paula's reply was, *I'll try.*
Meet me this afternoon... please... it's important. At the Trafalgar.
I can't...
You have to...

As she walked towards the hotel at half past four, she stopped dead in her tracks. It was getting dark, but she could make out the figure of her father coming towards her. His head was down, he hadn't seen her. Her heart felt as though it had stopped. She couldn't move, but then her instinct to avoid him kicked in. She ducked into the doorway of Marks & Spencer. She held her breath. Seconds passed, and he hadn't gone past her. She ventured out. Perhaps he had turned back? As she reached the Trafalgar Hotel, the brightness of the lights in the foyer relieved her. She would wait there for Paula. But then, at the reception counter, she saw the rear outline of her father. Her hand went to her mouth, and she took a step backwards. He was leaning forwards, talking to the girl. She had smiled at him, had laughed as though she knew him. He took something and headed to the lift.

He was up to something. He had to have a girlfriend there. Evie walked towards the reception desk as the lift doors closed.

"Excuse me, have I just missed Mr Riley?" She pointed to the lift.

The girl smiled again and nodded. Evie went to the far corner of the large hall and half hid herself in a large chair. She would wait for Paula and tell her this latest appalling news. She was still in shock when she saw Paula walking into the hotel. Evie stood, relief flooding through her, and was just about to call out to her friend. But it all happened too fast for Evie to reach Paula, who strode without hesitation to the lift.

Had Paula forgotten their arrangement? Paula was clearly meeting someone, but not her.

Evie waited five minutes then pulled out her phone and dialled the hotel reception. She watched as the girl picked up.

"Hotel Trafalgar?"

"May I speak to Mr Riley? He's staying at your hotel." She spoke quietly, her hand cupping her mouth.

"One moment!"

Evie's heart beat out of her chest.

A girl's voice answered, "Yes?" It was Paula. "Hello?"

Evie had never wanted to be so wrong before. Her heart leapt to her throat. She'd know Paula's voice anywhere. Paula with her dad? Her dad? Paula? Her brain went into crazy auto mode. Could things get any worse? Now, in a second, she knew what had happened. Whenever Paula was infatuated, everything else got forgotten.

As Evie left the hotel, with more presence of mind than she could have believed she was capable of, she called the dozy receptionist again and, assuming an older voice, asked for a copy of the hotel bill to be sent to her email address. She was Mr Riley's secretary, and these were his instructions. And, once outside the hotel, she pulled up her collar against the rain and started to walk to the station. But then she turned back and decided to wait for as long as it took for them to reappear. Two hours went by and there they were! Kissing goodbye. She took out her phone and photographed them outside the hotel, with Trafalgar in red neon, and sent the photo to her email account. And hardly a second later, she emailed one copy of the photo to her father, and another to Paula.

CHAPTER 4

2003

As she had run like a mad thing towards the station, a police car with flashing lights had passed her. One of the officers had looked her way, but it had been raining. She had looked away and it had carried on.

Evie was breathing hard. A woman with shopping at her feet looked up and stared. Evie pulled her sleeves down over the bruises on her wrists, crossed her arms and looked at the floor. She pulled her school tunic down over her knees. She didn't want questions or offers of help. It wasn't meant to be like this. It wasn't. The train pulled out of her small village station and towards London, passing through Eastcote, Rayners Lane, Hammersmith. At Hammersmith, a swarm of people got in and filled the standing area. After Barons Court it went underground, the lights went off, flicked on again, went off again.

As the Piccadilly Circus sign slid past the window, she stood up, pushed through the throng of people and got out onto the airless platform, making for the long escalators. She kept her head down as she looked around for a ladies' lavatory. It wasn't until she was up on the main concourse that she found it.

Entering a cubicle, she pushed the schoolbooks into the bin reserved for sanitary things. She knew the contents would be burned and would leave no trace. She changed into the jeans and jumper she had carried in her bulging school bag and stuffed the tunic, tie and shirt behind the cistern. She paused for a second with the blazer, then ripped off the identifying pocket and decided to keep it as a jacket. She might need that. It was cold. Catching sight of herself in the long mirror near the door, she thought that at least she no longer looked like a schoolgirl. She only had her pocket money savings on her, though, and no idea how to spend the next few hours, let alone where to go for the night.

Leaving the station at the Shaftesbury Avenue exit, she was immediately enveloped by crowds, crazy crowds of tourists and commuters. The air was different here, and she struggled to breathe. Cars hooted, and taxis pushed through the crowds of pedestrians. Going with the movement of the crowd, she walked up towards Cambridge Circus.

She had to put something more solid between yesterday and now. They would soon be looking for her. And she could never ever risk going back. She remembered the police car that had passed her. She looked for a coffee shop and, seeing one down a side street, pushed open the glass door and looked around. No-one moved or looked up; no-one was interested in her. Going to the counter, suddenly ravenous, she asked for a coffee and, "One of those please," pointing to a chocolate muffin. The girl, Evie was relieved to see, didn't blink.

"Milk?"

Evie nodded and took it all to a table in the corner furthest away from the street.

Halfway through the muffin, two policemen who had evidently just finished their shift sauntered in, handcuffs on belts, flat caps in their hands. Out of habit, they scanned the café. Evie bent down as though to rescue something from under the table, risking a peek up as she did so. A girl with bleached-blonde tufty hair came over to her, blocking her view of the police.

"Here, give me that…" She nodded towards the muffin.

"No!" Evie moved to cover it, but the girl was quicker and snatched it from the plate. "Get your stuff. Come on!"

"No! Who are you?"

Their voices were attracting attention now.

"Suit yourself." The girl shrugged, turned as if to leave and pointed to the backs of the policemen.

"Wait, wait!" Evie changed her mind, left the coffee and, head down, followed the girl into the street. She grabbed Evie's hand and almost ran up the street to the far side of Soho. It was only then that she paused.

"Why did you do that? Who are you?"

The girl, leaning against the wall to get her breath, bent over, stood up and laughed while looking Evie straight in the face.

"You don't get it, do you?"

Evie looked at her. She was a bit older than Evie but not much.

"I saw you come in. You was running from something. Something you done?"

"No." Evie felt herself redden.

"Liar."

"I've got to go."

"No, you ain't." The girl pulled Evie towards her by the lapel and, with a laugh, challenged her. "It's a school blazer, innit?"

Evie saw that the girl's nails were bitten right down.

"No."

Evie pulled away and ran back down the street they had just walked along. Taking the first left turn into a tiny alley, she flattened herself against the wall and waited, thinking she had given the girl the slip. Seconds later, the girl appeared again.

"What do you *want?*" It was Evie's turn. "Why do you keep following me?"

The girl lit up a smoke. "Want one?"

Evie shook her head.

"Suit yourself." The girl inhaled. "I saved you there." She gestured with her head.

"I haven't done anything. You're wrong."

"Yeah… yeah."

Evie was figuring how to get rid of this girl. How could she trust her? It was true that she had helped back there, in the café, but what was to stop her getting Evie into more trouble than she was already in?

The girl's pride seemed to be piqued and suddenly she announced, "I gotta go."

She shrugged again and walked away just as suddenly as she had appeared in Evie's day. It was odd, given what had just happened and how short a time, perhaps fifteen minutes, they had been in each other's lives but, with the girl's departure, Evie felt as though she had been abandoned in a desert without water. Bereft. She took a deep breath to steady herself. Had they noticed she had left home yet? She doubted it. Maybe later? What would they do then?

Evie looked at the women milling around outside the Apollo Theatre, all with short hair, smiling faces and little handbags, and she suddenly wished she was them. *Actually, though, no I don't*, was her next thought. She was never going to be like them. She had never, it seemed to her, done the right thing, been in the right place or been like them. And she knew, even now, that she didn't like boys. She would not be waiting for a husband like them.

The lights were coming on, streetlights, house lights. Soho smelled of food. Evie had nowhere to sleep that night and the tiredness that came over her at that thought made her slump down in the doorway of a shuttered loading bay, now closed for the night. As she slid down and semi-squatted, her hands over her face, she heard, "It's you, innit?"

Evie looked up. It was the girl with the blonde hair.

"You can't sleep there. Come on!"

And, for the second time that day, she followed without knowing where she was going. The girl in the Doc Martens walked with a long stride, headed out of Soho over to Regent Street, down a side street, through a little alley and, without looking round for Evie, seemed to disappear. Caution was returning and Evie was unwilling to go right up to the place where the girl had disappeared. What if it was a trap? She could hear voices, some low, and then silence. The girl poked her head out, this time with a smile, and beckoned Evie in. Slowly, Evie turned into the recess in the alleyway and, once her eyes became accustomed to the half-light, she could make out quite a large space under the archway with probably half a dozen people in it.

"You'll be safe here."

Safe? Safe! Evie wanted to scream at her. What did she know about being safe? How could she be safe anywhere, ever again?

"What's yer name?"

"Pauline. Paul." The name came out without hesitation.

"Paul. Yeh."

Evie waited, but the girl did not release her own name. The night before, Evie had been in a bed, her own bed, in a house in a village; now she would be spending the night with six strangers in a dark arch cavern without knowing if she would see morning. A cigarette was passed around.

"No." Evie passed it on, thinking it was an ordinary cigarette. The smell was sweet, the smoke trapped in the small space. The third time it came round, Evie took a puff, then a deeper one. Her head swam. She leant back against the brick wall, glad of the respite from thinking about everything. She was handed an old sleeping bag and lay down on it, but the smell hit her, making her retch. She sat up again. But what choice did she have? She would have to get used to it, for tonight at least. She could hear snoring. Someone was talking in their sleep, another farted. Evie could hear the traffic rumbling past, people shouting. Her eyes were adjusting to the gloom. It must have been a storage place. It might have led to a cellar, but she couldn't tell. The floor had fag ends all over it. She prayed there were no needles. She edged herself nearer to the wall. She needed to sleep and closed her eyes but, instead of sleep, the events of that day swam round and round in her head.

CHAPTER 5

Evie had trusted Paula from her first day at the convent. Boarders arrived a day before the day girls. Other children's voices could be heard around the echoey building. But then the day girls came back to school as well. There was excitement in the air, the nuns calling for 'hush!'. It was at once overwhelming and exciting. Evie looked around the thirty girls in her class, all of them strange and new to her, and wondered whether they all knew each other.

"Evie Riley, stand!"

"Yes, Sister."

She stood, looking as though she expected to be shot.

"For this term, your guardian angel will be Paula. Paula, stand!"

Paula turned and smiled over at Evie. In that single moment, life changed for Evie. Relief rippled through her, she drank in the beaming smile that was the day girl Paula, the laugh that *was* Paula, and school began to be bearable; she would not be alone. Paula, tall with curly brown hair, shrugged her shoulders as she looked over to Evie. Evie could see that Paula had no idea what a guardian angel was. But Evie knew what an angel was – and that was Paula.

Each week of that term, Evie had to write a letter home; it was always much in the same vein. How, even with Paula as her angel during the day, could she write that she cried herself to sleep every night, that she was hungry, that she wanted to go home?

On Saturday mornings the post would be shared out, envelopes held high each time a name was called. Letters from families, loving parents. Evie always waited, hoping, feeling foolish and ashamed when her name was not called out.

But then, one Saturday, she did hear her name called. Hiding her excitement, Evie took the letter and walked off to read it. Between opening the envelope and straightening out the letter, she imagined it would be all about home, how much they wanted her to be there, and how exciting Christmas would be. Her heart sank as she read:

Dear Evie,
Your father says you must behave well and not show us up. Do well in your lessons. We have to go away for your father's work, to Switzerland, but will be back by Christmas.
Love Mummy

That was it?! She wished then that she had not received the letter and tore it into tiny pieces.

By half term she had heard nothing more from anyone at home. Out in the field at break, Evie heard the others saying what they would be doing; some were going away for the week. Her toes were curled tight in her shoes. She prayed no-one would ask her. It was clear from that letter that she would not be going home.

"What are you doing, Evie? Getting out of here? Jailbreak?!"

There was laughter at that. She joined in but was dying inside.

On the way back into school, Paula said, "You can come to ours if you like?"

Evie's face lit up. "Really?"

"Yeah, why not?"

"What about your parents, won't they mind?"

Paula let out one of her huge laughs. "You're weird. Why should they mind? Of course you can come."

A cloud came over Evie's face. "I'll have to ask my parents."

"From what you've said, I should think they'd be glad!" Paula hadn't meant it unkindly. "Just tell them. Write them a letter or whatever you boarders do."

Life with Paula was that easy. Evie scribbled the letter before class. She'd post it off and that would be that. Now she had something wonderful to look forward to.

Half term came. Paula didn't live that far away, and the two of them waited at the nearest bus stop.

As the bus approached, Evie was giddy with the sense of freedom; even the air smelt better now. She had been stuck in that convent for a month and a half and now she was out!

"Come on! We're here!"

The girls jumped off the bus and ran down the tree-lined road to the side. *It's a broad house*, thought Evie, *like it's smiling, windows either side of the front door.* Paula knocked and knocked till it was answered. Evie held her breath; would her dad be angry?

"Hold on, hold on!" And he flung open the door and hugged Paula, looking over at Evie at the same time.

"Oh Dad, this is Evie!"

"Well, welcome, Evie; welcome, bubele!"

And he held out his hand, smiling warmly at his new guest.

"Thank you, Mr Johnson."

"Bill, it's Bill, please."

The house was warm, there was a smell of supper from the kitchen, and Mrs Johnson came down the hall to meet Evie too.

"Well, enjoy your half term with us and we are really glad to have you. Paula will show you everything."

All this warmth and colour made Evie feel in that instant that her life at home was like a black and white film compared with this. Paula's brother John joined them, and everyone talked over everyone else; it was like being held in a hug that wouldn't break.

That night, she and Paula talked for hours after they were meant to be asleep. Twin beds and a side light.

"Is your dad always like that?"

"Like what?"

"Well, friendly. Not cross."

"Why should he be cross?"

"Well…"

"What's your dad like?"

And it all spilled out, Evie saying more than she had meant to, and certainly more than she had to anyone ever before. It was the first time she had ever spoken about her father.

"Sounds like he doesn't want you." Paula was not one for tact.

"Yes, he does, of course he does. It's just that I'm always doing something he doesn't like."

A late plane went over the house.

"Four engines."

"What?"

"It's a Boeing, four engines."

"How do you know all that?"

"Because… Evie… I know what I'm going to do with my life. I'm going to be a pilot!"

With that, Paula turned over, but what she had said prompted a thought with Evie.

"I wish I was that certain. All I know is I'm going to university – that's my escape route. I want a different life. It's the only way."

"Wow, then what? Teach like the nuns?"

Sarcasm was another forte. There was always a mocking, taunting tone to Paula's voice, even when sleepy.

"I'm going to make films."

Where that thought had come from, Evie wasn't sure, but once she'd said it, she knew it was exactly what she wanted to do. Make films that take people away from their dreary, sad lives, even if only for an hour or two.

"Night."

"Night."

CHAPTER 6

Evie woke before the others with the small amount of light that came in through the arch. She could make out the other sleeping bags and eased herself out of her own sleeping bag and stretched. The stone floor was hard and cold. She was about to make her way outside but tripped over an outstretched hand she hadn't seen.

"Sorry."

The owner of the hand wasn't happy. Evie had trodden on an old wound.

"Sorry," he mimicked hoarsely, half asleep. The sound of a man's voice, and knowing that the man was between her and freedom, made Evie sweat.

"I am. I didn't see you."

And with that, she managed to bypass him and run outside. She saw how dangerous it was to be carrying a school bag now and ditched it in the first bin she found going down Haymarket. There was nothing much left now that she couldn't put in her pockets. It was early morning, before the commuters had arrived. Streetsweepers, who spoke no English, wore what looked like ex-army beanies and did their job at an even pace didn't look up at the people who crossed their path. Cafés were opening. Shutters were going up. She headed on towards Trafalgar Square and then through it and down towards the Embankment and the river. It was chilly this early and she pulled her woollen hat down around her ears. She found a bench and watched the working tugs, dredgers and pleasure boats ease themselves in and out of their moorings. Gulls squawked as they flew low over the still, murky river. She watched a gull pecking the mud that low tide had revealed. Her stomach rumbled, reminding her that she hadn't eaten for nearly twenty-four hours. She had £16.50 left of the savings account money.

A man in a raincoat sat down at the far end of the bench and looked her way, a newspaper in his hand. Evie fled upriver, running now. She slowed when she had no more breath and risked a look behind her, but the path was clear. He hadn't followed her. She walked on. The silhouettes of the buildings against the morning sun were all unfamiliar. It was an odd freedom. But then she saw a shape to the left, inland of the river, that she did recognise. St Paul's. She approached it more with curiosity than anything. She chose a corner pew at the back. It was all so confusing; religion had only ever meant restriction, fear, double standards, reprimands, terror, blame and, above all, the fear of Hell if you had crossed the line, but here felt alright.

They would have found the blood on her duvet by now. Probably thought that it was hers. But something nagged at her. She knew it hadn't been normal blood. But she couldn't remember, however hard she tried; the events of that night eluded her. They had gone. What *had* happened that night? She fell to her knees and began to pray.

"Our Father, who art in heaven..." But the words stuck in her throat. She felt stupid praying in the emptiness.

Evie thought of Paula. It was a habit to think of Paula. They had always confided everything in each other, or she thought they had. But she knew now that Paula had betrayed her, that much she did know. Paula had been part of her for so many years, and now that part of her had been torn away. There might come a time when she could cry for this, but for now she had to be strong. A pigeon flew close by her and Evie could hear the air shift as it did. Where to now?

She retraced her steps, the sun more overhead now, all the way back to the suffocation of Soho. Perhaps she would see the blonde girl again? Was that even a good idea? How did she know who to trust?

A siren sounded and she flinched, uncertain whether it was an ambulance or police car, and ducked into a doorway until she heard it pass. She looked down and saw that she still had her school shoes on. They would have to go unless she wanted questions about her age.

She found herself back in Piccadilly Circus. She looked up at Eros. She had never seen the statue in real life. It was so small. Cars drove by. She imagined more grime gathering on Eros' tiny wings with each puff of exhaust. Evie almost collided with a vending stand. She had turned too quickly, the sun bright. She put her hand out to steady herself.

"Sorry." The reflex was still there. How silly she sounded.

"Want one?"

The vendor was a young boy, not much more than her age, she thought. Hard to tell though. He held out a magazine. Evie looked at it, then at him, shook her head and walked further on. From a place of safety, she turned to look again. She could see the words *Big Issue* on the cover.

Soho seemed to draw her back in, almost suck her in, and before long she found herself drifting around Greek Street, down to Dean Street and back. At the end nearest Piccadilly Circus, there was a church, St Anne's, and outside was a stand with a big arrow pointing to the left. Was she turning into her mother? Always touching crucifixes, lucky charms, thinking priests were gods. Why was her mother so pathetic? Why couldn't she take charge instead of leaning on a God who wasn't there? Or, if he was, he must be laughing. There was a large red-brick building with large windows and a big pair of peeling blue double doors that needed new paint.

Centrepoint. All are welcome.

She almost changed her mind about knocking. But, before she could, a portly vicar in long black robes and cheap horn-rimmed glasses on his way home from the church was asking her, "Can I help you?"

Evie recoiled and stepped back. "No, I…"

The vicar said nothing more but waited. Evie felt caught now, but the hunger she felt overtook her and she looked back at the vicar.

"Can I get some food?"

The vicar rang the plastic doorbell; the door was unbolted from the inside, the chain released and finally one part of it opened. The helper, seeing the vicar, stood aside for both him and Evie.

It smelled of something Evie could not place but would get used to: used bedding, old cooking, old exhalations of substance abusers.

They walked to the back of the building where the kitchen was and where there was the biggest fridge Evie had ever seen. She looked around, uneasy now that there seemed to be no-one else in the building. She looked back but the door was shut again. She refused the offer of a chair while the vicar prepared a large sandwich made from stuff from the fridge. Evie didn't care what was in it. She hadn't eaten for over a day.

"Here, eat this. I'll make some tea."

She ate it, holding it in two hands, keeping her eyes on the vicar, never putting it back on the plate. It hurt to fill her stomach so fast. The vicar stayed on the far side of the table as he put two mugs of tea down. Evie was still standing when he took the stool.

"So, what brings you here?"

"Nothing."

The vicar took his cue. "What we offer here is a bed for three nights, if that would help. I don't need to know anything from you. Anyone over sixteen…"

Evie felt the iron sleeve come down again. She was fifteen. She'd be outside tonight if she said anything now.

"…is welcome. No drugs or drink and you can have supper here. Does that sound good to you?"

Evie nodded. Would they check and see that she wasn't sixteen?

"Come back at five-thirty."

He stood and moved with the intention of leaving the building, but it also meant that he would have to pass Evie. She was quick now and reached the door first. It was still unbolted. Despite his kindness, she fled. The knowledge that she had a place to go that night gave her an uplift though.

She spotted some old boots in a pile of rubbish put out to be collected by the dustman and pulled them free. They'd do.

"Evie!" she heard someone call, or thought she did. Diving into a shop doorway, she waited, holding her breath.

"Evie!" And again, "Evie!"

Who was it? The voice was getting nearer. It was a man's voice that she didn't recognise.

There it was again: "Evie!" But this time she heard it for what it was. A two-tone call for '*Eve-ning*' and then a drop-off '*Standard!*'.

"Are you alright?" a woman asked, seeing the terrified girl shivering in the doorway.

Evie fled. She couldn't risk being recognised, not by anyone. That *Evening Standard* call could have been someone calling her name, and then she would have lost everything.

Turning left into Denman Street, she saw on the right an old red-and-white helical barber's sign, and something clicked. She still had enough money, if only for a while.

The bald man, Greek-looking, pointed to the sign as she went into the shop. *Men's Barber*. His face indicated 'moron'. But she wasn't about to give up. To put herself at the mercy of an all-male shop took all her courage, but the day was warm, and the door had been left open.

"Can you do that?" She pointed from his head to hers.

"Heh?"

"I want my hair shaved off."

A woman, probably his wife, came in from the back through the plastic fringe curtains, and heard the exchange.

"Why you do that? Pretty girl like you?"

"That's why." Evie took out the £5 she had put in her separate pocket. "Will you do it?"

She kept her eyes closed the whole time the Greek shaved her head, making the odd comment as he went. She didn't want to change her mind, she had a beanie in any case, but now at least she did not look like the schoolgirl who had left Reston.

It felt cold as she walked back into Soho, really cold. She pulled up the collar of her jacket but, with the boots and now the shaved head, Evie stood taller, and her stride was longer, more certain. She knew that she would at least try to find her way back to St Anne's that night. As the doors opened, the group on the street flocked in one by one and, with a slight feeling of being in two worlds, Evie camouflaged herself well. Inside, the young man she had seen earlier was checking people in.

"Name?"

Evie winced and shrank inside herself. There were three ahead of her, which gave her time to think.

"Name?" he said to her.

"Jack."

"Jack?"

The man looked at her, took stock of the bald head and accepted that she would never be 'Jacki'. Food was on the go in the room near the kitchen, where Evie had had the sandwich with the vicar. Mabel, with swaying hips and apron tied round her ample form, brought the massive pan of stew over to the table. There was something odd in it. Nice. Evie kept her head down, not looking to right or left.

Afterwards, it was more awkward. It was not time for bed, but the meal was over. What now? What were you supposed to do? Again, she found a corner and tried not to be noticed. She would sit it out and at least sleep in a bed. Having expected safety, though, she instinctively knew this was not it. You had to be on your guard here. There was a smell of old disinfectant. Despite the warnings, she saw drugs being exchanged, money passed over. She looked at the tall boy, Neil. He was the ringleader, and she tried to sum him up. How did he get a Ralph Lauren logo on his shirt? How safe would it be to go to sleep? Were there separate rooms for boys and girls, with locks on the doors? She looked around, pretending to look for the lavatory.

"Yes?" The man who had checked them in was watching her.

"Where do we sleep?"

"You can't sleep yet."

"No. I know. Or at least, I don't want to. But where are the rooms?"

The man laughed. There was something frightening about his cold eyes. "Ain't no rooms. Beds." With that, he turned his back on her.

She kept all her clothes on when it came to night-time, but she had managed to keep a knife from supper and kept it under the bedclothes. Just in case.

During the following days, she saw no-one she recognised. She went into every newsagent to read the headlines, to check them for news of Reston.

When it came to the third and last allowed night in the shelter, the fear of having nowhere to go after that night overwhelmed her. She couldn't think straight. At the tap on her shoulder, she reeled, ready to defend herself. She looked up. It was the blonde girl who had saved her in the café when the cops had come in.

"Thought it was you. What happened?" The girl indicated Evie's new look, pointed to her bald head.

"Oh. Yes."

Evie felt her head. What was there to say? At that point, the desk man came over to her.

"Jack…" Evie looked up.

The girl looked at Evie, waiting to the end of this conversation.

"Jack, is it? What happened to Paul?"

Evie was enough of a rookie at all this to feel her colour showing.

"Don't need to tell me."

"No."

"What yer plans?"

Evie shrugged.

"I'm on the list… council flat."

"Oh."

All this was new to Evie. She really had no idea how to understand it all. She didn't know what to do, where to go or who to trust.

"How much money you got left?"

"Spent it all," Evie lied.

"*Big Issue?*"

At that point, the girl got bored being with Evie. She was biting her nails. She looked around and then suddenly moved to another part of the room. It was the second time that Evie had heard the name *Big Issue*.

That night, with the coarse, grey, woollen blankets scratching, Evie didn't sleep that much and, the following morning, was tipped out onto the streets with nowhere to go. She'd dreamed that night, tossing and turning, and when she woke she couldn't shake off the feeling that something had happened in her dreams. Bits and pieces kept coming back to her, but what she wanted was out of reach, left her feeling jumpy.

She had dreamed of her parents, she thought, and then a police car rushing past her as she had run for the tube station. But these small snippets did nothing to calm her mood. How bad really was the mess she was in? Standing on the pavement in Dean Street, not many people yet about, the cleaners sweeping up debris and putting it in their carts, early commuters making a beeline for their workplaces, everything seemed muted, caught between the night and the early morning.

The day ahead was too big to work out. It was beginning to rain, and she pulled up the collar of her jacket. Her stomach rumbled. She needed food. And she needed a place to sleep that night. And what about in between? She ran through all the options she would have had in her old life. The cinema, friends' houses, shops, school, none were an option now. What did people do? She checked how much money she had left; after the haircut, she would have to eke it out. Not yet desperate enough to check bins, she saw that the club opposite, the Groucho, had boxes of uneaten food waiting for collection.

Dashing over the road, a car hooted. She stood back and then made straight for the crates. She stuffed her pockets full of rolls, slightly overripe bananas and packets of cheese. It was exciting, like thieving but not, and it meant she could keep going for a bit longer. She could afford to buy a bottle of water on top of this. It cheered her a little, but the rain was coming on now. She turned around to walk away.

"Evie? Is that you?"

She didn't know the voice, didn't dare turn round. She had no idea who had recognised her. But the words were enough to send her hurtling up the street, beyond the stranger's reach.

CHAPTER 7

Gasping for air, she kept on running till she reached Piccadilly. Stopping in a doorway, she looked around but couldn't see anyone following her. She walked up Oxford Street, and into Bloomsbury and on up to Clerkenwell. She liked the look of Clerkenwell; there were some trees here and a little green. Perhaps she would sleep here and not go back to the Strand. It didn't feel quite so intense. There were some market stall frames left from the day. Some of the streets were wide, but not like Piccadilly.

Turning her back to the passers-by, she counted out what was left of her money and decided she could get a sandwich and something to drink. She took her food, such as it was, to the little green and found a bench which seemed safe enough. It was odd now how people looked at her, with her shaved head. She liked the fact she was no longer a target for men. Her uncle, her mother's brother, had always looked too long, stood too close.

Evie looked intently at the mother with her small child. Had that small child ever been her? Had her mother played with her in the park like that? Evie shook off the crumbs of the egg-and-cress sandwich and, like robots, the pigeons pecked and fed. Suddenly all energy drained out of her, and she could not have stood up if her life had depended on it.

As the evening drew in and people got sucked out of the capital, she found her own sheltered doorway with a big metal surround, a deep recess. Perfect. She allowed herself a smile. Everything was relative. She shrugged. There was even a discarded blanket nearby which she drew around her as the evening air brought with it chill and damp. She allowed herself to doze, then fall deeply asleep, her ordeal overcoming her. She entered a sort of dream state where two girls, about eleven, walked hand in hand across her vision. She thought about Paula. Did she wonder what had happened to Evie? Did she feel bad? Evie smiled despite herself; Paula wasn't like that, things were never her fault. Had Paula been round to her parents' house? It was odd to think that somewhere not that far away, all this was going on, and she, Evie, was here in a doorway.

She pictured her mum, still with that last image, beaten, grey. Would she be looking for her? Would she expect her home? Evie tried to see her mother taking decisive action, but she couldn't; Rosemary never dared cross her husband. And what about her father? Would he dismiss Evie's absence, saying she was probably at a friend's, and do nothing? And what had he made of the Trafalgar Hotel, the photo with Paula? What was he thinking now? When had Evie ever had evidence that he had cared about her? Loved her like Paula's father had loved Paula. Might her father have gone to the police? She tried to think clearly and only calmed when she realised her disappearance would not wreck his world. If she had gone, then so did his guilt around her, and around Paula. But was he afraid of that photo? And what she might do?

In Evie's dream, her mother was moving her blankets, making her warmer, but then it felt cold; she pulled the blanket back. The blanket was ripped away, and with that

Evie sprang awake. It wasn't her mother, it was the ugliest face she had ever seen. She was now fully awake. She hit out, scoring him on his face. He punched her on the nose; she was stunned, he was angry. Why?

"Help!"

Nothing. No passers-by. This couldn't be happening – but this man was after money, not her.

She felt for her purse, held it out. The man snatched it, leaving Evie huddled in her blanket. She began to cry, and then couldn't stop. She felt her stomach would come out. Gradually, light began to seep into the sky, lighten the dark clouds. People walked by on their way to somewhere, some looked at her, most did not, no-one stopped. Her swollen nose had bled; it was in her vision. Then a woman stopped, crouched down to her level and asked, "Can we help?"

Who's 'we'?

"Do you want to clean up inside?"

Evie pulled back. The woman, comfortably middle-aged and dressed in ordinary clothes, had a lovely voice.

"I don't think it's broken. Must have been a bad night?"

Evie nodded.

"You need help?"

Again, Evie nodded. This woman felt safer than anyone she had yet met in the last few days. Evie was conscious that the woman had not stopped randomly, but was holding her keys, trying to get in through the doors. She led her into her office on the first floor and into the kitchen at the back of the building. She mopped and tended to the bruising and bleeding. There were piles of magazines all around the room, done up in bundles ready for collection. *Big Issue*.

The woman saw that Evie recognised the magazine, and went on over a coffee to explain how it all worked.

"You see, you could make your own money from this. It's

a sort of business, a way out, or," and she smiled so warmly it felt like a soft rug, "a way through. Whatever brought you here. I don't need to know, it's OK. It's OK. But this gives you something else. Do you want to look at one? See what's in there?"

Evie leafed through and read some of the pages. There was something inviting about the woman that made Evie want to lay down her burden, tell her everything. But something stopped her.

Instead, she said, "I need to sleep somewhere. I've got nowhere to go."

The woman seemed to deliberate with herself.

"I usually point people in the direction of London Connection, in Piccadilly…" Evie was about to say she didn't want to go back when she continued, "But I happen to know there is a good squat two streets north of here. It would buy you time."

With the coffee done, the woman walked in silence with Evie towards the squat.

"It was an old disused lime brick factory, meant to be condemned, but planning issues held up the decisions, so, for the time being… it's a… squat."

There were some people still asleep, some awake. All knew this woman, so, for Evie, she was a passport in.

"Look here, there's a space here."

The woman introduced her to the girl nearby, Pink.

Evie said, "Hello."

The girl nodded, said nothing but looked Evie up and down from a distance. Pink was tall and thin; her legs are skinny, thought Evie, and there are dark bags under her eyes. And her short hair was dyed bright pink. She wondered why she didn't wear jeans like everyone else, not a short kilt. Besides, her tights had holes.

"Got any money?"

Evie shook her head. "You?"

Pink shrugged.

"What do you do for money? How do you get food and stuff?"

Pink shrugged. "Thieve mostly." She handed Evie some bread.

"Thanks."

"You on the Jesus trail?" Pink indicated with her head. "She tried to get me working for her."

"Who?"

"Kate. The woman you came with. *Big Issue*."

"Didn't you want to?"

"Nah, can't be bothered."

There was enough of Reston in Evie to see that stealing would be the worst thing for her. What if she was caught? Police? And then what? They would find out who she was and the whole ball of string would unravel.

"How long have you been here?" Evie looked around, felt the damp in the building.

"Not long. No-one stays long."

"Where shall I put my things?"

"Just find somewhere." And then Pink had an afterthought. "I'm over there, there's a space near me."

Evie looked over at the corner, the brickwork bare, the large black pipe running along the wall higher up dripping water.

"Thanks." And then, almost out of earshot, "I like your hair."

She placed her stuff in the corner, but at a good enough distance from Pink. Undoing her sleeping bag and smoothing it flat, but holding on to her possessions, such as they were, she was pleased at least that she knew where she would be sleeping. For a small second, she saw again the twin beds in Paula's house.

Pulling her coat tightly round her, she called out to Pink, "Going out for a bit."

*

The next day, she made her way back to the doorway of the little office that the *Big Issue* was using, trying to get it off the ground.

Kate explained the system, the badging up, the paying forward, the pitches.

"Don't worry, it will all make sense. Start small and see how you go."

Over the next few days, Evie began to feel she was not as far out of her depth as she had felt before.

She had a place to stay for a while, but then again, she had almost no money. And she needed a bath.

After the formalities, the false name and the squat address, Evie handed over her precious £5 that she had put into the lining of her bra; it was all that she had left after the attack when the purse had gone. She took her first bundle to sell. Ten copies, £1 each. She went to the pitch just near St. Paul's where she had wandered in that first day. She thought she would be selling, but instead she began to push and beg, her hand out, forcing the exchange. Why was it so hard? It was like the normal people she had always seen were now behind a pane of glass. That first day she only sold six copies, but still it felt better than the day before when she had nothing to do. She remembered the diary she had always kept; it was still at 'home'. Would it be found? Would it be read for clues as to where she was, why she had run away? She didn't want it read, but it would be anyway. Writing down her thoughts had always made her feel more real. Something stirred in her, an idea. She had made £6 back and spent the real profit of £1 on a ring binder book with lined pages and a blue biro. It was nearing six o'clock and Evie could no longer force the *Big Issue* on indifferent people, not today; she would get back to it tomorrow. Instead she walked back to the squat. She was the first back, it was empty, but this time quiet in a good way. She began to write in her diary, nothing incriminating, and still her name was Jack, but this time she wrote about the forty-eight hours she had just endured. She had to make sense of it. The book was small enough that Evie could keep it on her, and at times during the day she would return to it.

After three days, Evie went back to see Kate.

"Sold them all."

Evie wanted congratulation; she felt she had achieved something solid.

"Can you wait a moment?"

Kate was more the businesswoman today; there was a desk between them, not so much the mummy, more the headmistress. Evie felt rebuffed.

Evie nodded.

"Well, come back on Monday and we'll have the next lot for you. We're a monthly at the moment, but if things go well, we'll publish more often."

Kate sensed a hesitation. "What is it?"

Evie stood. At that moment, Evie's diary fell out of her pocket on the floor. Kate was already standing ready to end the meeting, so she was the one to pick it up. Evie was about to snatch it back.

"Is this a diary?"

"Why?"

"No reason. It could be helpful."

Who to? thought Evie. She snatched it back. She knew Kate wanted to know what was in it.

"OK then."

There was nothing in it to give her away. It was just about the day, mostly, and the nights. And trust. And fear. And being ignored. And attacked. There was silence in the room for the next ten minutes or so. Evie could hear people in other offices, doors opening, shutting, telephones ringing.

"Hmm." Kate looked straight at Evie. "It's very interesting."

Evie shrugged. Kate handed her back the diary.

"Come back on Monday. There's someone I'd like you to meet."

*

On the walk back to the squat, Evie walked the long way round, past the imposing old Mount Pleasant Sorting Office. In the next street, she came across a library and remembered they had newspapers as well as books. The librarian wasn't too happy having a skinhead in the library, they were always trouble, but she was the junior here and her boss didn't seem to mind so Evie was shown to the newspaper section. Big swinging arms of broadsheets on metal binders. She knew the date she had left Reston, but she needed to know what had happened. This would give her a chance of knowing what to do next.

"Do you have local papers too?"

She might just as well have asked for caviar for all the look the girl gave her. *What next?* was all over her face.

"What area?"

"There's three. Halifax in Yorkshire, Exeter in Devon, and Reston."

"What was the last one?"

"Reston."

Evie could hardly say the name; she felt as though she were calling the police in by saying the name out loud, but she couldn't back out now.

Leaning closer, she repeated, "Reston. Middlesex."

"I'll see what I can do. There's the nationals to start with."

Evie scoured through *The Times, The Telegraph, The Mirror*. Nothing in the main articles, nothing in the 'news in brief' bits. Nothing. The librarian girl came back with the locals. She flung the weight of papers down on the table. Evie looked round to see if she had attracted any attention. Pretending interest in the first two, she focussed on the *Reston and District News* for the whole three days in question. Saturday nothing. Sunday, of course, no. Monday, which was the first possible day to mention something, no. Evie read with her finger tracing each and every article and thought that she was drawing a blank here when she saw on page ten an article headed *Mystery Man Found*.

Evie's heart skipped a beat. He was apparently a 'mystery man' because he had nothing in his pockets, nor his clothes, to identify him. *Police are asking anyone who can help to identify a man, possibly in his 40s, found by the bus stop*, etc., etc.

But there was nothing about her, nothing about someone running away from home. Wasn't that news? What had happened to the man 'found'? Who was he? She shrugged, nothing to do with her anyway.

"Finished?" The girl looked up at the clock. "We're closing now."

Evie's head was swirling. Why hadn't there been anything about her? No mention of her going missing? It was a small place, a local paper, and still she wasn't worth a mention.

*

Evie talked to Pink mostly. She was about her age. It was a week of being in the squat before Evie risked asking the question.

"Do you feel safe in that skirt?"

There was a pause before Pink turned to face Evie.

"I don't mean anything by it... it's nice... it's just that I wouldn't..."

Pink looked at her but didn't answer.

"It's just, I think..." she added, hearing how that might have sounded like criticism, "that I never feel safe."

Once she'd said it, she felt she might have confided too much.

Pink shrugged. "See yer!"

It was like that in those early days, no-one relied on anyone else. They had a common cause, but different reasons for being there. The squat's entrance was boarded up with spare floor planks and from the outside it wasn't obvious that there was an entrance, let alone what it led to. Lights were candles, washing was done elsewhere in public lavatories, or cafés.

Food was brought in and eaten, but not cooked there. Mice shared the space with them, sniffing the scraps.

By now, Evie looked very different from the girl who had boarded the Piccadilly line train. With her shaved head, her men's boots, no-one would immediately have recognised her. But it was the way she was that had changed the most. Her shoulders were up, her head down, her eyes cautious.

Whereas before, she would have responded with politeness to a stranger's enquiry, for example, of how to find the way to somewhere, now when she sensed any approach, she rebuffed it before it happened and walked away.

There was enough time in the day, and sometimes by candlelight, to keep writing her diary. More and more she looked forward to it; she could talk openly there.

She was amazed to find, as she dated the page each day, that almost a month had passed, and she had survived something she would have considered impossible before.

Was Paula feeling guilty? Even now, it felt unreal. Had that really happened at the Trafalgar Hotel?

Evie had bought a new Sim card in a second phone, a simple one. She had kept her old phone though, just in case. It had the text messages still on it and the photos of her father and Paula.

She would keep those. She missed Paula as you would miss your heart if it was ripped out, but when she thought of her, she knew that she would have to get used to knowing she would not see her again.

Evie had grown to like how her shaved head felt, except for the stubble as it grew back. When the stubble changed to something softer, downier, she headed back into Soho. The barber's was still there, the Greek was still there. He smiled as she went into the shop this time.

"Heh, you back again?"

"Sure am."

There was a different tone to her from when she had gone in before.

"Heh, you wait, yes?"

Evie shrugged.

When the Greek had finished cutting the hair of the podgy man in the chair, he patted both sides, held up the mirror so the customer could see the back.

"Heh, you look a meelion dollars, yes?"

There wasn't much to ask when it came to Evie's turn, he brought out the electric razor and shaved every follicle he could see.

"You no pay for this?" He held out a lotion.

"No, no. Leave it now."

Evie stood up, she had no wish to be his favourite niece

or to be told that she too was 'a meelion dollars'. She'd find somewhere new next time. She paid and left and didn't look round as he called down the alley, "Heh, see you again, heh?"

Now back in Soho, it felt a bit like going back to an old school, a familiar haunt, although it had only been a month or so since she had arrived here from Reston. She wandered round and found herself subconsciously following the actual route she had first taken – the coffee shop, the run across Soho to Regent Street, back to Greek Street. She saw no-one that she knew, none of the people she had slept in the shelter with. Pigeons had left droppings everywhere. She walked back down Shaftesbury Avenue, always noisy, taxis hooting. It was just then that she saw on the right, where they hung out T-shirts, shirts and scarves on large, round hanger stalls, someone she thought she knew.

From the back view she looked familiar. Then she saw the girl take a T-shirt, then another, stuff them into the inside of her jacket and run towards the Circus. It was the blonde; her hair wasn't so blonde, but it was her. Evie ran to catch up, but then the guy from the shop gave chase and for a terrifying moment she was part of the hunted again. She pulled aside, studied a shop window, and watched to the left of her what was happening. She couldn't see for the crowds. The man returned empty-handed, swearing under his breath. Evie was exultant; the blonde had got away with it. She turned to follow where she thought she must have gone, down Regent Street and over to the arch that she remembered.

"Hey, hey!" she called.

The girl did not look round.

"It's me!" She caught up with her. "You remember me, don't you?"

The girl pulled away from Evie's hand on her arm but all the same, her face relaxed as she recognised her.

"'Course I do. Yeh. How's things?"

"OK. I'm up in Clerkenwell. A squat. Got into the *Big Issue* thing."

"Yeh? Who are yer now, Paul or Jack, or is it Bill?"

Evie laughed. "Does it matter?"

"I'm Dee Dee."

They were almost at the archway, and Evie marvelled at how invisible it was until you were almost on it. Dee Dee ducked inside. Evie followed, taking her time to adjust to the gloom. There was no-one else there; it was more a night-time thing. Just her and Dee Dee.

"Want some?" She passed a gin bottle over. Gordon's. It was already open, a third drunk.

"Nah."

Dee Dee drank as though it were lemonade and she had a thirst to slake. They sat in silence for a while.

"Sure?"

"OK then."

Evie took a swig. It was her first time with gin and she reeled at the taste and then at the hit, but kept quiet about it, sitting in the dark with the bottle. Before she passed it back, she had another, larger slug. Before long, the world felt softer. She and Dee Dee were mates. All that sort of thing. Between them they finished the bottle. Dee Dee chucked it aside; it clattered but didn't break.

"You sleep here still then?"

"Yeh."

"Where did you run away from?"

Dee Dee shrugged. "No-one asks that."

"Sorry."

Then, after a while, Dee Dee added, "Got a flat coming."

Evie remembered that Dee Dee had said that before. Perhaps it was just something people said like 'on the list', then 'got a flat', then 'didn't work out'.

"Where? How d'you get that?"

"Put yer name down, that's all."

"Could I do that?"

Dee Dee shrugged. This was a levelling of a playing field and to Dee Dee, Evie was still the junior, even through the fug of gin.

"Won't you miss the others? The ones here?"

Dee Dee considered this, as though for the first time. "You could come if you wanna?"

"What, live in it? With you?"

"What do you think I mean? Don't even know your name, but you could."

It was a decision made in a minute and one that Evie would look back on as a turning point.

"Yeh. Where?"

"Down there… near the river. Cool."

*

Before she left the area, Evie chanced one last visit to the Clerkenwell Public Library and the reference section. She now knew where the papers were kept and didn't have to cross paths with the librarian, just a nod and a half-point to the relevant section was all she needed. She felt now, given that time was beginning to pass, that she might, just might, be alright. So, leafing through the *Reston and District News* was more a default procedure this time. This time, looking at the back issues, one month on from when she had fled Reston, she did not get as far as page eleven. On page three, a larger article, a quarter of the page this time, read, *No clues in local murder*. Murder!

She read through line by line, still wanting not to find what she knew she would. There it was: *A body was found... bus shelter... head injuries... no identifying documents found... and if anybody has any information*, etc., etc.

Still nothing about her. But the nagging connection was there, if only she could remember. Leaving the papers where they were, she ran out of the library and round back to the green. She must have looked strange. An old man asked her if she needed help.

"Fuck off!"

This was all like a bad dream. There would be no good ending. Her thoughts racing, she walked around for a while, catching sight of herself in a shop window. Quite tall, thinner now, shaved head, boots. It wasn't enough to save her; she could still be recognised. She would have to take steps to completely change who she was if she had any chance of escape from her past. Her eyes were still brown, should any description be posted, and she still had her fingerprints intact. And they might one day give away who she was.

CHAPTER 8

Evie had moved now into the flat with Dee Dee, trying to make her bedroom feel like home. But she needed more money and made her way over to the offices to collect the new month's batch of the *Big Issue*. She stood with the group in the front hallway of the building instead of going into Kate's office as before.

There were three in front of her and as Kate saw her, she asked, "How many?"

She answered, "Twenty."

Kate paused and said, "Can you wait till I've handed these out? I want to have a word with you."

Evie shrugged. It felt a bit like school. She needed the copies and decided to wait. The line was seen to, the hall empty. Kate smiled.

"I was talking to Ed; do you remember I said I would talk to him? After I read your diary?"

Evie nodded, unsure what to expect.

"Well, I just think it fits with what we're doing." She indicated the pile of magazines in the corner waiting for later distribution. "You actually describe what life is like… on the streets. You write well."

Evie waited. Kate was unsure how fast to go with her ideas.

"What would you say if we put some of what you've written in the magazine? I think it would help people know what it is to be in this position. Most people don't have a foggy clue."

"I don't know."

Kate had never known Evie's real name or actually anything that would identify her, but she could sense that Evie pulled back at the thought of exposure.

She went on, "It would be under any name you chose. No picture, no identification of the writer at all. I must stress that. No-one would know it was you. Sort of *Twenty-Four Hours* was my idea. Are you up for this?"

"Would you pay me?" Where this came from, Evie had no idea. The boldness of demand was new to her, but then again, so was hunger.

"We could. But not much. How about £10?"

"£12."

"OK. We could do that. But promise me one thing, don't change how you write your diary just because people are going to read it. Keep it real. Keep it yours."

Evie nodded and, after that encounter, Evie felt less invisible.

"Thanks. There's one thing, though, it can't be my name. Ever. I don't want to be found. And we'll do it in cash, yeh?"

Evie didn't think that much more about this for a while. She bought another diary book and began again.

The first time, the following month, when Evie read her *Twenty-Four Hours* extract, she looked around her to see if anyone had seen her. She told no-one what she had done. It was only Kate who knew. That was enough.

The £12 went up to £15 as the magazine began to flourish

and that £15 meant that Evie had something to build on, something to fall back on. She bought some food for her store cupboard.

She thought of Paula and how they would look at shops at the weekend. She began to cry, then slammed her hands down on the kitchen counter.

"No! No! No!"

She didn't see Dee Dee come in.

"What's up?"

"Nothing." She wiped her face, forced a smile.

"Yeah."

That's what Evie like about Dee Dee; she knew things without facts.

Evie laughed. "I'm glad I'm here."

She looked down at her hands, still flat on the kitchen top. They were rougher than when she left Reston. She turned them upwards towards her and suddenly it was as clear as day: her fingerprints would have to go; one day they would let her down. She would actually *be* someone else from now on.

She was done with crying. And looking over her shoulder.

It was late summer now, and the sun had that hint of autumn as it closed in for the evening. But for now it was beautiful and, the next evening, after hawking the magazines around, Evie strode out in the direction of the flat. It was still a joke with Dee Dee that she still didn't know Evie's real name.

Evie's spirits lifted with the sun warming her skin; she had the beginnings of a new life. She would see to it that she kept writing. She had to cement this new life in a new reality, really, really leave it all behind. Her fingerprints needed to go.

The last part of her walk took her by the old church. There was something Evie loved about the old stone with verdigris and lichen; she loved to touch it. The grass was long; no-one ever seemed to come here. Making her way over to a stone seat under the old yew, she took out the matches.

Could she do it? How painful was it? She struck the first match and held it close, then closer until she felt the heat. Her flesh smelled as it lightly burned, first one finger and then, biting her lip to fight the pain, the other nine. Ten burned matches lay on the ground and tears came unbidden; the pain was so immense. *It will go*, she kept telling herself. *It will go*.

Evie stood up and continued the walk through the little cemetery; it was clear that there was a new burial, a new headstone. The grass had grown long, but Evie found her way over to the far corner and, kneeling, read the legend.

Vivienne Jasmine Wheeler, taken too soon, loved forever.

Ugh, Evie felt the jerk of tears, *loved forever*. And then she saw Vivienne's year was her birth year.

It was like a sign, surely? Thank you. Thank you, Vivienne. Evie laid her hand on the new stone. "Thank you."

As she left the cemetery, something felt very right. She would become V. J. Wheeler; she would be someone completely new, start again. Viv, she could be a Viv. All she had to do was apply for the birth certificate and no-one ever would drag her back to the past.

CHAPTER 9

2017

Viv slept badly and woke with the hangover feeling that something had happened in her dreams that she could not recall. Amanda had stirred something in her. She was not the first film-maker to come knocking at her door, but she was the first who had not come through either Nancy or Hugo. Why and how had that happened? Hugo was quite laid back about it. Perhaps he would rouse himself in time to take his cut. Viv pictured Amanda's face, her faultless ivory skin, and those blue eyes. It was, she thought, the blue of the wonderful thermal basalt pools in Iceland that she so longed to visit. There weren't many people who made Viv uneasy nowadays, but Amanda had. And it bothered Viv. But it was more than that, and as she worked her way through the morning's emails, making the calls she could no longer avoid, it came to her. This was one of the moments when everything came together. She *had* to seize the opportunity. All the moons were aligning. She had a chance. And she was truly afraid she would blow it.

When she had written *Riots Inc.* years before, she had seen England through the memory of having lived rough on the streets for two years, through her fear of narrowly surviving, smelling the hostility between different factions and different classes. Most people were too busy with their own interests, on the train, in cafés, in meetings, you name it, to lift their heads and see wider. But it was different if you were on the outside; you saw it alright. The days and nights spent wondering where she would find a bed, or be attacked, seeing people's faces and their reactions had all become etched in her mind.

Fights broke out without any warning. Someone off their head on drugs would wake up as they were robbed and teeth knocked out. Spoils from stealing during the day would be scrapped over. Food banks were commonplace now. This was England as people came to the West End to see plays, chat over supper, return to the shires. This was England. There would be riots.

There would be actual riots, but it would only be the big ones that got written up. Otherwise they were quickly put down by police with truncheons. This was the place she had written *Riots Inc.* from. It had been taken up, applauded in Hampstead, the Roundhouse had contacted her, and that had largely been that. Until Amanda. And what Amanda had done was reawaken that sense of urgency, that awareness that England was once again a divided, angry country. Amanda had woken her dormant fear of a polarised country where rich and poor were two different tribes.

As though by telepathy, just as Viv was about to call her and suggest a second meeting, a message on her phone came through from Rosberg. Viv steadied herself, but her speeding heart and shaky fingers betrayed just how personal this was.

*

Their second meeting, having been suggested by Amanda, was in her own offices. Viv was not averse to this, a little wrong-footed, but not averse. It would be interesting to see how big a project Amanda's production company was, get to know more about her. It was Battersea. SW. She found the address easily enough, a short walk from the mainline station. It was one of those consciously arty buildings with red and blue door bars, windows where there should be walls, studio suites facing a courtyard. She felt a pang of curiosity. Here was a community of like-minded people. Not much traffic, no flight path, on-demand buses. The main door had the names of all the occupants under a Perspex cover. She scanned down, not recognising the names – startups and independents – and it was with the smallest flicker of pride that Viv saw Amanda's buzzer. She pressed Rosberg Productions and took a very deep breath; a few seconds later, she was surprised it was Amanda herself who answered.

"Come on up!"

Viv glanced to her right; a camera had given her image away. She needed to be more careful, especially now. She could not rid herself of the feeling that she was being spied on. The hallway was polished and well kept, no flowers, but some magazines of a trade nature on the table in the middle. Viv found Rosberg Productions on the first floor to the back. The door was open. Amanda rose from her desk on the right to greet Viv, a smile on her face. Amanda was dressed in a black wool dress, slim, precise, exact, manicured.

"Coffee?"

"Black."

As Amanda poured the coffee, Viv rose and walked to the windows and lifted one of the Venetian slats to peer into the courtyard. A small fountain, lily pads, a wooden bench all surrounded by similar Venetian blinds. Amanda's perfume – light, lemon, flowers, fields – hung in the air.

Amanda placed the two coffees on the light wood table between them. She gestured to the easy chairs at the far end of the spacy studio. It was a world away from the club with its dark interiors. Viv chose to sit with her back to the door should anyone unexpectedly barge in. It was an ingrained habit. Amanda was in the opposite corner of the black leather couch. She spoke with animation.

"Have you had further thoughts about my offer?" Amanda's tone was gentler than before.

She found the way that Amanda kept her gaze until the full stop of her sentences unnerving. Viv had long ago developed a way of breathing at the comma, before the sense of the sentence was clear; this was at first unconscious but then she became aware of its power. Amanda came to the point.

"Well, do we go forward? It made a very big impression on me when I first read it. It seemed prescient – for its time. As you know, I liked its rawness." Amanda drank her coffee and continued, "But I thought it was a work of its time, that that time was over. But it is not. We are again a divided, angry country and you are very right, there is that feeling of barricades building again. When the summer comes, that will be the test – will riots break out all over again?"

Viv listened intently.

"But if you want to know what I thought about the book, your book, I would ask you a question instead."

Viv looked straight at Amanda, returning her gaze.

"How did you know all this? Where were you as a person when you wrote this? I need to know more. You are the most interesting author I've met in a long time."

Amanda wondered, not for the first time, whether she had taken a step too far, too quickly. Flattery usually worked for her, but Viv visibly bridled at the question. Viv wanted to tell Amanda the truth, she wanted, for the first time since she had fled Reston, to fill in that missing gap. She wanted to tell her who she was, to tell her about Paula and how she felt she could never trust anyone again. She wanted to tell her how she had begun writing, at night with a candle in the squat, how she cried with loneliness. But something held her back and she studied Amanda's face.

"What are you thinking?" Amanda laughed, noting the scrutiny.

Viv, wrong-footed, apologised, "I'm sorry, I…"

"…Was trying to decide whether you trusted me?"

Viv reddened. "Well, yes. I'm sorry. It's a bad habit. My belief is that the book speaks for itself; although, another time, perhaps, I could answer your question more fully."

"Of course. Every artist has that right. I think I was merely… intrigued."

Viv caught Amanda's eyes.

"There is much that I will tell you, but there are also gaps in my memory. I have no idea why, but there are gaps."

They finished their coffee.

"I have thought about little else; the casting, the locations, the style. I have people in mind, good people."

Amanda mentioned more names. Viv felt reassured, buoyed up by Amanda's enthusiasm. An assistant came into the room and left.

"If – and it is still if – you made the film, there would be conditions. No publicity shots of me, no biogs, nothing. My name on the credits I would insist on, but no intrusion. I think you knew that?" Viv added as Amanda did not register any surprise.

"That would be understood. The film will be good enough, trust me, to prevent that line being taken."

"Which of your films is your favourite?"

Amanda suggested *The Last Encounter*. Viv laughed nervously.

"Oh. Yes. That would be good."

Viv's stomach rumbled; had Amanda heard?

"Shall we talk more over lunch?"

"Is it that obvious?"

Viv laughed and Amanda's face softened.

CHAPTER 10

I know who you are, I know…

There it was again! Viv recoiled and slammed the laptop shut, as though it were a live animal. Viv had a rule not to open untitled emails, but she was raw from the day before and she pressed 'open' without thinking.

Oh God, first the club, now her email. How did he, if it was a he, get her email? She turned off her mobile and folded the shutters on the windows. The letter sender knew her email. Viv couldn't think straight. It was all she could do to still the terror that was taking hold of her.

She went out on to her balcony; the air was chill, and a wind was coming from the east. She took deep breaths and, walking to the end of it, she caught sight of her own palm prints in the concrete. She remembered how she'd found Don in the local pub, and he'd agreed to rebuild what had once been there. It suited the place, he'd said. He remembered the flats from years before, so for him it had been a personal pleasure as well as a job to redo the balcony. He'd always loved rivers; his dad had been a tugman. It hadn't been that big a job; Viv had just wanted a nice, smoothed-over concrete area. Still with his belt on, the trowel and plaster in either hand, he had stood up and, after admiring his handiwork, took in the view of this magnificent working river with its history, its beauty, its traffic, and beckoned Viv out. He was ready to do the last bit before stepping back in. She stepped out gingerly to the dry area.

"There you go, perfect!"

Don stood back and Viv admired the perfection that he had brought to an odd, unfinished, rough bit of the long balcony.

"Thanks, Don, it's great."

"Go on then." With a movement of his head, he had indicated that she should leave her imprint in the corner. "It's tradition! For posterity!"

"I don't want to be remembered," was her quick reply but she covered the moment with, "well, not like that!"

"Yes, you do. Everyone does. Every bus shelter has names on it. Put your hand in the corner before it dries."

She winced at the words but squatted down and, in the far corner, she laid her palm flat, leaving the imprint of her small hand, but not the fingertips. It was as they were talking, Don reminiscing about his dad and the life he had had not that far from here when it hadn't been posh, that the quick-dry concrete set hard. Viv heard Don, but she was thinking at the same time that her fingerprints – or rather, her lack of any discernible fingerprints – would be there forever as evidence that she had once been someone else. Burning them for three excruciating minutes had seen to that and now the skin had become hard.

*

By the next morning, the thoughts of the previous day had not left her, but she was glad now that she had agreed to go out to meet Hugo, her editor, for lunch. Viv brewed some coffee, her favourite Colombian, but today she struggled to taste it. She thought of Amanda. Had she left the possibility of working together clearly enough on the table? She scrabbled for her phone, charging on the kitchen counter, but just as she was about to call, an email from Hugo came in confirming lunch today.

Fine. Good.

She would call Amanda later.

She had worked on her second book with Hugo, Hugo posh boy. Editor Hugo. Viv liked him. He thought the world was his playground; Viv had soaked this up and absorbed something of the autocrat from him. They were odd together, but, in another way, made perfect sense. She was glad to be away from her Google searches, which had begun to unsettle her. *He's always invigorating, a good laugh,* thought Viv, *and I could do with a bit of that right now.* Hugo always brought a whiff of the estate with him. It gave her a feeling that her world was steadying up; she knew it was an illusion but a welcome one.

She made a mental note to put Blu-tack over the camera on her laptop. Even Mark Zuckerberg recommended that. She wasn't crazy or paranoid – just terrified.

*

Working on her weights after the coffee, she felt her tough biceps with pleasure, her strong thighs from the squats. Mostly she wore clothes that covered rather than revealed her shape; it was enough to know that she was strong. She could cope, she had coped with worse, she would get topside of this, she would.

The rest of the morning was taken up with admin for her latest book *Growing Pains*. By ten past one, she was in Hugo's club Boodles. She knew he'd be there a bit before one; it didn't hurt to keep him waiting, not with his sense of entitlement. The club was, as Viv already knew, a stone's throw from Soho at the top end of Pall Mall, just past the statue of Charles de Gaulle.

Two worlds. She kept that much to herself as she wandered in to the flagstoned hall, pausing only to give her name to the doorman, half hidden behind the oak booth.

She gave Hugo's name, and the doorman indicated where he would be found, at the back in the dining room. Nothing much phased Viv nowadays and she enjoyed the private joke of straddling two worlds like this. As she entered the dining room, she was met by a waiter ready to escort her, but Hugo had seen her first and strode over with the languid stride that only people not under pressure achieve.

"Hello!" He looked genuinely pleased to see her and, not for the first time, she wondered why he liked her. He gestured to take her seat. He was about to offer the menu, but Viv waved it away.

"One course, Hugo, you know me. Just order what's best today."

He was not affronted, he was used to Viv now and accomplished the order, adding the Club claret without further consultation.

"Well, Mr Wheeler, and how is the world of royalties going?"

"Fuck off, Hugo!"

"Well, at least I know why I invited you. It was to have the pleasure of your insults! There's something different about you today..." He cocked his head to one side, studying her with amusement. "What is it?"

"Your defective eyesight!"

The wine came and Viv, still thinking about the concrete moment with Don, was glad of it. It shut down the inside discussion about how odd it would be if and when it was discovered that she was not who she said she was. She made a mental note to make a good cover story for this eventuality.

"What did you want to see me for?"

"And that too."

"What?"

"Wheeler never beats about the bush!"

Hugo had given in to the need to find a job at the moment he discovered there was no-one left to play with. He had asked his friend Jamie on a jaunt to India, spur-of-the-moment-type thing, only to be told that Christie's would not release Jamie for that length of time. "Oh!" It was Hugo's Damascene moment. He was bored, and quickly, through contacts, of which he had an inordinate amount, found himself a job in one of the leading literary agencies in London. Viv had heard him recount this story and wondered, not without a hint of awe and jealousy, how easy it was for some. On the plus side, she argued, he actually had natural talent for what he did. He was still very attractive, around thirty-five, Viv thought. Slim, dark, slightly pointy face, with large grey eyes. He never seemed to take life that seriously. But then, he didn't have to.

"So?" she prompted again.

"I have an offer for you. A big one." He let that sink in. "It's an American publisher, a major one." He looked at Viv's inscrutable face. "It's to write the story of Nelson Smith."

"Nelson Smith?"

Hugo nodded.

"*The* Nelson Smith? Why me?"

"*Riots Inc.* has caught their eye. Anti-society, rebellion. Need I go on?"

The lamb arrived and Viv, as always, felt a frisson of gratitude. The memory of having no food for days on end was something, she noticed, that had never left her.

"There's a catch, Hugo. I know you."

She didn't look up but waited for him to struggle with that one.

"Nelson Smith stands for something that's getting bigger every day in the States now. Black civil rights has never gone away. You know that. I don't need to tell you – sorry. So it stands to reason that this book would be…"

"A weapon in their armoury?"

"Well, yes."

Hugo was never comfortable with confrontation, and he could feel one coming down the road towards him.

"I have always told you: no pictures, no publicity. The work must speak for itself. I just write."

"Have a think about it. I would imagine the film rights would fly off even before the book was published."

Hugo half looked up to see Viv's reaction. It was certainly a carrot. At the mention of film, Viv's mind went back to Amanda Rosberg. And her smile.

"I've already had film interest. *Riots Inc.*"

"Oh?" Hugo plainly did not believe her. An eyebrow shot up.

"Believe me or not. But I might do it. There would be the same conditions. I'm talking with her, so I'll keep you up to speed, but no publicity. You knew when I came to you that was off the table."

The lamb shank, which had tasted good, looked unappetising now; cold and a little fatty on the plate. Beyond the reach of mint sauce to make it taste palatable.

Hugo began the sort of questioning only journalists normally used. He changed tack.

"What inspired you to write *Riots Inc.*? I often wondered. More convincing, if you don't mind the comment, than any of your other books. Is it your favourite?"

She was reminded of how Amanda had made a similar approach. Viv took advantage of the wine waiter's attentiveness to recall how much Hugo knew of her past. How much had she told him?

"Well, you know…" She shrugged.

"No." Hugo looked straight at Viv in way that made her at once uncomfortable but made her laugh.

"You're impossible. No, well, you know, it's just the way society could go. Wouldn't take much. Breakdown of law and order."

She looked at him. "Don't you notice these things? The way people are if you knock into them? Or if you ask them the way? The lack of time and space people give each other now?"

He looked perplexed.

"See, that's it, Hugo, my boy, you don't live the way ordinary people do, the way I had to."

She realised she had almost gone too far. Hugo waited.

"It's all in the book. All you need to know."

Over coffee, Hugo suggested that they took the afternoon off from books. Viv could choose what to do and he would go along with it. One condition, though, she would tell him what she had meant by 'I had to'.

"That's a big ask, Hugo. You know that…"

Hugo looked at her for a long time. He had never fully figured Viv out. She was a high earner for him, his second largest client, but he didn't know anything about her past and not that much about her present. Walls shot up if he went too close.

Viv leant across, almost conspiratorially.

"Hugo, we work well together. You know we do. You are the best agent I know. But, and don't take this the wrong way, you aren't my publicist concocting a marketing story."

"Ouch, that's my wrists slapped!"

During the exchange, Viv could tell, as she always did with Hugo, that there was a moment that he would not respect her boundaries.

"You've always been a total ingrate, haven't you, Wheeler?"

"And you have never lived in the real world!"

It was part of their love/hate dynamic. Viv stood up.

"Thanks, Hugo. As ever – thanks. I like the proposal but only without strings. Get back to me, and give my best to Nancy, I miss her."

As Viv exited the dining room, she collected her coat from the doorman and walked down Piccadilly. But it wasn't Hugo's offer on her mind, it was Amanda's.

CHAPTER 11

When she surfaced the next morning, Wednesday 14th June, her first thought was of Amanda. Sometimes the complete silence of living by the river, no planes, only the wheeling gulls, unnerved her. Sometimes the space was too big. She remembered their lunch and talk, and the thought of working with Amanda cheered and warmed her.

The kettle boiled, she pulled the cafetière along the counter, spooned in the coffee and poured, inhaling the richness. But then, still in the kitchen, she flicked on the rolling BBC news station with the remote. On the television, she heard 'firemen', 'several days', 'unknown number of residents' and walked round and back into the huge sitting room. She was transfixed. Images not just of firemen and residents filled the screen, but of the luminescent wall of flames licking vertically up twenty-four floors of Grenfell Tower, like a mad, hungry, devouring beast just broken out of captivity. Pictures of dazed people with blankets round their shoulders and Lily Allen crying into the interviewer's mic, "They won't tell us how many there are, why won't they tell us?" All this was building to a crescendo around the flames. The firemen were in the building, up ladder extensions, everywhere, hoses going.

Why didn't they get water planes like California? But still the flames burned. Black silhouette images of people waving from the top floors against the yellow and red flames about to kill them. Who were they? Viv cancelled her plans for the day and remained glued to this unfolding drama of how the poor were viewed not just by the local council, but by the government of the day.

No Prime Minister May in sight. Just like George Bush in New Orleans. No fire sprinklers, no-one heard fire alarms. It had started just before one in the morning, no real chance of survival. As the day wore on, it was clear too that the construction of the building with its cladding and padding and gas-filled flammable interior, designed to reduce running costs, had played a leading role in how fast the fire had spread. Cladding that, for example, you would not find at the Dorchester, or Buckingham Palace or the Houses of Parliament. Watching this unfolding disaster on News 24 was the decider.

Life was too short. She called Amanda.

"Have you seen Grenfell? We *have* to do the film! And soon."

"Of course. I know. That's good news. I'm glad." Amanda was almost purring down the phone.

Viv wrapped herself in her duvet and curled up on the sofa with the television.

*

Amanda, for her part, watched the Grenfell news unfolding and knew the parallels Viv had been talking about. This was exactly what they already felt. She knew they needed to move forward. It meant no turning back. What was also going through her mind, though, was how odd it was for a writer of Viv's stature, and success, to have no biog, no trail, nothing before *Riots Inc*. What she was thinking was that if it had been her, she might have concocted a false biog that would have satisfied people like her. Why had Viv not done that? Amanda's excitement, her delight at landing the film rights, or nearly landing them, was tempered with this background thought as she went through the motions of her day. Did Viv not realise this blank would raise questions? What did it hide? Well, from her conversations with Viv so far, she knew better than to think she would elicit anything that would satisfy her; she would have to do some investigating herself. It was, after all, she told herself, just due diligence. Having come this far, she was cautious enough not to want anything to trip her up. She made a note to call her old friend, Linny, and get him to call Births, Deaths and Marriages, sleuth around.

"Linny, you can do me a favour?" Her clear voice went down the phone.

"Favour, yes, but paid favour."

Amanda laughed. "Well, worth a try!"

They both knew the score; they'd been friends since university in Oslo.

"I need to know about V. J. Wheeler. What is her story before she hit success as a writer? Where does she come from? I just know there's a big, big gap, and before I sign papers, I need to fill this in."

Amanda had meant to leave this with Linny for a day or two, so she was surprised to see an email ping through that afternoon.

This is a possible answer, or beginning of an answer. V. J. Wheeler's birth certificate was last applied for in 2006. When Viv would have been eighteen. Only, it wasn't V. J. Wheeler who applied for it. It was Evie Riley. This made me curious, so I checked Deaths and Marriages. Deaths record V. J. Wheeler as dying in 2006. Let me know what more you want?

Normally composed, not much ruffled the exterior of Amanda Rosberg, but this information did. The question was, was it important enough to do anything with, or should she leave it well alone and make a film that would further her career – with the risk that it could trip her up?

Before she thought better of it, she emailed back to Linny. *Great work. Thank you.*

A further email from Linny. *Do you want me to go on?*

Amanda stood and paced her office, checked her image in the mirror as she turned and sat back down again at her desk.

"Well, Vivienne Wheeler, do I?"

Two calls came through, her mind was distracted for half an hour, and by the time she returned to Linny's email, she knew the question was in two parts.

"Do I want to unearth the secrets of V. J. Wheeler before we make the film? And, if so, why is this so important suddenly? And if so, will it get in the way of..." And here she noticed the doodles she was drawing with her Mont Blanc pen on the page. But the second part of the question was more pressing. She knew that she wanted Viv in her life, film or no film. They had a connection that was more than work. She had been lonely for too long without knowing it or minding about it, but meeting Viv had changed all that. Should she just trust her, and wait for her to reveal her secrets? Would finding out Viv's past make it impossible for them to be together? And what would Viv make of her trying to find out behind her back? Would this ultimately be unforgivable? To clear her head, Amanda went for a walk. Battersea was not the most prepossessing of areas to walk in – hard pavements, traffic hurtling by, air pollution becoming worse by the day – but

Amanda pressed on, her stride settling into a rhythm which brought some calm to her troubled thoughts. For better or worse, and without judgement, she had to get to know her Viv, with all her secrets – and it couldn't wait. By the time she re-entered her office, her PA had gone to lunch and the office was quiet.

Linny, she emailed, *you have done tremendous work. Please email me the address and contact details of Evie Riley's family. Then, I will get back to you if I need more. Amazing work. Amanda x*

CHAPTER 12

Sitting in the back of the taxi on their way to lunch, Viv glanced over at Amanda. She was hard to read, but she was, without doubt, the right person to trust with her book. This film was a risk, but it was taking Viv to a new dimension of success. The letter delivered to the club never left her mind though and Viv wondered whether a deal with fate was being offered. Was becoming more successful because of the film going to provoke whoever sent that letter to take action against her?

"So, what do you think?" Amanda broke into her thoughts.

Viv looked over at her. "I'm sorry, miles away."

"You are a mystery, Viv Wheeler!"

Amanda's laugh was light, as was the touch of her hand on Viv's. Viv did not pull away and surprised herself by saying, "Amanda, it's a yes. I've struggled with this, but I want you to make the film."

"That's wonder—"

"I'm sure."

Amanda had chosen nearby Chelsea, a buzzy French restaurant near the Royal Court where the two of them would not attract overly much attention. Viv scanned the place as she went in and noted with relief that it was a reasonable blend of cultures here in Chelsea. The rich, the entitled, the arty and the visiting from out of town who liked its proximity to the tube were all there. Viv and Amanda drew no attention as they found their table in the far corner, on the Cliveden Street side. Viv sat with her back to the rest of the room. Conversation from the table a bit too close next to them wafted over.

"You have no idea how difficult it is to find the exact marble…"

"Have you tried…"

Viv glanced over; the two women, almost identical with their long blonde locks, were leaning into each other, intent on the conversation, their hair almost in the soup.

"Of course. Everywhere. In the end, we retained a consultant sourcer to find it."

"And have you? Found it?"

"In the end, but even now as I look at it in a certain light, it's not an exact match."

The first course came. Viv was finding it hard to concentrate, even with Amanda there, as more came from the nearby table.

"The room really wasn't good enough."

"But you were overlooking the bay, darling."

"I know but there was only one bathroom."

"Surely that was the point of your trip?!"

Amanda, keen to keep Viv's attention and nurture this fledgling relationship, broke across this with, "Did you hear what happened last night? A twelve-year-old black boy in Camberwell was shot by the police. He wasn't even armed."

"Parallel universe," was Viv's comment, indicating with a tilt of her head the next table as she took another gulp of the wine.

"Exactly. It is how and why these things fester. It is exactly because that happens and," here she indicated the next table more clearly, "while *that* goes on. Don't you think that's it? Not indifference exactly but completely different worlds side by side? The gap between is like the space between retreating tectonic plates."

Viv suddenly had an unnerving flashback to that first evening alone in London where she had watched the theatre goers flocking in, chatting and laughing in their floral dresses and navy jackets before she had found some doorway to sleep in. It was that divide still.

"It's more dangerous than they know."

Amanda poured a glass of wine for them both and held the glass in the air without touching. There was a question with the toast, an inflexion and a hope.

"To our project. We must engage the finance, next step, we'll do that together, yes? I think we have something..." Amanda tilted her head slightly. *Almost a coquette*, thought Viv. *On purpose?*

Amanda reached over to Viv's other hand, gave it a soft squeeze.

Viv smiled. "To our project."

Was it all happening too fast?

After a pause, Amanda continued, "I know so little about you, Viv. You fascinate me. I know your work, I like you, but you have so little footstep. Tell me about you."

Viv flinched at the word 'footstep'. Had Amanda Googled her?! She made a mental note to search her own name, see what came up. And Google Evie Riley too, from her second email account.

"I think you first."

"Well, I come from Norway." Amanda stated it simply in answer to Viv's question, and now the inflexion in her voice that Viv had first noticed fell into place. "My parents left, but they returned. They cannot leave. It's their home... but for me, history, it was suffocating."

Viv noticed the nuanced syntax.

"I grew up hearing the stories of the war mostly from my grandparents, the occupation, the crimes of the Nazis."

Although Viv did not wish to terminate this conversation or stem the flow of information, she couldn't help herself and parried with, "So did France, so did Slovenia, so did many countries."

She shrugged. "But it was our family, people I knew. This makes it different... to, well, just history."

"Do you miss Norway?"

Amanda looked away and when she connected again with Viv, her eyes were misty.

"Only the trees. I miss the trees. Before I left, I planted a row of pines on the edge of our land. Tiny. So high. But they will grow and one day. If I go back, they will be worth seeing. You will have to come to Norway!"

Amanda was immaculately groomed. Viv wondered if she visited a manicurist on a regular basis. Or did the manicurist come to her home? Viv tried to picture that. Pale grey silk cuffs to the black dress, they suited her. Elegant.

"I know what violence like that does to a people, to a country."

"When you read about Camberwell, where do your sympathies *instinctively* lie?"

Amanda was stopped in her tracks by Viv's question. "That's the problem. Both. I want change and I fear it."

With Amanda's mixed answer, Viv's heart sank as she realised she had thought they were on an identical page, but they weren't quite. Viv's response to Camberwell was to fan the flames of the riots, cleanse and burn, build again. There was nothing temperate about her thoughts, but it was too early perhaps to share the extent of them with Amanda.

Amanda continued to probe. "Have you always lived in London?"

Viv took her time, a sip of her drink, before she answered, "More or less." She pictured the newspaper she had found that had eventually noted that there was a *Girl Missing*.

Amanda smiled. "And do you have family?"

"I left home many years ago, like you."

"And you have always been a writer?"

Viv nodded, that would be enough at this stage.

"And you live alone?"

"That, Amanda, at this stage, might be a question too far!"

Viv managed to convey this slamming door with more charm than was familiar to her. Enough was enough. Viv was not ready for this – take the book or not was her feeling.

"Is making the film contingent on this biographical information?"

"Well, no. Of course not. But we need to get to know each other to work with ease." Amanda put down her fork. "Don't you think?"

"Well, here's a way. If you were driving along a country road and saw a wounded or dead animal at the side of the road, what would you do?"

"Excuse me?"

"You said we need to get to know each other…"

Viv did not over-egg it, she had a quizzical look on her face as she waited for Amanda's answer.

"Well, I suppose…"

"Don't think about it – first thought."

"I would probably be going to an appointment so I could not afford to stop. I would call the emergency services. And you?"

"I would stop and if it was in pain, I would kill it. If it could still live, I would nurture it."

Amanda was not about to be wrong-footed, although somehow she felt she had come out of that question badly. She would make other enquiries about Viv. Viv was attractive but there was mystery to her.

The bill was placed on the table. Viv reached for it and her card at the same time.

"No, no, this is a working lunch. This is mine."

"No, Amanda, I insist."

But Amanda caught the waiter's eye, holding out her card. "Settled! Shall we go?"

They stood. Amanda edged out from the table, which meant that they were standing so close they were almost touching. Viv could smell the soft scent again.

She moved towards the exit, but they were just leaving the restaurant when Viv heard, "Excuse me, excuse me!"

Viv felt a light touch on her arm.

Amanda was ahead of her, heading for the door. Viv turned and saw a woman's face, about her mother's age. The woman was looking so intently, as though scanning.

"I think I know you."

Viv feared what was about to come. "No apologies necessary."

Moving away, or trying to, she was spoken to again.

"Yes, from Reston."

Viv's head flooded with fear. For a second, she felt blind and deaf to the woman and glanced round to see if Amanda was in earshot. Had she heard what the woman had said? For a split second, she wondered if this woman was her letter writer.

She pulled her arm away, then heard her own decisive tone saying, "I have to go."

And she walked towards the door, leaving the woman staring after her. Amanda had, in fact, waited just inside the restaurant, by the dark plush curtain, rather than outside, and she had watched the encounter.

"What was that?"

"Oh, nothing."

"Didn't look like nothing. Did she know you?"

"No."

Amanda looked back at the woman, who held her hand up in farewell as the two left the restaurant.

"How odd," mused Amanda.

"Think nothing of it. I have to go now."

But as they walked with speed across the square, with its plane trees and unlit string of lights, the Royal Court behind them, and began to walk down Kings Road looking for taxis, Amanda put her arm in Viv's. Viv felt, rather than heard, Amanda's indrawn breath as she pulled Viv closer without thinking, the encounter in the restaurant forgotten for now. She looked up. Two policemen in flat caps were hauling a young man, who was resisting, dragging his feet, out of NK and into a police car at the kerb. A young girl, another Chelsea type with long blonde hair, expensive shoes, her quilted Gucci bag with the gold chain strap open, empty on the ground. She had a blanket around her and was being comforted by a PC. A knife, held in a plastic bag, was in police possession. The boy's hands were handcuffed in front of him. Viv caught his expression; it wasn't anger, it was despair; he was a defeated attacker. Amanda put out her arm as though to stop Viv going nearer but there was no need. For a second, they stood stock still, very close, then turned, walked through to the street behind Kings Road.

An attack in broad daylight. Anger and rage surged back into Viv. Although she had not witnessed it, it felt as though she had.

They shook hands; Amanda's hold was firm. Should they kiss goodbye?

"I'll send the contract over to Hugo."

Even in this affluent area, Viv noticed the stained sleeping bag in the doorway, the occupant away and coming back that night. She noticed too how food banks were an accepted cultural norm. In Chelsea! When did that happen? How could that possibly be acceptable? Women with their designer carrier bags walking by food banks. Chained Alsatians waiting for their owners. How long can that go on without something erupting? It was still a fine day and, striding out, she told herself a walk would help her to sort out her thoughts. Crossing over Chelsea Bridge to the south side, she paused to take in the sweep of the river. The view was impressive out towards the City buildings with their distinctive shapes, but it had an immediate, depressing effect on Viv. This was a solid wall of male invincibility. She shuddered. Over on the south side, she traced the river and felt comfort in the less conformist atmosphere.

It had been an early meeting, a pleasant lunch, hardly time for another stop but the Founders Arms, perched right on the river, was polyglot enough to be inviting. She wandered in, then out with her top-up whiskey to the farthest bench. It was cold; she put her collar up. All she could smell, though, was the beer. City types wanting to avoid their own area often came here long before five o'clock and drank way too much. She always had hated the smell of beer. The sunlight was watery, sad; she closed her eyes and breathed in. Something like a waking dream, perhaps a memory that the beer created, came to her, or was she imagining it? As before, when she had had a feeling she could reach back and retrieve the memory that was missing, she felt that the beer was part of it and concentrated hard on the smell to find that first connection, but this time nothing further came.

"Is this seat free?"

The question jerked Viv out of her reverie. Fear was in her face as she faced her questioner, a harmless middle-aged woman with a small child.

With one stride, Viv was out of there, back on her walk down river. That part-memory had not been an imagining, it was a part-remembering. She was sure of it. There had been an attack that night connected with the smell of beer.

CHAPTER 13

Amanda was familiar with London like the back of her hand, but suburbia was unknown territory for her. She chose to drive rather than take the underground as it left her feeling more in control of whatever choices she would have to make that day. Driving down the A40, the satnav brought her to the area she was looking for. She pulled up slightly away from the house she presumed the Rileys lived in. She noted that the parking was still unrestricted here, unlike London where you had, it seemed, to pay to breathe some days. The houses were not terraced; some were semi-detached, one or two on their own, but all the same, there was a feeling that this was a sprawl of a village, part of the vast London overspill. Little thought had been put into these houses, leaving it to each occupant to differentiate themselves with a choice of paint colour, or front garden design. She paused outside the Rileys' house but walked on by as an upstairs curtain moved. She had set out with clear purpose, but now she was suddenly afraid of what she might find out. This is where her Viv had come from. She could still turn back; no-one would be any the wiser if she did. But with sudden resolve, she turned on her heel and headed back to number twenty and rang the doorbell. The monotone ring echoed inside the house, the uncarpeted hall echoing. Amanda waited. She rang it again and almost immediately she heard footsteps, soft footsteps, approaching the door. The chain was released, the door opened but not fully, and Rosemary's lined face appeared.

"Yes? Can I help you?" she asked without any expression.

"Mrs Riley?"

Rosemary pulled very slightly back, a frown on her face.

"I'm sorry, may I introduce myself? I'm Amanda Rosberg, I'm looking for a friend of mine, Evie Riley?"

The question in that sentence suddenly fell into place for Amanda. She was indeed looking for Evie Riley.

Rosemary looked down and was pushing the door closed as she replied, "She's not here."

Amanda held the door with her hand. "Please. Please may I come in and talk to you?"

"No, no, that's not a good idea."

But there was something so clean, so honest, about Amanda that Rosemary relented and opened the door, gesturing for Amanda to come in.

The house was cold; there was no cooking smell, no sign of activity, nor of anyone else being present.

"Can I get you something to drink? Tea, Miss Rosberg?"

Rosemary stayed looking at Amanda; she was curious.

"Amanda, please. Yes, thank you, tea would be most welcome."

On the edge of knowing facts she would not be able to unknow, Amanda's nerves needed settling. As Rosemary made the tea in the kitchen, Amanda was aware of the sounds of the kettle, the water, the cups on the metal tray, but she was looking around the small sitting room and picturing her Viv here. There was no dust, no crumb of dirt, nothing out of place; the ornaments on the bookshelf in balance, the coal in the scuttle ready for the cold weather.

"Here we are."

Rosemary placed the tray on the table and poured tea for her visitor. Amanda saw with a degree of shock that Rosemary's wrists were both bruised, a dull brown in the places where someone had held her, not recently, but far too tightly.

"So, how do you know Evie then?"

Amanda had expected this question and knew how difficult it would be to answer in any way truthfully.

"I was in her class at school."

Rosemary looked more intently, almost squinted. "I'm sure I would have remembered you."

There was doubt, Amanda saw the query in Rosemary's eyes, but an eagerness to be wrong too.

"But only for a term."

"Oh."

"I lost touch with her and she's not on Facebook and so on. We were good friends for a short while."

"Have you come far?"

What Rosemary was thinking was that Amanda had indeed come a long way out of her usual life, by the look of her, to search for a friend of so many years ago.

"She always wanted to ask me home, but it never seemed the right time, I don't know why. Did she ever speak of me?"

Amanda was appalled at the ease of her own inventiveness; she had no idea she could lie so well.

"No. No."

They drank their tea in silence. Every morning, Rosemary's waking thought was of her missing daughter, but she tried and tried to divert herself during the day, so that her loss was manageable, bearable. Now, though, with Amanda talking of her daughter as though she would walk back through the door at any minute and find the two of them chatting like old friends, Rosemary was beginning to feel unstable, teary. It was reviving memories she preferred not to have yet could not detach from now that they had been reawoken. Evie felt real again. She rose with the tea tray, about to leave for the kitchen. Amanda could see that the situation could get out of hand, and then the opportunity to elicit information would be lost, probably for good.

"Please, if you could let me have her present address or at least phone, or email, that would be amazing, and I would leave you in peace. I'm so sorry for the intrusion like this."

"I can't..." Rosemary took a deep breath and admitted, "I have absolutely no idea where she is." She stood, turned her back on Amanda and, looking out on to the neglected back garden, with weeds growing through the patio stones, she told Amanda, "She left when she was sixteen and..."

Amanda heard the front door open with a key, and a man's steps coming through the hall towards them. She sensed Rosemary tensing. As her husband Douglas came in, his formality allowed him to greet Amanda and to be superficially charming. It was when Rosemary explained that Amanda had come to find Evie that his manner changed, and, thought Amanda, not that subtly. He moved to the other chair and explained that they could not help Amanda and that she should probably leave now. Was she from the press? He remained standing to emphasise the fact that the visit was over.

"How long have you been here?"

He looked across at his wife as though trying to establish just how much she had said. Douglas's mobile rang. He took it out and glanced at it, was about to leave it ringing, but something made him answer it.

"Excuse me." And with that he left the room.

Something kicked in and Amanda took hold of Rosemary's hand. She insisted that she needed to know why

Evie had gone missing. Rosemary wasn't sure; why was this 'friend' so desperate?

Douglas came back into the room.

"I would like you to leave. You are upsetting my wife."

But Amanda's presence had given Rosemary courage. Amanda had brought Evie back to life for her and she was not about to let go.

"Douglas, no-one knows. It's unbearable... Please wait, Amanda."

She left the room to return with some newspaper cuttings of the local paper.

"Look."

She pointed to the picture in the paper that she herself had supplied, asking if anyone had seen Evie. Even with the passing of fourteen years, allowing for the severe change of haircut, it was her Viv looking back at Amanda.

"And then there was this, we always thought it was..."

Douglas reached over and tried to snatch these papers from his wife's hands, but Rosemary was quicker, and she handed them to Amanda. No-one, not even the police, had made this link, and Douglas was not about to let it be made now. And certainly not by someone he didn't know.

Rosemary had the other cutting on the table. *Local garage owner murdered.*

"It was the same time... No-one ever knew what happened..."

At the suggestion of Reg's name, Douglas's tolerance of this meeting had reached its limit.

"Miss Rosberg – time to go. Please."

He remained standing while Amanda gathered her bag and coat from the sofa.

"Thank you, Mrs Riley. I hope you find her one day."

She left her card under Rosemary's teacup.

Rosemary had warmed to Amanda during their talk. She had felt so alone all these years.

"Well, yes, perhaps."

The oddness of that comment disappeared in their movements to the front door. Before she was at the gate, Amanda heard Douglas raging against his browbeaten wife. That was a red flag alright.

As Amanda walked the hundred or so yards back to her car, she tapped the name and date of the newspaper cuttings into her phone and found the nearest library to research further. She blessed the computerisation of records and newspapers; it allowed so much more to be stored than in the days of keeping physical cuttings. Scrolling around, she found mention of the garage owner Reg Dawson strewn over a few weeks following his disappearance, but only that one mention of the missing schoolgirl Evie Riley. What she found intrigued her. Here was a man already known to the police because of being implicated in receiving stolen goods (not proven), but also a man who managed to have his character vouched for by one Douglas Riley! What on earth was the connection here? After that, it seemed that the trail had gone cold, no-one was in the frame for a murder, and there was no mention of anyone looking for the missing schoolgirl. And no-one had made any link between the two.

The day was getting on but there was still enough time, since she was in the area, to call in on the police station which served the wider area. There was a forbidding Perspex shield and push-button system to keep you at bay; no feeling that you could walk in and, as an innocent citizen, be served and protected. The film-maker in her noticed how it made her feel about the police.

As Amanda waited for the tinny voice to speak through the intercom, she martialled her reply.

"Could I speak to someone with regards to an ongoing case, please?"

"You'll have to email in your request."

Amanda pressed the buzzer again. "No, I have to speak to someone here today. Please."

There was a click as the door released and she walked to the counter and another Perspex shield. The PC behind the counter motioned for Amanda to walk to the side to be let in there.

"Thank you."

"Yes?" The PC frowned, managing to convey that time was a factor in Amanda's query; she hadn't got all day to deal with it.

"DCI Armitage used to work here? Fourteen years ago?"

His name had been quoted in the newspaper article.

She looked blank. "Before my time."

"He was working on a murder case, Reg Dawson?"

Another blank look. The front buzzer went again.

"I'm sorry, I can't help you."

She was about to leave when Amanda had a brainwave. "Has anyone here worked that long that might remember DCI Armitage?"

The PC disappeared to attend to the query at the front door and was trying to be as civil as she could under the pressured circumstances, and she was about to repeat that she couldn't help when she remembered that there was an archive file on the main computer.

"Hold on!"

She disappeared again to return with a phone number for the now retired DCI Armitage.

"Thank you so much, you've been most helpful."

"I shouldn't do this but—"

And Amanda made her exit through the airlocks out into the outside world again.

DCI Armitage's number was a landline. It rang as she walked along the street and was answered almost immediately. Amanda ducked into a doorway so she could hear better against the traffic, one hand up to her other ear. She managed to explain that she was looking for information as to what had happened to Reg Dawson and Evie Riley. In retirement, a call like that can be flattering. In an instant, Geoff 'Bingo' Armitage felt relevant again, stood up from his armchair and suggested, as she was in the area, she could call round, and he would fill her in as best as his memory allowed.

*

He was a big man – *fond of his food*, thought Amanda – and filled his doorway, and his smile showed how pleased he was to meet her. He showed her into their well-carpeted sitting room, which was flooded with sunlight.

"My wife's out shopping at the moment – Tuesday. How did you find me? How can I help you?"

And Amanda went over the information she had, and something made her frame the query with, "Any news would be so good," and then, hardly daring to ask, she added, "was there any connection between those two events?"

The clock on the tiled fireplace chimed four o'clock. Geoff took a deep breath.

"I think it was coincidence. Nothing more. People talked, of course, because in a small place, like Reston was in those days, it was odd to have two events so close together. What I do remember was that there was a delay in the forensic results coming back as there was a technicians' strike. It meant that good leads went cold, and it also meant that the chances of solving a big case like that were very much reduced. We made enquiries in the area and, of course, with the Riley family.

Found a bus pass at the site if I remember. It led to nothing, but the main bit of evidence we did have was, or would have been, a good lead, but it wasn't enough to build a case on. Couldn't prove anything."

"May I ask what that was?"

"It was a pair of green leather gloves, two gloves both there at the scene, drenched with Dawson's blood. Had distinctive shamrocks on them. We had a school secretary claiming they belonged to Paula Johnson, but then Paula, and her father when we interviewed him, denied they were her gloves. There was nothing further to go on."

"Were they kept as evidence?"

"They were. Of course they were. You've got the golden twenty-four hours, possibly forty-eight, for all the best leads, the best hope of solving a crime... After that," he shook his head, "after that, you scale back your work, and then next thing you know, you're filing it as a cold crime."

After a moment's reflection, he added, "There had been recent sexual activity, I remember that."

"Do you know where Paula Johnson can be found?"

"No, I'm afraid not. The family went to live in the States not long after, for the father's work I think. We didn't treat it as suspicious at the time, but now you're bringing it up again... it's all very odd. If anything further had come to light, we would have wanted to question Paula again. She was very much a person of interest at the time, I do recall that."

"And Evie Riley?"

"Poor girl. Just disappeared. Another statistic. There was always something about that missing girl that made me feel we had let her down, couldn't put my finger on it though. So many kids go missing, don't they? There was pressure to leave it alone, and that," he leant forward, spreading his hands, "was that. I feel sorry for the parents, well, the mother anyway. I'm not sure about the father."

For the second time that day, Amanda thanked for the help and stood up, her hand out to say goodbye, but Geoff held her hand, his mind elsewhere.

"There was one thing. Probably nothing to do with anything and certainly nothing we took any further, but when I spoke to Mrs Riley on her own after I'd seen them together, she seemed sort of grateful to have me there. She'd been very mousy when they were together, wouldn't say boo to a goose. Kept looking at her husband, checking. She leant forward to cut the cake – she'd made a cake, even – and I saw the bruises and red marks up her arm. I made a joke of it, 'Been in the wars then?' But she pulled her sleeve down and sat back on the sofa.

"'No. It's nothing.' She said it quickly. I've been around and I knew what that was. Without her properly telling me, my hands were tied – pardon the pun! 'Who did that to you? Your husband?' I asked her straight out. It had to be the husband. At first, she wouldn't say anything, but then she started crying, shaking, nodding her head. What she told me made my blood boil. He was one of those men who show their real self behind closed doors. What was relevant to the case though was that he had, she told me, once broken Evie's arm. He was a good old-fashioned abuser. And," he went on, warming to his story, "that does affect how we see Evie. She was one man's victim. Was she another's too? 'We'll need you to make a statement, Mrs Riley,' I said to her. 'Oh no. I can't do that,' she said. And it was just then that the key was in the lock and old smiley walked in. Without her help, we couldn't do anything. But without a doubt, violence went on in that house that no-one ever reported."

"So Evie had been hurt too? Do you think that was why she ran away?"

"Who can tell? Anyway, I mustn't keep you."

"Well, thank you again. Oh, I have one last question, did Paula and Evie know each other? Did they go to the same school?"

Geoff thought about this for a moment. "Now you come to mention it, they did go to the same school. Not sure if they were close friends though."

"Oh well, thank you anyway."

CHAPTER 14

Geoff's mind was buzzing now in a way that it hadn't for some time. It had always bothered him that he hadn't managed to close that case properly. And he couldn't rid himself of the niggle that there was a connection he had missed. They had checked the girls' phones, of course, he remembered that. But what was odd, he recalled, was that both of their phones had been at the cinema in town that night, but both of the phones had gone back to Evie's house.

Only, when they had questioned Evie's father, he was adamant that Evie had returned home alone that night drenched from the rain.

Geoff decided to keep that information back for the time being, he didn't want to add to the impression of incompetence.

Amanda walked down the short, crazy-paving path, careful not to knock into the potted shrubs either side of the entrance, headed for her car, and then back home to Battersea. As she let herself into her mansion flat near the park, she breathed a sigh of relief at returning to familiar territory, and to the knowledge that although Viv would feel hurt, betrayed even, if she knew what Amanda had been up to, she would have no real reason to be afraid. Amanda realised that one of her biggest fears had been that she would find that Viv was implicated in something awful, life-threatening, and that that was the reason there was so much secrecy around her, and that that was the reason that she had changed her identity and erased her past. But even though Amanda had met Evie's family, she knew no more about her than she had that morning.

What had happened to change Evie into V. J. Wheeler? What had she been running away from? Being able to establish that there was apparently no terrible mystery, that she was just a runaway from home, lifted Amanda. She began to hum softly to herself. Amanda had heard of amnesia through trauma and was convinced by Viv's lack of memory, so why, if there was no terrible secret, could she not recall? What could she not recall?

Amanda had not liked the father, Douglas, one little bit. It wasn't just that he had been hostile to her personally and ejected her from the house as though some terrible virus would lay hold, no, it wasn't just that. She pictured him again in her mind. Good-looking, angry. She saw too his wife's face. She had been afraid of him, and it had only been Amanda's presence that had lent her courage. She was sure of that. Was he just a good old-fashioned misogynist with his own damaged past? Or had the speed with which he had virtually pushed her out of the front door been fuelled by hiding his own secrets? As she settled behind the wheel, and her thoughts stopped whirling about like a kid's snowstorm toy, what she felt was a surge of pity for Viv, of love, protective love, for Viv. She felt sure now that, in time, Viv would come to trust her enough to tell her what she knew. She just prayed that it would not come to light before then that she had been nosing about behind her back.

CHAPTER 15

Geoff's wife had the five bags from Sainsbury's to deal with. She struggled noisily from the front door down the hall and through to the kitchen.
"You could help!"
Geoff heard this as though from a distance. Usually he would be up and doing it, without Jane having to ask.
"You could help!" she repeated.
"Sorry, love." And he was through to the kitchen.
"A bit late!" Jane turned to her husband of forty-two years. "What's up? You look as though you've seen a ghost."
She continued to rummage around the orange bags for storage cupboard items. Geoff's attention wandered, and he returned to the sitting room. Amanda's visit had at first flattered him. That case she was interested in had been the biggest of his career, just coming at the end of it, and he had not managed to solve it. All coppers want the big one; well, he'd had it and bungled it, so it had all dredged up some very mixed feelings. He went to the bookcase and took out the box of cigarettes stashed away for special occasions. He'd promised Jane to give up, and he had, except for now. He went over to the window and opened it to let the smoke out.

He stood looking out at the neat, small front lawn. Anger and irritation surged up at the thought that he had lost his opportunity to have his name on the record books. But as the nicotine served its purpose, he calmed and remembered that not only had the forensics been on strike, but when the strike was over, they had actually lost some of the evidence, namely the green gloves which had been at the time a critical lead.

All that had been brushed under the carpet, and, in a way, he had been part of that. If the public had got wind of the state of affairs, all hell would have broken loose. But with that happening, it had been impossible to put together a CPS case and it had had to be filed as a cold case.

Amanda's flattery had breathed energy into his memories though. He hadn't given it much thought before today, but now he had a mix of emotions as he realised he had not forgotten one single detail, and perhaps it was time to go over it all again to see whether something had been overlooked that could have solved the murder of Reg Dawson. Perhaps he should look again at the father, magistrate and all-round important bigwig good guy; he was linked to both people, after all, mixed up as he was with that sordid little amateur ring of borderline paedophiles. All that business had come to light and should have been prosecuted in its own right; he couldn't recall why it hadn't been. But the girl, Evie, had she really been a simple runaway and had they given up too easily on her? Or had she been a victim of this? Was it all connected? Douglas Riley had, after all, vouched for Reg when the stolen goods charge had come up.

"I've finished now. Geoff, can you make us some tea?"

He noted she chose not to mention the smoking just yet.

"Yes, love."

And as he waited for the kettle to boil, Geoff's energy returned, along with the thought that perhaps he could reawaken this case, retired or not. He filled the teapot, forgetting to put the teabags in.

Something at the time – irritation, regret, something, anyway – had made Geoff copy and keep a set of the entire notes of these two cases up in the attic of their tidy little house. Should have handed them in, he knew that. If upstairs had got wind of it, his pension would have felt the pain. Odd though, he reflected, what had made him do that. He wasn't given to whimsy, but all the same, had he known at the back of his mind that he should have done more? Well, now perhaps was his chance to put that right.

He had been on the brink of retirement, and he had promised himself he would go on thinking of it in the long days ahead of him, but never had. But now, Jane heard the metal retractor steps being pulled down and Geoff's tread going up to the loft that was only ever visited when a suitcase had to come down.

*

With all the adrenalin coursing through him, and now having to kick his heels, Geoff made an excuse to Jane the next day and took the short train journey to Reston. He saw the station name pass by the window and, just before it was too late, dived out of the doors; he would have a look round the village and see if anything else came to mind. He walked the half mile from the station down to the centre of the old village where old Dawson's garage had been. In his mind, it would be a boarded-up derelict now, a crime scene fallen into disrepair that no-one would touch. But as he got nearer he could see how wrong he was. There was a garage there, a buzzing one, with three men working on a car on the forecourt, two more waiting to be seen, bright lights, everything clean, a radio playing. He stood there for a moment, taking in the new scene, till one of the men crossing from the office to the working area called out, "Want something?"

Geoff walked over and, smiling, admired the garage. The man shrugged, it was just where he worked, that was all. It was an awkward moment and Geoff's instinct to always find out more led him to confide in the man how he knew of the garage.

"It was called Dawson's then."

"Yeah, I know, we got loads of calls, all the time; my dad said it drove him mad."

"What sort of calls? Who from?"

Again the shrug. "I don't know, just blokes, customers." The man paused, turned back as though a thought had struck him. "Odd though, they wanted to speak to Reg, personal, but they were never after getting their cars mended, I remember that. Look, got to get back… Who did you say you were?"

"Geoff Armitage."

They shook hands, Geoff enjoyed the feeling of grease on his hands.

*

The train journey home took longer than planned as the train was left standing between stations; apparently there was some obstacle on the line. He walked down the tube carriage and parked himself in the corner where hopefully no-one would disturb his thoughts. He needed time to think and remember what had actually happened that night. *Had* he missed anything? Could he have done more to find Evie Riley?

First thing he remembered was the call out for the dead man, Reg Dawson. They hadn't known his name at the time, but that's who he turned out to be. Then there was the witness, the one who had found the body, needed a bit of calming down – Edwards, Sylvia Edwards. Very agitated, more worried about being late for her job than seeing a corpse! They had taken her in for questioning, but she hadn't been much use after that. Renshaw had got there first with Paul Creech, the graduate intake boy, and filled him in. Time, evidence, etc., etc. There hadn't been anything startling, he had been dead probably eight or nine hours, no ID on him. Green gloves with a four-leaf clover cut out on the back had been found, possibly not even linked to the murder. The usual shattered glass from the bus stop timetable, old chocolate wrapper not thrown in the bin, the black plastic bus pass that he had not at first noticed. Then a memory made him smile, almost laugh. The woman in the opposite seat gave him a sideways look. He remembered the detail of that bus pass.

"Bingo, blood on it. In the bag!"

Geoff remembered his excitement had risen when he saw this; it could have been a good lead. Again, he'd passed this to SOCO, the Scene of Crime boys, but before he did, he had taken a photo. It had clearly been murder, the bloke's head had been stove in. Nasty. Either it was another man and Reg had been gay, or it could have been a woman in self-defence. Either was possible as the bloke had had his flies open, after all. In all his time in the Reston area, there hadn't been a murder, so this was a big one and he had just hoped they could keep the case; it would be a feather in his cap if it all went well. He stayed till the SOCO boys had done a full job and the body taken off to the mortuary.

Half an hour after this discovery, Geoff had driven back over to Reston and then on again to the crime scene for a second look, and it was then that he had noticed the garage just by the old village pump was still closed, no cars on the forecourt, no lights. Nothing odd about that, it was Sunday after all.

He recalled something he had heard in the pub, that the owner, Mr Dawson's wife, had left with the children. Perhaps it was shut up for good? Perhaps that was all connected?

He'd personally checked around for the owner of the gloves and talked to the owner of the bus pass. And he'd been told that the owner of the gloves was Paula. But when he talked to Paula, she had been with her dad and they both flatly denied they were hers.

"I did once have some a bit like that, but no, they aren't mine."

DNA tests on them had revealed no DNA from her; it was corrupted with Reg's blood, so a dead end there. He was proud to remember that he had taken the girl's mobile to check. It showed that the mobile had been at the bus stop. Could be useful or innocent, he didn't know yet. He instinctively knew there was some involvement, but Geoff couldn't as yet prove anything.

Dr Warren, the toxicologist, had talked at length about his findings. Reg Dawson had been intoxicated, he was a smoker, liver damaged, recent sexual activity, left-handed, needed the dentist again, had a recent scar up his right arm, and his hands were used to handling oil.

What Geoff had wanted, though, was fingerprints to see if they came up with anything because, as yet, they had no certified identity for their stiff. Their first grip on the case had been when Renshaw came up with a match on the national database. The initial earlier charge of handling stolen goods was enough for him to have been entered on the national database, and that gave them their match.

"Bingo!"

Dawson, the garage man, had once been questioned and charged with handling, but the matter had been dropped. If he remembered, and something was nagging at him, there'd been some question about underage girls. Geoff tried to recall if he remembered how this had been dropped. Oh yes, it came back to him now, he'd had a good word put in for him by the magistrate, Douglas Riley.

They had driven first to the garage, and it was indeed still very much closed, not a sign of life. They asked around the other shops; all shook their heads and said they hadn't seen Dawson that week, and yes, they did know that his wife and kids were gone, but no, they didn't know where he was.

Their excitement had mounted. Off in the car again.

"Where to?" asked Renshaw, who sensed that this could be good for his promotion chances.

The other passengers in the train were getting restive now and broke into his thoughts.

"When are we getting going?"

"Does anyone know why we've been stopped here?"

They were distracting Geoff, but he personally was glad of the downtime to put himself fully back in the picture. He put his coat on the seat next to him.

That was when he had first come across Rosemary Riley. She'd been terrified to see him. Much like that film-maker had said, but he could see that all she cared about was the whereabouts of Evie. She couldn't look Geoff straight in the eyes, always offering tea or plumping up the cushions or checking in with that damn crucifix.

Then, without warning, she had crumpled as she said, "Everything is wrong."

Anyway, by the time he left the Riley house, he had felt in his gut that Evie was somehow involved with the bus stop killing. He had asked to see Evie's mobile but no, that was a dead end because she had taken it with her. But Evie was nowhere to be found. He remembered going up to see Evie's room, thinking that perhaps a hairbrush would give them DNA, but when he looked at it, it was pristine, clean and tidy. Rosemary saw his disappointment.

"It was me," she said, "I tidied it, ready for when she comes back."

Well, thought Geoff, *I've seen that before. Pity though, DNA would have clinched it probably.*

He remembered they had been suddenly swamped with work. Another police station had closed and dumped their work on them. It was a matter of prioritising cases and that had been his responsibility. If there was nothing immediate coming through, he'd check in a month to see if anything had turned up, he decided. If not, he'd enter it on the cold crime list and wait. First thing in the morning, he decided to put Creech on to a limited twenty-four-hour intensive search of the case; he promised he would see to this. Only, that night his wife had given him shepherd's pie, a bought one, slightly past its sell-by date. And Geoff was confined to quarters the next day and, what with how bad he was feeling, he forgot to call the station.

He knew Jane wanted him to forget all about policing; she felt they had earned a retirement and what she wanted was a cruise. Somewhere warm. Geoff smiled at this; they would do it, but not just yet. Jane fancied a Mediterranean cruise. She had been a very loyal, long-suffering wife and as he pictured her, he remembered something else. She had comforted him when news of the forensic team's strike came through. Without forensics, they couldn't do anything with this case. He felt he had let everyone down, but she had told him firmly otherwise. Forensics had let him down. She was right, of course, but it didn't help how he felt. Filing it under cold crimes was always a failure of sorts.

He was still of the mind that the murder of Reg Dawson, done the very same night that this girl had gone missing, had done what murder always does – stir up a million unrelated secrets from all connected and unconnected with the case. And he had reassured Amanda Rosberg that Evie's disappearance and Reg Dawson's murder had been entirely unrelated, and that it was more likely that Paula was in the frame if she ever returned to England. Now he wished he hadn't done that; he was not so sure. Budget cuts didn't run to trips to the States just for questioning. But all he had had on her was the gloves and the phone, and they had gone missing from the evidence vault. Was that forensics too? Had they not returned them after testing for DNA?

He wasn't sure now that he had been right to say all that to Amanda. He recalled their conversation. It was odd, looking back, that he had never seen a photo of Evie Riley other than the one in the newspaper, and he was unsure why that had been. The parents said they hadn't got any. But now that his mind was back to it, he remembered that when he had asked for a photo, the wife had started to get up and find one, but it had been the husband who had wanted none of it and motioned with his hand that she should stay sitting. And she had obeyed without a word. And then came what he had thought at the time was an unrelated event, but now he was certain, even though it had been dark and raining, that he had witnessed Evie Riley running away. It was only now, as the film played in his mind, that he remembered seeing a young girl and she hadn't minded getting wet. The girl had half turned her face away as the headlights lit her up. At the time, it hadn't meant anything, but now… now he wondered, had that been Evie Riley?

All his untidy feelings around the resurrection of this case now focussed on trying to put it right. He should try to find Evie Riley and determine once and for all what part she had played in Reg Dawson's murder. If any. Whether she had been his victim and whether she had defended herself or whether it was something else entirely. Reg had had sex with someone. Had it been Evie?

The train lurched, stopped, then started again, the sound of cheering broke through his thoughts. He'd leave it there for now. Soon it was his stop, and he wandered home. Geoff thought about Creech. Bright young Creech. He'd be the one to talk to. See if anything had moved on after he'd left.

*

The next day, Geoff managed to track Creech down. Geoff had had half a thought that he might have left the Force and gone on with his writing, become one of those turncoat authors using all the police knowledge he had to become a bestselling author. He'd never thought about it before, but it was possible. Geoff made a few calls, Googled Creech's name.

"Bingo!"

Creech had been bright and, above all, ambitious. He'd ended up with the Met. And doing well. Geoff felt a pang of envy and acknowledged that his own time was past, and all the what ifs and what might have beens had now settled in the armchair. All the same, he arranged to meet up with Creech to see if his memory tallied with his own.

As Geoff travelled by tube up to Victoria Embankment, joining the District line at Hammersmith and then round to Westminster, he felt his energy rising. He felt alive again, more relevant; early retirement had been more Jane's idea than his. They had almost booked the cruise straight off but hadn't gone, and then settled into a sort of boredom that neither dared question. But here he was, and it felt as though things could happen. The buzz was palpable.

He'd arranged to meet Creech in a coffee shop just down from the Met's imposing headquarters. *Another time*, thought Geoff, *another life*. As he went to the coffee shop, he immediately recognised his old junior, still slim and trim but with an air of authority about him now.

They shook hands with genuine pleasure both sides. As their coffees arrived, there was a bit of catch up on both sides, more on Creech's than his, as more had happened, Geoff noticed.

"So, what is it then, Geoff, that brings you knocking at my door?" Creech checked his watch and smiled. He still had a boyish charm.

"Do you remember, just before I retired, that murder that we were never sure was victim or perpetrator? The one that looked like a tramp but had a garage in the village? Reg Dawson?"

The name brought recognition.

Geoff went on, "And that girl that disappeared about the same time?"

Creech nodded, stayed silent, straightened his coffee cup in the saucer. And Geoff explained how Amanda had come asking questions, and it had stirred up both memory and regret that they hadn't solved it.

"That was the time that forensics went AWOL, wasn't it?"

"That's my point, that's my point. We accepted at the time there was nothing we could do because the gloves had been lost once the strike was over, hadn't been returned to evidence. But what if," and Geoff leant in as though the café might hear, "what if they came to light? Wouldn't that change things? Could we not then open up the case, chase up Paula's DNA, re-examine the phone records of both girls?"

"Why is this getting to you? You should be out on the golf course!"

"Well, pride is one thing; it always sat badly with me that the big one got away. But over the last few days I know it was something else too. We failed that runaway, Evie Riley. We failed her. And I want to find her. A friend of hers came to see me, asking questions, and it's stirred it all up again." Geoff paused.

Creech prompted, "And…?"

"Well, here you might remember better than me. Do you remember when we searched Dawson's garage and his home, and we talked to the wife who had walked out on him, that we unearthed something very unsavoury?"

Creech looked at his coffee, added more milk.

"It wasn't just the filthy calendars, the private stash of magazines, you know what I'm saying… It was more than that. We took his computer away and it was more than clear from that hard drive that Dawson was in some sort of neo-paedophile ring. There were names on there, photos. You were the computer whizz, you looked at it. Why didn't we take that further? Clear prosecution for that. And, come to think of it, what would have happened to that hard drive? Where did it go?"

Geoff had not meant to make this an attack on Creech, and he could see that, defensively, Creech could shut up shop on this one now and he would have the position to close it off. Geoff needed to bring the conversation round again, see if he could get what he wanted from Creech. Geoff called to the waitress before Creech could intervene.

"Two more coffees, please."

"Look, I have to be back in the office in ten minutes." His voice had changed, become more official.

"That all came out wrong, Creech – Paul – I was just

thinking aloud. But the prosecution for the paedophile ring, do you remember why that came to nothing?"

In the gap of time with the waitress clearing the old cups, putting down the two new ones, it came back to Geoff. The Super had been breathing down Creech's neck, wanting to pull him out of examining computer material – "Silly waste of time" – and get him on to some other nameless bit of enquiry.

More gently this time, Geoff said, "It wasn't your fault at all, was it?"

Creech shook his head, looked around. "Look, this is difficult for me to talk about; I'm still in the Force. Little was written down, I do remember that."

Geoff knew now what his next course of action would have to be, and he didn't want to over-alarm Creech at this stage.

"These coffees are on me. It was good catching up. Very helpful. And don't you worry."

A flicker of something crossed Creech's face but he decided to trust his old boss. They shook hands and Creech, looking very smart, crossed the road and returned to the office, while Geoff, in his soft windcheater jacket and weekend trousers, walked back to the underground station.

He would call into the station before any alert could be sounded.

Geoff then called Renshaw who, while doing alright, had not risen to the dizzying heights of Creech. Renshaw had been Geoff's sergeant on this case. A good worker, Renshaw was. Reliable. Not gifted but good. He had been transferred and was now working in another division. After the pleasantries and brief chit chat, Renshaw asked what he could do for him, which relieved Geoff as he wanted to get to the point and down to business and waste no more time.

"I need to look at the old evidence of a case again. Reg Dawson's murder. It was one that we worked on together and I know you can get access. I want the numbers of two mobile phones, and if they have turned up, I want to see some gloves, but in particular I need to look at a computer hard drive and any notes made on the contents. Can you do that for me?"

Renshaw whistled. "You don't want much, do you? That could cost me my job."

"Would it raise eyebrows if you had a good reason to do this for yourself? Like believing a possible link had turned up?"

"Well… that's the only way it could happen. But what link?"

"Check out Douglas Riley, magistrate and all-round suspicious person. He just keeps turning up on the edge of trouble."

"Who's he?"

"He's the father of the girl who went missing, the girl who might or might not be implicated in Dawson's death."

"No, Geoff. I'd like to help but it's too dodgy, there's no real link there."

"What if you suspected his name was on the hard drive? Would you be failing in your duty if you did not check this out?"

"Look, Geoff, leave this with me. I don't know if I can do this. It'll be dodgy, but it's possible I might be able to make it work, but only if I do it. You can't be anywhere near. I'll call you tomorrow."

PART II

CHAPTER 1

Amanda had decided to press on with building finance for the film. It was true there were still nagging questions in her mind, but for now she felt there was no need for these to stop the film being made. It was exciting for her, as well as for Viv.

"You are so right. We need to move forward with the film but first we need finance, backing. I'm off to New York in ten days' time and…" Here, unusually for Amanda, she stumbled as she reached the point of her call; her voice became softer. "I'd like you to come with me."

There was a long pause before Viv answered, "Oh. Oh yes. Of course."

She had no passport; she had never flown and most certainly she had never been to the States.

"Great idea."

Clicking off from the call, she wondered what she had just agreed to. How much on both sides was work, and how much personal? She shrugged. What the hell. She would go through with it, it felt like fate. But a sudden thought came to her, and she stopped in her tracks. How would she get a passport?

At the time of becoming V. J. Wheeler, she hadn't considered that she would be scrutinised all over again. How could she manage a passport? And in such a short time? And get some decent clothes?

She passed a great hour or two in Portobello Market looking for some clothes other than black, she liked the lack of pressure there, then down through Acklam Road to the more raucous expression of the West Indian culture, the food, the cheap scarves, the hanging out, the reggae music, the pot. She paused at the clothes stalls, held out the arms of a jacket, let them go. Seeing a beer stall on the right, without hesitation she ordered one.

As Viv downed the cold liquid, it felt like it was slicing the icy sides of a ravine. Then, with no conscious prompting, another shadow memory she couldn't get into focus engulfed her. It was the smell, not so much of her own drink, but the stale smell of all the other beers of the day all around her. She'd had that feeling before at the Founders Arms.

She drew her jacket closer round her. She was breathing heavily, panic rising, didn't want to attract attention but her impulse was to get away and get hold of the memory. This interplay of past and present was happening more often now, it was unsettling her. And then, with dazzling clarity, she connected the smell with rain. She closed her eyes, unwilling to let this thread go. It was raining hard, she was wet…

"Are you OK, missus?"

A huge, kind hunk of a young man was checking. He wasn't to know that he had interrupted anything. A second later and she might have put it all together.

"Fine. Thanks."

With a degree of equilibrium restored, she realised that she had accomplished nothing in the way of new clothes here in the market. She shrugged; she'd go as she was, they could like it or lump it, this was who she was. Just as she was leaving, she caught sight of herself in a long mirror, by the side of a stall. She looked older now. Standing back from her image, she studied herself again but could not look for long. In her mind, she had the self-image of being tall, slender, but here was the contradiction to that. It wasn't the clothes that were wrong; the clothes were the clothes. *It's me. I don't want to look. I don't want people to look. At me.*

*

Getting a passport was an exposing and risky situation. As panic clouded her thoughts, she thought perhaps she could go along with the trip only to say at the last minute that her passport had been stolen. No, Amanda would begin to doubt her.

"Lose the hat!"

The photographer assumed it was no problem, but it was. She did as she was told though, she had no choice, and emerged with the photos, and got them signed by Nancy, who remembered when Viv had first argued her way into representation all those years ago and had been delighted to handle the final negotiations of film rights with Amanda. Nancy had no suspicion that V. J. Wheeler had once been Evie Riley, why would she?

Viv decided to do a walk through at Victoria and get the passport sooner than waiting for the postal system; it would have the date of issue on it, but Amanda need never see that, and besides, she might assume, if she did see it, that it was a second passport. It hadn't been an easy process, they had asked for the original birth certificate, and Viv had come up with an elaborate story of a house fire, again unwittingly authenticated by Nancy, to explain why Viv only had a doctored copy of her birth certificate.

*

On the plane, when Viv had been handed the three-times-folded-over sheet of information that Homeland Security needed filling in, her stomach had clenched. This was her first time in America, and she was full of fear. She took a deep breath, saw that Amanda next to her was calm in her approach to this form; no panic, no drama. With her Mont Blanc pen, she proceeded to put the letters of each word in the designated computer space. Viv looked out of the plane window, still managing the panic of being trapped for six hours. She asked the stewardess for a small bottle of wine. She felt rather than saw Amanda look over at her – was that a criticism? It was grey and unwelcoming as they began to land, the rain passing horizontally across the windows. Of course she was feeling sick, sweaty at the list of questions, but she couldn't afford to let Amanda to question why she was behaving oddly. Not now. Not now that she had come this far. As though sensing something, Amanda looked across at Viv and the moment seemed to hover like a bird, before Amanda looked up, placed one hand on Viv's and placed a kiss on her cheek. Viv slightly turned towards her, then turned away.

For a fleeting moment, Amanda remembered Reston, Rosemary and Douglas, and felt guilty at having somehow betrayed Viv's trust and prayed that Viv would never have to find out. On the other hand, Amanda argued with herself, her actions had only been due diligence.

Rummaging in her case, Viv found the old Bic and proceeded to commit the fabrication of who she was to paper once more. V. J. Wheeler, born in Clerkenwell. Her age – no problem there, that would not be a lie. But her birthday would be. Viv was born a Scorpio, but her new identity made her a Libra. And so it continued. She had memorised all the details of fabricated parents, various addresses that she would need and so it was with elation and relief that she came to the last question. What is your reason for entering the USA? She smiled as she remembered Peter Ustinov's answer: 'Sole purpose is to overthrow the government.' Funny then, but very not funny now. Viv prayed that all these details would pass muster when they landed.

Once in the airport, Viv tensed at the sight of armed police with their truncheons at every turn, their guns visible, walking between the desks, an air of aggression seeping out like sweat. Viv had gone to the restrooms immediately before the queue began. She prayed silently that no questions would be asked, no samples of anything taken, her documents approved. It felt enough to just get through the demands of this journey without arousing undue suspicion. Amanda went first. Her document checked and approved, she moved towards the recognition camera, the iris scanner. Viv followed, she handed the form to the official who, without looking at her face, shoved it back aggressively.

"Complete this form again!"

For a second, she felt like the escapee who hadn't made it over the wall.

"It is complete!" She shoved it back, feeling the tide of anger rising.

"Incomplete."

By this time, the official holding out the offending paper was pointing to where she should stand, outside the queue. *Have they lost all ability to communicate?* Viv looked around, no sign of Amanda now, only a female policeman approaching her, emanating attack, her hand on the gun on her hip. Viv once more tried the full sentence approach querying why she had been shoved aside with no satisfactory solution.

"But why?"

At this point the cop pulled her gun from her belt. "Over here, ma'am!"

How could the use of 'ma'am' sugar-coat this assault?

Rapidly finding her feet in this unfamiliar situation, Viv commanded the cop, "Put your weapon away. There is no need for this and a poor advertisement for your country. This is my first visit. At least have the courtesy – no, the intelligence – to fully explain how we get through this next step!"

While knowing she was countering with an aggression that could land her in water that was too deep to survive in, she could not pull back now. She had encountered worse. The weapon was restored to the holster and the cop explained that all the questions were one line out. It had to be done again.

"At last. On one condition. I will not return to the end of the queue and stand for a further two hours. Once completed, I will find you and you will restore me to the head of the queue."

There was clearly something cathartic for the cop in meeting counter aggression. She nodded assent. Viv texted Amanda to go on without her. She would be a while. She knew the address and would meet her at the hotel. All this was with an assurance that Viv did not feel. Eventually, emerging to the curved pavement outside the terminal, she felt awe and disappointment at the same time. It was odd, having seen so many films, that New York and the line of yellow cabs did not seem that new to her. Everything looked disappointingly familiar.

*

They met at six in the Atlantic Bar of the Roosevelt Hotel on 45th Street. Viv felt aeroplane tired, stale, English, but there was Amanda, sitting at the bar under the row of low concave lamps, looking dew fresh. Her stomach flipped. Viv had a habit of countering the feeling of wrong-footedness with aggression and heard herself accusing Amanda, before they had even ordered a drink, of abandoning her at the airport. Amanda let it run; she had to manage this. Viv was her product, without her she would not raise the money for the film.

"Tell me your favourite drink," she purred and, turning to the barman, "two whiskies, please. Glenmorangie?" This last question was to Viv.

Viv nodded, annoyed with herself that she was pleased Amanda had remembered which whiskey she liked. As they sat there, with a piano player playing at the very far end of the massive, low-ceilinged bar room, the drink did its work and evened out their differences. Viv began to feel just a margin less of a fish out of water. It was still surreal, being here, though.

"Reasonable flight." It was more a statement than a question. Amanda had been to the States many times. "So, what happened back there? At immigration?" She drained her glass, laughing, turned to Viv. "Enemy alien?"

Viv shrugged. "We're here now, aren't we?"

It was embarrassing to admit what had happened. She felt nine years old again.

"Shall we eat here or find somewhere else?"

"Here's good."

Viv could feel she was beginning to find her rhythm. The restaurant was all chrome, low lights, deep carpet.

"So, what's the plan – tomorrow? Who are you planning to impress?"

"We have two meetings, one morning, one afternoon. The afternoon one is the more important, so let's use the morning as a run-through. Perhaps for all that it will go more smoothly. The morning is with someone I've only recently made contact with. Made his money on Wall Street. Only thirty-five. Wants to break into big-time producing. Hal Mossiman."

"And the second?"

"Ah, now, they know what they're doing. Financing films is their main investment."

"Corporate versus pirate?"

Amanda laughed. "We're going to get along." She placed her slender hand over Viv's as she had in the plane. Amanda let her gaze linger on Viv for a few seconds. "I like you." A light kiss. "Very much."

The food was welcome. Viv had held back from the desiccated carbohydrates of the plane. The wine on the plane followed by the two drinks at the bar were probably enough, but a glass of red with her lamb tipped her over the edge and suddenly tiredness such as she had never known, even on the streets when she had gone days of weariness and napping, engulfed her. Amanda still wanted to know why Viv had taken so very long to join her. She would not have thought anything of it had it not been for the knowledge she had gained about Viv. What had she been doing? But when she had asked Viv, it had sounded like an accusation, and she could see that Viv had been embarrassed.

It was late. *It feels later*, thought Viv, as she scanned the room of late-night diners. Viv checked her watch, half eleven.

"Why are you checking the time?" Amanda smiled to soften the accusation contained in her question. "Do you have to be somewhere?"

She leant towards Viv, reaching for her hand again. Viv moved to reach for the linen napkin but was unsure what to do with it, and replaced it, crumpled.

She had had no need of it, she knew that, but everything was feeling wrong suddenly.

"We should not argue."

Not for the first time, Viv noticed Amanda's way of chairing their conversations, summing up their experience. She looked away and out of the window; there was not much to see except the lights of Manhattan against the almost black sky.

"We aren't." Viv bristled; her tone was short.

"Well, discuss then." Amanda laughed, softened her approach.

"Today has been exhausting – shall we leave it at that?"

"Of course, of course."

Amanda leant back and beckoned to the waiter. "Two brandies, please. Cognac?"

The soft-shoed waiter appeared to have wheeled himself into view. Viv nodded. Unused to drinking brandy late at night, but more unwilling to show it, she acquiesced.

"I prefer whiskey, but…"

Amanda was about to recall the waiter.

"No, no, it's fine. Cognac." She thought of Lloyd for a second.

Viv played with the unused dessert spoon and fork. Amanda began to raise her glass, but Viv was lost in thought, her eyes closed. She took one sip, then slowly another, allowing the warmth to run around her body like a race car round a track. She wanted to feel Amanda's lips on hers. She raised her brandy glass and drank it in one, no swilling it around, no delicate sipping. Finishing her own brandy, Amanda suggested they call it a night; it had been a long day.

Viv stood first, held on to the corner of the table.

Amanda stood up too and held out her hand to steady Viv. The kiss came gently, swiftly. Viv's world paused and in that moment she knew she would always remember that kiss.

CHAPTER 2

Viv had slept in a way that felt almost unconscious. When she woke the next morning, she struggled to separate reality from the intense dream. Had she recalled something vital again?

She saw from the bedside electric clock it was just five o'clock in the morning. She lay flat on her back, staring at the ceiling, trying to make sense of it all. She had drunk too much yesterday. Then her hand touched another. She jumped, sat upright, ready to strike, but what she saw was Amanda, now asleep herself. She was fully clothed – but what the…? How had that happened?

Viv moved away, out of the bed, angry at the intrusion, drawing her bathrobe to her. The mix of emotions was so utterly confusing that she pretended not to know what she had just seen. Returning from the bathroom with a glass of water, she saw that the light had become stronger through the curtains. Should she shake Amanda awake, send her back to her room? What was she doing there? How had she even got into her room?

Just as she approached the bed, ready to rouse her, she looked down on Amanda's beautiful face and the well of loneliness in Viv suddenly became acute, unbearable.

Amanda stirred, and, now half awake, was embarrassed for a brief moment.

"I was worried about you…"

Seeing Viv's puzzled face, Amanda gestured with her head to the adjoining rooms' door by way of explanation.

"I'm sorry, I didn't mean to scare you, I was just checking on you."

Viv reached over to kiss her Amanda. A brief pause and they connected gently.

"I have to go, prepare for today."

As Viv stumbled about the hotel room preparing herself for the day, she remembered the dream that had left her feeling so ragged and scribbled down her thoughts before she forgot them. It reminded her of that odd moment at the Founders Arms, and then at the market, and now it wouldn't leave her alone, like spring bulbs anxious to force their way up to the sunshine.

She knew this was important. *I know exactly what you did.* Were these two things connected?

She walked to the shower and let the hot water run down her face, her back, her arms, and hearing it go down the sluice, she hoped that she would now leave the dream behind her. Only, it didn't leave her and after some time in the shower, she knew with a certainty that what she had dreamed had been total recall. She *had* known Reg Dawson. And Reg Dawson was vile. And she had managed to get away. But why, if she had got away, was she still afraid of that man? The dream had done nothing to erase her unease; instead, it had magnified it. Amanda knocked on the door.

"Coming! Give me five minutes."

Viv would Google Reg Dawson and see what that uncovered.

*

"So!" This was Amanda, looking slender, unhurried, purposeful, waiting for Viv in the high-ceilinged, marbled lobby. "Let's just go over this…" Over breakfast, she pulled out some papers in a clear folder. "Our first meeting is with Hal Mossiman. He's eager, like a puppy, we can try out our approach on him before Tordstein and Elder in the afternoon. Hal is two years out of Harvard, bright, has two films in ongoing production, but they have yet to be released so, in a way, he doesn't have a track record. He has to prove himself to us. So," and here she turned to face Viv, "what do we want from him?"

Viv was a writer not a producer. She shrugged. "You should know that."

It came out curt, but Amanda rolled with the punch.

"I do. We need three quarters of a million dollars, half up front and half in six months' time. All we need is finance, we do the rest, but this is where the lawyers come in – and I have a good one up my sleeve. Shall we go?"

The question was almost rhetorical. Amanda, in business mode, was up and moving towards to the revolving door of the hotel, moving towards the first cab on the rank.

"Fifty-eight on 5th."

Not that far away.

Much of Viv's conscious energy was taken up with not appearing to be the rookie she actually was, and not letting jetlag creep up on her. Cool was the order of the day and on the ride there she chose to leave the conversation to Amanda and the Puerto Rican driver. Pictures of his wife and Our Lady stuck on side by side on the dashboard. A rosary swung from the mirror. The car smelt of warm leather and pastrami. The building was like many on 5th Avenue whose main intention was to impress and be impermeable. They did, however, navigate the gatekeeper and the view from the window on the forty-second floor was just of sky. They had rocketed up to the penthouse floor.

Hal had put everything on show: the choice of area, the choice of office, the size of desk, the choice of questionably original paintings that lined the main wall. If, thought Viv, they were the originals, she and Amanda should watch his profit margin.

He walked around his desk, hand out.

"Miss Rosberg? Miss Wheeler? Please sit down."

Amanda noticed his mild tan but was unclear whether he had recently holidayed in the Caribbean or whether he favoured a spray tan. He pressed a buzzer and as the girl came in, he ordered coffee for them all without enquiring as to whether that was their choice.

"So..." He beamed at them both, showing teeth that had been not only well organised, but bleached to a fine degree. "Tell me about your film. Does it have a title yet?"

Amanda and Viv began speaking together. "Well, it's—"

Amanda followed the awkward moment with, "Shall I?"

And as she took ownership of the story, Viv's story, Viv felt as though her insides had been stolen from her without permission. It was ridiculous, of course, she knew how they had arrived at this moment and she was being unreasonable. But she needed to control where and how her story went, even in talks like this. She took advantage of the coffee, knowing she would need more than one today to keep going.

She took a long look at Hal Mossiman and decided that he wouldn't know a good story from a bad one, all he wanted to know was whether he could pin a big name to it. Amanda had managed to combine a sort of précis, along with a detailed flavour of the story and where the film sat in the market. She made a mental note to talk to Amanda later, but for now she could see that it was a simple transaction with Hal, who alternately leant forward over the desk, showing his expensive watch, and sat back as though he were in a producer's chair.

He listened through to the story then shot out, "Comparisons? Rivals? Anyone attached to it?"

In the pause that followed, his eyes went to Viv, trying to sum her up. He plainly wasn't that comfortable with arty types, certainly not pent-up aggressives who wore ambiguous headgear. He preferred the nuts and bolts of production, percentages, box office. Americans.

Amanda was no newcomer to this scenario and handled the responses with ease, but at some point she was aware that Viv was feeling like a spare guest, so, turning to bring Viv into the conversation, she asked, "And, of course, you would be interested to know that much of this book was the direct experience of the writer?"

A chasm had suddenly opened up under Viv's feet. What was Amanda playing at? They'd already had that conversation. Nothing personal. Hal appeared to want more from her.

"And would you be part of the promotion on that level eventually?"

Viv decided, whatever the financial risk in this meeting, not to defer any more control issues and shut the question down with, "Miss Rosberg understands that I do not do publicity."

Hal's heavy black eyebrows shot up; it was rare that he met with such a stonewall at the first meeting. After all, they were wanting the money, he could find other films.

"What Viv means, Hal, is that this is a film that promotes itself with the everyday evidence of unrest and violence."

"Sure."

There was an awkward silence. Hal pressed his buzzer.

"So, can we leave this proposal with you?"

Amanda was standing now, Viv as well. Hal's hand was out. They shook hands, not one of the three entirely sure how the meeting had really gone.

Hal's parting shot to Amanda was, "You either have a marketing story here," his head inclined towards Viv, "or a real problem on your hands. Your call."

The second meeting, scheduled for three o'clock, gave them time for a quick bite to eat.

Over chicken noodles, Amanda began, "Viv, you have to give something, you know…"

She hadn't meant her tone to sound so peevish, but she could see that a complete blanket embargo from Viv would not get them the backing they needed.

Viv carried on eating. "Like what?"

"Well." Amanda shrugged. "Like, for example, what it was like to live on the street, give them some idea of the danger and the rawness of that life, give them some colour, they're just money men with no imagination… please? Make it up if you have to!"

As Amanda reeled off this plea, Viv looked at her, taking in the gulf between them.

"I'd be telling you as well, wouldn't I?"

"Look, don't hold it against me that we have had different lives. Get real, sell yourself."

This was Amanda not just in business mode but, she realised as she heard her own words, in personal mode too. She was, in that moment, irritated by what she saw as pretence, feyness. She couldn't stop herself, despite what was at stake in less than an hour.

"You need to show people who you are, who you were…"

Still nothing from Viv.

She leant forward over the small table. "Well, who *were* you, Viv? Who *are* you?"

There was now a tension between them that had not been there before. Viv felt there was something that Amanda was not saying to her, and they needed to clear the air before the next meeting.

"Well, what is it? Speak up."

"No." Amanda laid down her knife and fork. "No, *you* need to speak up. I have gone along with, understood, whatever, your need for privacy, but now, after that meeting this morning, I begin to feel it is a charade. It is getting… in between us."

Amanda's colour had risen. The knowledge that she had of the Reston Riley family visit had stayed with her and she longed for Viv and her to be on the same page. Why couldn't Viv just come clean? Or did she genuinely not remember? Was there some drama? And was this amnesic cognitive dissonance?

The waitress came over. "Everything good?"

"Yes," they replied in unison.

The waitress shrugged.

"Charade?!"

"Yes, a cover if you like."

"You know what you make me feel like at this moment? Like a pimp's toy. Dance, little monkey, dance! I won't do it."

Little more was said. Amanda checked her watch and, deciding to risk that the downtown traffic would be light, she had to say something now or the moment would be lost.

"I work best with honesty, total honesty. I've laid out my cards such as they are for you to see but all I get is a stone wall. Why? Don't you trust me?"

Viv said nothing.

Amanda continued, "If I'm honest, it is not just about the work, the film, the finance, whatever – I like you and, well, it feels like you are somehow rejecting me. Just say now if you don't want to proceed."

The ambiguity of this remark hung in the air, too delicate to touch for either of them. Amanda called for the bill. She had suddenly had enough; the Nordic calm was caught in a storm of her own making.

She pulled back, found her credit card and just at that moment, Viv, talking over her and the waitress, oblivious for the moment of her surroundings, began, "I can't. I would. I want to... but I can't remember... well, I can remember some things of the past, of course. But I know that what I can't remember is important – and dangerous."

Amanda waved the waitress away, the electronic transaction going through.

"Just... some things, of course, they are in the book, but before that sometimes I recall, but then I wonder if it is fantasy, imagination, hoping... Anything but terra firma. I think I don't want to remember. Whatever it is, I can't. I've tried." Viv had gone further than ever before. "Enough for you?"

They left the restaurant, hailed a cab and made for downtown in silence to meet Troy Tordstein, with Amanda thinking she might have made a huge mistake bringing Viv. It wasn't working. She would do the talking, again, and do the best she could – but what the hell was Viv bringing to the table? She'd paid her air fares, her hotel, and for what? The bloody work would *not* speak for itself! She seethed in silence, mollified only somewhat by realising that all the expenses were tax allowable.

The offices of Tordstein and Elder, across from Wall Street and discreetly tucked away in Carlisle Street, were quite different from the flash of this morning. Instead, there was wall-to-wall discretion, a smaller office, leather everywhere and a smooth assistant who appeared to wheel them into the meeting.

"Good afternoon." Troy Tordstein, tall and blond like a quarterback, held out his hand to each of them in turn. Viv noted that there was not one shred of evidence in the room that this man was involved in the film industry. Just like this morning but less flashy. Probably Brown's. What Troy was involved with was discreet old money.

Amanda began her practised, polished pitch. He was attentive, he appreciated her professionalism. Viv, sitting silent, noted that Troy was not that engaged with the story of the film, tapping his fingers soundlessly on the desk. He was more interested in the line-up of director and headlining stars.

Amanda, this time, was not about to give Viv an opportunity to embarrass her again and maintained her flow, so much so that she was not prepared for Viv's interruption.

"May I add something here?"

You could have heard a pin drop.

"Please, go ahead."

Neither he nor Amanda could guess what was coming but they were all ears, for quite separate reasons.

"This book – this film – this book, that I have put my heart and soul into – and much of my own experience – I wish to be made exactly according to how I see it. But we all know that this is not possible. I have given my trust to Amanda on this occasion, and she will, I know, produce you an award-winning film."

Neither Troy nor Amanda knew quite how to take this new direction. Was it relevant? Did it add anything to the mix?

"It is not easy for me to do this; in fact, I have never done it. If you had lived surviving by your wits alone, you would know exactly what I mean, and quite how big a deal it is to trust in this way. I want you to take her, us, this film, that seriously."

Troy looked at Viv with new interest. *So, she isn't just the sidekick, she can talk*, was what he was thinking, and suddenly he could see opportunity, dollars.

Viv sat back in her chair; she was done for now but caught the expression on Amanda's face. A mixture of relief and pride. In the back of the cab afterwards, Amanda turned to Viv.

"I'm so proud of you – for that in there, in the meeting. It clinched it for us. I know it did."

Deflecting the warmth, Viv rejoined. "Please don't patronise me. I'm not a child."

It seemed to Amanda that if their relationship proved to be ongoing, it would be at the cost of two steps forward, one step back. She feared that she was already falling in love this prickly woman.

CHAPTER 3

It was six-thirty when they walked into the dining room of their hotel.

"We should celebrate!" Amanda looked sideways, an invitation in her smile.

Viv hoped that her face was giving nothing away. It seemed that, despite herself, she would soon be made to remember the particular events that she had been running away from. Was that a good thing? Was she ready for that?

"We did well today. If Hal comes good on his promise, we have two-thirds of the money we need to make the film. And if Troy is with us, we most certainly can put a start date to this film." Aware of the need to make the link between book and film, give credit, she added, "Your name will be up in lights!"

Viv snapped back, "Why? Why, after all I have laboured to explain to you, would you say that? Why would you think that was an enticement to go further?"

Viv's colour was up, her face like thunder. Having signed the contract, she had given away her power to have any real say.

Amanda paused. "That was thoughtless. It was a figure of speech, that's all. I will honour all we agreed."

She moved from sitting opposite Viv, came and sat next to her in the upholstered high-back seat. She put her hand on Viv's.

"I'm sorry. I didn't mean to frighten you. I did frighten you, didn't I?"

It was one of those moments that was impossible to come back from. Amanda's instinct was to protect this difficult woman. From the outside, she was aware that she herself might be the one who looked as though she needed protecting, but it wasn't so. She put her arm, then both arms, around Viv. Viv moved apart, her emotions, thoughts, were in turmoil as Amanda released her hold.

Viv beckoned the waiter.

"A double whiskey, please and…"

Amanda added, "A glass of red wine."

Amanda broke the silence.

"There is a total mystery to you though, Viv Wheeler, and I do mean to find out. But only when you are ready, of course."

She was being duplicitous in her anxiety for them both to be on the same page, her guilt and unease to be assuaged. What would Viv think if in fact she realised that Amanda had half the puzzle solved? Should she tell her?

Amanda decided to lead the way to confidences being shared by talking about herself. Viv listened, her anxiety receding, and she was entranced — no, seduced — despite herself. She loved the swoop of Amanda's voice, the flattening of the vowels, knew that she would probably always love hearing it. She imagined that she could go to sleep like a baby listening to her voice. How could anyone fall in love this fast?

"My parents, well, I, was born in Norway, but my father was Russian. Russian Jew. My mother was Norwegian. My father could smell danger a mile away and we left to come to

England." She laughed. "That's why I sound English like you. You *are* English, aren't you?"

Viv nodded and despite the amount of whiskey she had put on board, she ignored her desire to get closer to Amanda with her own confidences. How could she possibly talk about her mum and her violent father who had left bruises on her mother and her own broken arm in places that did not show to the world?

Instead, she heard herself saying, "My parents died in a car crash in France when I was sixteen. From then on, I had no home."

Viv had no idea where this new fabrication had come from.

Amanda's face registered horror. She remembered Linny's emails. She remembered Rosemary Riley.

"Why don't we take these drinks up to my suite? Let's skip food, I am dog-tired now, it's time to relax."

They took the wide stairs to the first floor. Viv wondered if this had been a private house once. She imagined the sweep down the grand staircase to the hall, and let her fingers drift along the beechwood stair banister. For a second, she felt beautiful. Those early pioneering Americans were so voluptuously romantic with their dreams. The Roosevelt indeed.

As they entered Amanda's room, Amanda kicked off her shoes, threw her jacket on the bed and flumped down on one end of the sofa without putting on any lights. Amanda patted the seat of the small French-style sofa next to her. Viv hesitated; she had had two days full of extreme fear and shock, colour and strangeness. She looked at Amanda and remembered the moment she had first seen her at the club. Some comfort, some warmth was what she longed for, but that wasn't new. She sat, at first on the edge and then sank back into it. They sat in silence, with the profile of Manhattan at night at once glamorous and calming. The Chrysler lit up with its metal tower glinting.

Amanda turned to look at Viv's profile. Was she falling asleep?

"Out of suffering comes the strongest soul."

"Oh no." Viv's voice was soft. Her eyes were closed. Despite herself, she was smiling.

"What?"

"Cliché alert – Khalil Gibran."

They shared the joke – it broke the ice.

Amanda turned towards Viv and placed a gentle kiss on Viv's lips, holding it there for long enough to establish that Viv was not resisting. There was something so familiar about Amanda, that although there was a nagging voice telling Viv she was moving too fast, she did not pull back but allowed herself to drown in feeling safe, protected. Her head swam. Amanda held Viv closely, stroking the back of her head like a baby.

Amanda's prayer was *please never let her know that I spied on her life. Please not now that I've found her.*

At that moment, a text pinged in from Geoff. Amanda reached behind her, turned the phone face-down.

"What was that?"

"Nothing." And then, after a pause, "I booked us an extra couple of days, I thought you would like to see New York. Do you mind?"

Viv didn't answer immediately.

"Well, is that OK? I can change yours back to tomorrow if you like? I'll stay on anyway, there's a picture I want to see at the Frick."

"I'd like that."

It'll give me time to sort out my thoughts, was what Viv was thinking, *know whether this is crazy or right.*

Amanda went over to the minibar and brought back two very small brandies.

"Here's to us!"

They drank in silence, knowing how the night would go.

"I'm so glad you came, that we're here."

Viv let the relief of not being alone flood through her, just for tonight, just for now, she told herself as the world receded. What she wanted was to be held close for the whole night; there would be no regrets.

*

As Amanda stirred, ready to move, Viv looked over and folded her arms across Amanda. To wake up with someone was almost enough for Viv. She wanted to drink in that feeling.

"I want to show you New York, I'm excited!"

A morning person, clearly, was Viv's thought, but there was a lightness about her today that allowed her to respond easily.

"What's on the agenda?"

"The Frick, of course… that is first on my list. Do you have any must-sees?"

She thought for a moment. "Ellis Island."

"Oh?"

"Yes. I've been fascinated about that for as long as I can remember."

That day and the next were light, exciting, giddy, and it felt as though the world was capable of endless expansion, whizzing through time. Art galleries, walking for mile after mile, wonderful food, and then the ferry over to the island from Atlantic City. The wind was blowing, the sun was shining, the sea splashing up over the guardrail. Viv was invincible.

She grabbed the arm of a fellow traveller. "Would you mind taking a photo?"

"Sure."

"Breaking the habit of a lifetime already?" Amanda was laughing.

The camera clicked.

"Thank you."

Viv took back the camera and looked at the result. She and Amanda without a care in the world, Amanda turning half to face her, her arm around Viv's shoulder.

"Thought we were doing a no-photos rule – what happened to that?"

"My photo, my camera. I'm safe."

CHAPTER 4

Back home in England now, Viv reflected that a lot had happened. And quite fast. Her mind was over-racing, and she knew from experience that this was not a good place to make decisions from. She cradled the warmth of the coffee cup and tried to still her mind. New York had been intense, a whirlwind. She had never ever felt like this about anyone and now it was so painfully precious, she was afraid it might just disappear. She looked again at the photo. She stroked her own arm, remembering the feeling of how it felt to be stroked like that. They had made love each night, tender and close. Closing her eyes, she inhaled the memory of their lovemaking, not a moment unremembered or regretted. Could she afford to let herself be subsumed in this way?

Amanda, she knew now, felt the same. It was love. They had gone to the Frick to see Vermeer's enigmatic *Girl Interrupted at Her Music*, had wondered how such a cruel tyrant as Old Man Frick had the sensitivity to gather these paintings together. But then, she reflected, there was control and menace in that painting as well as innocence.

"Was it all just ego?" Amanda had wondered.

They had taken a boat to Ellis Island, and it was Viv's turn to be overwhelmed.

"What a cost to being American," she said after they had seen the museum with its donations from accepted migrants of tooled leather work, fine needlework, which spoke of a defined cultural heritage.

What a cost, indeed, she thought, as they stood in the echoing magisterial decision hall, and she felt herself to be one of these migrants who had travelled steerage with just hope to keep them going.

The flight home had felt precious, but Viv knew things would change the minute they landed. Would Amanda feel the same once they were back in their London lives? It was a thought she couldn't voice but told herself she had coped with worse. She would be fine. Over and over she told herself she would be fine. She would be fine.

The view from her flat which never changed, apart from the odd new building across the river or down towards the working outflow beyond the city at Dartford, Gravesend. The morning light was thin, reedy, as though it could weep thin, pale-yellow tears. She let out a breath; she should get that app that tells you when you are holding your breath from tension, and in whose company, what thoughts, made you constrict the life out of you. That'd be interesting, wouldn't it? She already missed Amanda as you would miss food or water but persuaded herself that she had just got too used to her company over the last few days. She would go for a walk, shake off this feeling.

She had schooled herself for the last fourteen years not to need anyone. Paula had seen to that. It still didn't make sense, what she had done to Viv. Viv couldn't put together how you could be as close as twins and not blink at the betrayal. Was that how Jesus had felt with Judas? It gave her a jolt to think about this, and, in turn, it made her think of her mother with her dread adherence to the church.

She realised just how deep down lonely she was, how desperately she wanted the love she had had with Amanda in New York to be something. But, and there would always be that small voice in her, would that let her down too?

Viv recalled her Portobello moment and wondered if *anyone* could have feelings for her. A small smile played on her face. She really had made a life for herself, made something of herself. The knowledge of having built an identity on the back of a dead person's birth certificate made her proud and uneasy in equal measure. She was, after all, Viv Wheeler. V. J. Wheeler, admired author.

She pushed the giant glass doors open, went out to the balcony, pulled her bathrobe around her; it was chilly this morning. She could smell the low tide, watched the gulls and birds busy with the muddy pickings. Her eye caught the palm print in the concrete. She remembered the letter, wondered if she was being watched, even now. Drew her bathrobe even tighter round her. Fear lurked like a bug in her gut. If only she could remember the one thing that was missing – why she had run away so suddenly and cut all ties with everything from her past. As much as being in her Wapping home gave her a feeling of safety, she knew that until she unearthed the sender, and the secret, she was not.

She drained the coffee cup and walked back to the small kitchen at the side of the living room, leaving it on the side to wash later. She entered her laptop as *Edward Evens* and Googled her old name, feeling sick as she saw with a jolt that there were four mentions, all detailing that she had run away. Well, she knew that, but she hadn't counted on it being so recorded, that was all. An odd feeling. She threw on some trousers, walking boots and a huge hooded black jumper instead of the fedora. Walking would clear her head. People she knew swore by meditation, but walking was her thing. Let the breath go through and the head quietens, that much she did know. She would Google Reg Dawson when she got back.

Five minutes later, she was down on the towpath and, as always, striding out towards the estuary. It was cold, but good, the air chilling and calming her. But a mile later and she was still feeling anxious, couldn't shake it off. Unusually for this time of morning, she saw a couple walking towards her, dressed for work, holding hands, he with a briefcase in one hand. It was clear from their closeness that they had shared a warm bed that night; the nearness of their bodies, something about the angle of their heads ever so slightly tilted to each other, the peace between them. They took no notice of this strange woman in their path as they moved as one to the side of her. Viv heard her own sigh and redoubled her speed and stride.

Amanda had not rung since they got back two days before. Was she inventing a relationship where there was, in reality, none? Was Amanda keeping her on a string for the sake of the film? *Oh my God.* Viv recoiled in horror at the thought of being played. The sun had broken through now, the cloud had cleared, and it felt warmer. She would walk on, forget the club this morning. But what to do? Suddenly the answer came – what Viv needed was to feel in charge of herself again. She would get out of London, on her own, a change of scene, that would do it.

Her plan was to drive to Dorset, stay by the sea, find a pub. She would put a rough bag of things in the back; it was all she would need. A couple of days and sea air and she would feel better, clearer. She would know what to do if she could hear the rhythm of the waves crashing up the beach. Hear the seagulls. She often thought that that sound was a childhood memory, and it was that that had made it feel so intimate, but it wasn't at all. She had imagined that that had been her childhood and had longed for it to be.

But once in the car, she had to pass the club in Arts Lane in old Bermondsey and couldn't resist the place. Say hello to Lloyd, read the paper and then she'd get down to the coast. She checked her oversized man's watch, plenty of time. She and Lloyd always had plenty to discuss and this time it included her impending trip to Dorset.

"One for the road."

"You sure?"

"Lloyd!"

He knew better than to push. He was fond of Viv, but they were different people. He knew where to draw the line but sometimes he knew she didn't. He saw her taking risks he wouldn't, pushing the envelope that little bit further than he would, and he wondered about her. He liked her. What he didn't know, and it might have influenced his decision to serve so generously if he had known, was that Viv had made a night of it the night before. Top-up time. So, it was three generous Glenmorangies later when Viv took to the wheel of her bottle-green MG and sped across and out of London on the M3, not exactly the right route but faster, and much of the day was already going.

The autumn sun was low. She pulled the sun visor down, felt for her sunglasses with one hand. Life was sweet.

Who'd have thought it? This thought came to Viv's mind as she sank into the low bucket seat. Hood down. *Who'd have thought it?*

She began to hum Etta James's 'At Last'. She caught sight of herself in the driving mirror and reflected that she was indeed, for perhaps a fleeting moment, happy. Except for the letter, with the unknown writer, still hanging over her. She marvelled at the freedom her life gave her. No dependents, no-one to ask when she would be coming back. Her right foot relaxed; there was so little traffic. She looked up, saw the birds wheeling around looking where to land for the food. *Like me!* She laughed at the thought; it was true.

In London she had the familiar anxieties, but here, blue sky, open road, her foot pushed down. As she let her thoughts wander, she recalled the years of looking into crowds, over her shoulder, checking, checking. She wouldn't swap that for this, but then an evil thought crept in. She sometimes missed the excitement of those years.

She glanced at the speedometer, 70mph. Her foot went slowly, slowly down, 80mph. She glanced in the mirror, fuck it! Something snapped as she paused at 98mph, then her foot released. 100mph! She hadn't felt so elated, so high, in a long, long time. All the moons… Then she heard the siren, saw the blue lights, and her life compacted in a frozen second. She pulled back, knowing it was too late. She slowed to 60mph, the police car overtook, slowed her down and indicated the pull in.

For a wild second, her urge was to wait, then pull out and off. Could she get away? Too filmic!

Instead, she pulled over to the hard shoulder. It seemed an eternity before the policeman settled his cap and made his way to her side of the car. The hood was down, he had no need to stoop to talk to her. Viv had her beanie on and as the cop was about to address her, just for a second he stepped back, hesitated with madam or sir, then settled on madam.

"Madam, do you know what speed you were going?"

She prayed the open air would let the whiskey breath dissipate. She chose not to smile, not to placate, not to breathe over him. He wasn't sure if she was defiant or foreign.

"Madam, you were doing 100mph."

He had hoped for a reaction, but Viv was not giving him one.

"Could you please step out of the car, madam?"

Viv made play of the structure of the sports car to cover what might have been interpreted as a hover or a stumble. The policeman whipped out the breathalyser. Viv's heart sank. Could she fake it, shallow breath? He inserted the tube the correct way, handed it to Viv, with instructions to blow as hard and deep as she could. He looked annoyed at the result, pulled out a second one, repeated the process.

"Don't play games, we've seen it all."

This time she had no option and as though on a slow release play, she saw the amber disappear and the red take its place.

"Keys, madam."

His hand was out. All she had was dignity; she'd keep that. All these years she had kept out of the clutches of the law, and now of all ridiculous times, and because of her own fault, she found herself riding mute in the back of the squad car with the back view of two short-haired policemen. She glanced back at her sports car, marooned on the hard shoulder. She had just her two rescue bags beside her. She could see the eyes of the driver in the mirror, steady, never flicking on to the back seat. By the look of him, he was the older one, his younger partner in the passenger seat. *Is it the short straw to be a patrolman?* she wondered. *Or does it at least get them out of the station?* She shrugged; who knew?

The road gave little away as to where they were, apart from the Fleet Services, until a sign off to Basingstoke appeared. She watched it all as though it were a film with the sound turned down. No-one would hear her scream or yell, no-one even turned at the sight of the police car. Gradually, the road became busier, more normal, until they got to Basingstoke. Viv knew that that was where whatever police station they were going to must be. The car wove through the shoppers in the town, through the police yard and pulled up just short of the back entrance to the police station. The car swung into the yard behind the massive concrete custody suite building, the twenty-four-seven station of the area. As they stopped, she tried the car door; it was locked. She had to be let out like a child. The men walked either side of her, ushered her up the steps and into the building.

Once inside, the older policeman handed over paperwork, half turned his head towards Viv and asked the younger colleague to, "Take care of it. Full notes, full samples."

'It' not 'her'. Viv's hackles had risen, everything in her was feral in this moment.

"Where can I get my car back?" she demanded of the older one before he signed off.

"All in good time."

"But where is it going?"

He walked off to the far end of the hall without replying and let himself in through a keyed number lock.

"Right, come with me." This was the younger one, and together they walked in the opposite direction and into a small cubbyhole of a room, with a further partitioned small area. He showed her in and closed the door behind him. The room was featureless, except for a wall clock showing half past three. Left alone in this blank cell of a room, she couldn't breathe for a second. She rose, tried to open the door but it was locked.

"Help!"

The sound of her own voice embarrassed Viv. She composed herself. *This will end and end soon*, she told herself. *Just breathe*. All the same, it was twenty minutes before the young policeman came back. She needed some water. She had a headache and was now bitterly regretting the extra whiskey.

She thought of kindly Lloyd. Viv's head was ringing with fear; it was all she could do to hear what the officer was saying as he read through her rights, explained the results of the breathalyser and what it would mean for her.

"We'll need a blood or urine sample and your prints."

Something snapped; she stood up.

"I won't do that."

"Madam," suddenly his neutral tone went to harsh, "it's the law, and we can enforce it. You were doing 100mph and you have been drinking over the limit. Now sit down."

He pushed the consent form towards her and opened the fingerprint kit in the small cupboard.

Oh my God, it's beginning, was Viv's thought as she went through the pantomime of having her non-existent fingerprints taken. She had always taken care to check whether they were growing back – the burning had been deep, but even so, she had kept an eye on this. She watched his face for reaction as he took her prints, but so far there was none, just recorded them ready for entry into the database. Had they regrown? Partials?

He handed her a urine bottle and nodded towards the compartment.

"It's this or a blood sample, your choice."

Her humiliation was complete. "No, take blood. I'm not doing that." She motioned with her head.

The officer called for the medic on duty but that meant a two-hour wait for him to arrive. *No matter,* thought Viv, *no matter.*

"Could I have some water, please?"

"Not yet – after the doc has been."

Again, she was left alone in the small room. She could see the small camera in the corner of the ceiling, but apart from that there was nothing to keep her company. No sound, not even traffic, no window, nothing, just a flickering neon light. She drank too much. If she hadn't been over the limit, none of this would have happened. She would have to cut back, she wanted to cut back. She closed her eyes, hoping for peace. She had been there for a whole hour; it was shredding her nerves. Is this what prison would feel like? She took a deep breath and then, unbidden, the petrol smell she still carried from the police car brought something back to her. When the officer had filled up, he must have let some dribble before wiping it off. Petrol, garages, grease, she felt a memory was being wrenched from deep inside her. She closed her eyes and shivered.

She had been at the bus stop. *The man was lurching at me. He had one eye that didn't blink. It was dark, raining…*

Something was just about to crystallise in her memory when the young policeman came in saying the medic had arrived early.

Viv rolled up her sleeve, went through the drill, clenched her fist and fantasised about what that fist could do to them as she watched her crimson blood drain away. It was a violation, that was what it was. She wanted to claw it back, just as she wanted to retract time. She definitely watched too many films.

He pushed the form across the table for her to sign.

"What am I signing here?"

"Just to say that you agreed to our tests."

"And… if I don't?" She was still struggling to come to terms with this processing.

"Well, we can always charge you, keep you here." He seemed to find this amusing. "Then, pending your hearing, you would be free to go."

"Let me think."

Viv sat down and let the choices sink in. The officer didn't often come across this response, but all the same, he went along with it, noting the time on the wall clock; it was nearly the end of his shift.

Viv lifted the biro and signed *Viv Wheeler*. Her mind was whirring; what was the penalty for a false name if it was revealed?

He walked her out of the building, clicking the entry lock shut behind her. She stood there, feeling like an immigrant with her two bags and unsure where to go. She would appear at the magistrate's court in Salisbury on the following Monday.

CHAPTER 5

The train to Paddington took just under an hour, but then it was on to the Circle and Overground. Still stunned by what had just happened, she watched the fields disappear and be replaced by identical little houses with no chimneys. She saw a garage closing up for the day; the guy was pulling down the rolltop shutter door with a long, hooked pole. She swivelled in her seat to keep it in view, knocking the knees of the old man opposite. She didn't respond to his tutting. That was it! That was it! That man had been Reg Dawson from the garage, he'd been in the papers in the library. Relief at the connection made tears sting the back of her eyes. That was it! She'd taken her bike to Reg – and that had been the beginning, all those years before. She knew it. She sat back in her seat, her eyes closed, desperate to pursue the images, the memories, that that garage had thrown up.

The bike, the garage, the cuttings. She had been attacked that night – of that she was sure now. Was he connected with both memories? She could see him, greasy, shifty, he'd backed her up against a wall, she hadn't believed he had meant it, and then he had, and then she had kneed him in the groin, and she had got away. That was it. She had got away. So that dream that first night in New York had been true. The smell was the same, she was sure of it. But he had been in the papers because he was dead. Reg Dawson was the link. Was there a second time and had she killed him? Was that what she couldn't remember? She was in shock, unsure what to do with the thoughts now racing through her.

That wasn't *it* though, it still couldn't have been the only thing, she wouldn't have run away like that, so fast, just because of being attacked. She had, even in those teen years, been tougher than that. There had to be more. Trying to draw out the memory was so fragile. What if she never remembered? Whoever wrote that letter either knew her or was a good researcher.

The train was now gradually being swallowed by grimy industrial buildings with no name and less beauty, the Tannoy barely audible about not leaving belongings. They were in Paddington. Viv's legs felt like lead as she stood up, as though the effort of walking would be impossible.

She waited to disembark after the other passengers and then unsteadily made her way to the underground, still with Reg nagging at her memory. She was reeling still from what she had just gone through; she could almost literally hear the clock ticking to the moment when she would finally be exposed for whatever had happened. She had to remember, she had to remember before the police knocked on her door or she was shamed in the press. It was rush hour now, something that Viv had always avoided like the plague, humans being treated like animals – no, worse than animals. No air, no space, she couldn't breathe. She had to stand on the Circle line, eyes closed, strap hanging.

And then, there it was again, that smell, beer, practically in her face. She knew with the desperation of a drowning man trying to reach the lifebelt that it meant something and breathed it in deliberately and deeply so that it could communicate with her brain. She retched, put her hand over her mouth. *Oh God, oh God, it* was *Reg that night.* She raised her arm as though to protect herself.

"Steady on!" The bespectacled young man was glaring at her.

"I'm sorry, I thought…" But before she could get the words out, she knew how stupid, how crazy she would sound. She turned her back to him, changed strap-hanging arms and tried to calm herself.

Her hand went to her forehead. She had to hold it in. Now she knew finally what had happened. Relief and panic. It was Reg, Reg had stunk of beer, he had come out of the bushes by the bus stop, she had been waiting for the bus after the cinema, and he'd attacked her – and, then for the first time in all these years, she remembered that he had raped her. She had been standing in the rain, then, oh God, she shuddered, looked around the carriage as though her thoughts were readable. He was on top of her. He was hard, rough, angry, ripped her skirt and he was in her. That is what happened. So vivid was the memory she knew it was what happened, without any doubt. And then her hand had felt concrete…

She reached for the central pole in the carriage before she collapsed on the floor.

"Steady on, hold up."

Someone was holding her elbow. She was about to faint.

"Thank you," she mumbled. "I'm fine. Thank you." She was cold, clammy; she turned to look at her saviour, heard herself say, "It was Reg. Reg."

And from the man's blank look, she knew she sounded like a nutter.

"Sorry."

She remembered feeling for the lump of concrete and bringing it down on his head until he went limp, and she had pushed him to one side. And then, standing over him, she had brought it down on his head not once but so many times. And she had missed the last bus. So that was it. Relief at knowing at last collided with dread at the consequence. The concrete, her DNA, it would be all over Reg, that was what made the clock tick so loud. That is what the police would find once the central computer reported back to Basingstoke – and that was what the letter writer knew. So abstracted was Viv that, crossing over the concourse to the exit, she walked into a man intent on his phone.

"Mind out!"

So this was it, she was at once a victim and a killer. That was what she had run from. That was why she was Viv Wheeler. She was trapped, she was that animal finally caged, gnawing at the metal bars to get out, desperate to smell the air of freedom.

How long before they came for her? She had an alien name, no fingerprints, and now she would, she imagined, have a record of some sort. And she would still have Evie Riley's DNA. How long before all these results added up, before they heard back from the central database? The no fingerprints would be a red flag she felt sure, but the blood, the blood had surely trapped her. Reg would have her DNA under his fingernails and elsewhere, and that would mean the end of her. Certainly the end of Viv Wheeler. She threw up at the side of the gutter.

It was late evening by the time she got back to her flat and she had, she congratulated herself, held it pretty well together till then, but her first move was to drop her bags on the floor and reach for the whiskey in the middle cupboard of the sitting room. She would cut back tomorrow – she already knew she had a drink problem – but it didn't stop her pouring until she reached the top of the glass. She sat there in the dark, figuring out what options she had left.

A binary choice of fight or flight now presented itself. Her heart was pumping now, she was shaking with the shock. She rushed into her bedroom, grabbed her passport, checked her pockets for her keys, her phone, and picked up the same holdall she had dropped by the door and left. She was not waiting for the knock on the door, no, no, no, that was not for her. City Airport was her nearest and there was just time to get one of the last evening flights out to Paris. She would think then, she would think when she got there, but for now she had to run.

CHAPTER 6

Viv grabbed a cab to London City Airport and booked a flight on the way. Waiting for the flight to be called just made her feel the past was happening all over again. She looked cautiously around, sat in the corner. Was this what her life was always going to be? Escaping, watching, being on the alert.

She pulled her fedora further down over her face, shielding it from the cameras. She had thought that was all behind her. The thought prompted her to turn her phone off, cancel the signal; she would get another Sim card just as she had done all these years ago. Her shoulders slumped, she was tired, her head was throbbing, but she was far from defeated. She was Viv Wheeler, right? She glanced up at the board and reached the queue first. The young man smiled.

"My, you're keen, aren't you?"

This was no time for chit-chat; she was not about to make memories if anyone should ask if they had recognised her. For they surely would. There would be a manhunt and the difference between now and before is that she would not just be any old runaway – she would be V. J. Wheeler. Possibly even a news item? She shuddered at the thought, kept her head low.

The plane was small, mostly full of businessmen on the last flight back. She didn't want to be remembered by anyone and kept herself firmly to herself all flight. By the time they landed in Orly, it was late enough for anonymity to be easier. People were tired, ready for bed, they weren't looking around. She would disappear into the city, take a cab north and find a small hotel in St-Germain-des-Prés that she had been told about by Hugo. It was late to book in, but the night bell was answered, and she was let in by the porter. After registering and surrendering her passport, she was shown to a second-floor room with no lift. The bedroom was not like a Hilton or an Ibis, and it would have been rather charming if Viv had been in a different mode. The bedframe was iron, the furnishings reminded her of a private house. It felt good to be here.

She locked the door, pleased to note the old-fashionedness of the large brass lock and the long key. The passport might prove to be a problem, as would the credit card, as far as a trail went but there wouldn't be a search party yet; she had time to figure that out. She was dog-tired. There was a full moon, a clear sky and Paris was beautiful even at that hour. The curtains weren't drawn, and she sat on the edge of the bed in the dark. She recalled seeing the Manhattan skyline just like this with Amanda. The skyline here in Paris, such as it was, was across the river. She pulled out her phone about to call Amanda but stopped as she remembered the Sim card still in her pocket.

She tried to sleep, but she saw the hours go by – two, three, four. She must have fallen asleep, though, at some point, as she woke with a start at nine, her mouth stale. Cautiously, she made her way down to the front door, hoping to avoid the concierge, the smell of coffee and croissants almost irresistible. She heard talking – the concierge was on the telephone – and escaped to the front door without meeting anyone.

She stopped for a coffee at a small café next door and, sitting outside on the pavement, the turmoil of the last three days settled, and her thoughts crystallised. For a second time, she would have to take another identity. French police were notified of each visiting passport after twenty-four hours. She didn't want to, but what else could she do? She would have to bury V. J. Wheeler as surely as she had brought her to life. The air was different here, full of wonderful smells of food and cigarettes. For a whole day she wandered about the city, along the Seine, looking down from the bridges at the dark, deep water, the *bateaux mouches* ferrying waving tourists, imbibing smells, trying to feel safe in another city. There would be no alarm yet, she had time still to make a plan.

She caught sight of a blonde woman; it reminded her she needed to say goodbye to Amanda. She bought another Sim card and went back to the hotel room and called. It rang for a long while. Viv panicked, wanted to cut off the call rather than leave a message, but just at that moment, the voice she loved to hear answered.

"Amanda Rosberg."

Viv's empty stomach flipped; her heart missed a beat. Viv was wrong-footed.

"Amanda Rosberg?"

"It's Viv."

Amanda's voice dropped. "Oh, Viv, how are you?" Then, "Is something wrong?" This last was because Viv had never been a casual friend caller.

"Yes, yes, of course. All fine, I…"

"Stop. Stop. What is it?"

After a struggle, Viv heard herself say, "I can't see you again. Go ahead with the film but for me, this is it."

"Viv! Viv, what are you saying? Tell me where you are!"

Viv had never heard Amanda anything but cool and in command, this was new and something in her tone allowed Viv to tell her where she was, swearing her to secrecy.

"Tell no-one. I am in trouble, and I have to disappear."

In that second, her doubts disappeared; she could hear that she mattered to Amanda.

"Don't be so cryptic, Viv. You can talk to me. Tell me where—"

But Viv had cut off the phone.

"Viv!"

Amanda redialled, got the answerphone, reached for email. *Please tell me where you are.* And then something she was not used to saying, let alone writing, *I love you. Talk to me.*

I love you. It was hard for Viv to read at the moment she knew she had to walk away.

Amanda called Linny. "Linny, don't ask me any questions at all. Please. Trust me. Tell me where this mobile with a new Sim card number is right now."

Amanda could not risk adverse publicity at this stage of the film.

"What are you involved in, Manny?"

No-one called her Manny; she bridled.

"I said, please no questions. I will owe you."

"You certainly will," was Linny's reply, completely unphased by their exchange; he was working on a major hack for the government.

CHAPTER 7

By the next morning, Amanda was in Paris at the hotel address of the mobile and had the concierge find Viv for her. Viv was halfway down the wrought-iron staircase to reception when she saw Amanda. She turned, about to go back up, but Amanda had seen her. She beckoned Amanda to come up to the second floor.

Closing the door behind her, Amanda searched Viv's face for clues as to how to proceed.

"Are you in some sort of trouble?"

"Have you told anyone I'm here?"

Amanda shook her head. Linny was the perfect friend. He never told anyone anything.

"How did you know where to find me?"

"It wasn't difficult."

Amanda was telling more half-truths than she was comfortable with but, at this stage, it seemed the best answer.

Viv went to the window and looked up and down the street.

"Viv, Viv, it can't be that bad, surely. What made you run here? To Paris?"

Viv shrugged. "It was anywhere."

Amanda stood behind her, put her arm round Viv's shoulder and this time Viv did not resist as Amanda drew her into a warm hug. After several minutes standing like that, Viv turned to Amanda.

"I got caught for speeding. 100mph, but it's worse than that, I was over the limit."

"Oh my goodness, you had me worried for a moment, I thought you were in serious trouble. We can sort that out if—"

"I am."

"Oh, Viv, darling, you are going to have to explain. You are not making sense. From the top. I won't interrupt."

Amanda lay down on the bed, her hands behind her head, and waited.

"When I was at the police station, something triggered the memory of all the past and it is terrible. You always thought, I know you did, that I was withholding, but I wasn't. I knew there was a piece missing. It all came back, just like that, once I was on the stinking train home. It all rolled out. For so long I have wanted to remember, but I couldn't, but now I have. I am not who you think I am. I'm not really Viv Wheeler. Viv Wheeler is dead. I was... am really... Evie Riley."

Viv searched Amanda's face for reaction; horror, perhaps. But all Amanda was feeling was relief that they were now on the same page.

"Then there was my father. I haven't been able to think about him for years, but he's so real now. So many memories are coming back."

Viv was not yet making sense, but Amanda waited impassively for more.

"He hit my mother and me, always angry and violent, one time he broke my arm, but he was always so charming to everyone, no-one would have believed us. I wanted to go to the police, but my mother just broke down at the thought that I would make it public knowledge. She always begged me not to. There was something missing in him, that protection thing, he hadn't got it for me, no top cover. But he should have kept me away from Reg Dawson. He knew Reg Dawson; he must have known what sort of evil man he was."

So, not dead then, was Amanda's private thought.

"Wait, wait, who is Reg Dawson?"

Amanda needed to hear this from Viv. She wasn't making sense, and why all this about her father? What had it got to do with what was going on now?

"He had a garage. My father sent me there to get my bike mended. I didn't know then that they were both Masons, I didn't put it together, and Reg made a lunge for me, but I kicked him and got away. He wanted to punish me."

There was a note of pride in Viv's tone here.

Amanda knew there must be more to all this drama, but so far it wasn't making much sense.

"But why did you have to run away like this? It is just speeding, isn't it? This happens all the time."

"No. It doesn't. Not like this. They took my DNA and my fingerprints." She held up her hand. "I don't have any… they will ask why."

"That's not the end of the world surely?"

"You have to hear me out. The DNA… they have it… and it won't be long before they find it on their database."

Amanda tried to make a joke of it. "You're not a criminal, are you?"

"I don't really know. I think I might have killed him."

It was Amanda's turn to be lost for words. "Killed?! Who?"

"Yes, perhaps. Reg. He died. I know that. I know too that he…" Viv turned away from Amanda; she was still herself so unused to these words. "Raped me."

Amanda walked over to Viv and held her shoulders. "It's OK. It's OK."

All she wanted was to get things back on an even keel. She had a film to make, she wanted Viv back but not like this. She had never dealt well with failure, victimhood and this, despite her feelings for Viv, was beginning to smell like it. She didn't like herself for being like this, but there it was. She wasn't entirely comfortable, but she decided to go with it as at last Viv was opening up to her about who she was. She reached for the red wine she had brought with her.

Pouring two glasses, she handed one to Viv.

"It's not so bad, darling. There is worse. It doesn't change how I feel about you."

"It will."

Viv was having to handle two conflicting emotions. Amanda was so clearly stating how she felt about Viv at the very time that Viv had no idea what lay ahead of her.

"There's more?"

Viv nodded. She had now to get it all out on the table. If this was a make or break with Amanda, so be it; she could still disappear.

"I had a friend, Paula, and that night we had gone to the cinema and after I caught the bus home, I still had her mobile. We'd been looking at photos and I forgot to give it back. Paula had lent me her green gloves it was so cold, and that night I lost them. It was dark and raining and I didn't know if the last bus had gone. Then… oh." And here Viv stumbled. The memory was new, still raw, still assaulting to her senses, shaming. Could she actually get it out in words?

"Go on." Amanda was remembering what Geoff had said about the gloves and Paula.

"He, Reg, he stank of beer. He attacked me, raped me. I

was just there on the pavement in the dark, on my back, and there was no-one around and I couldn't stop him…"

Amanda put her arm around Viv. "Go on," she murmured softly.

"…And then I felt this concrete, huge stone, and I brought it down on the back of his head. Again and again until he went limp. I remember after crouching down right by him, I hit him again. I think I must have killed him. That's why I'm in trouble. That's what I couldn't remember. The police will put it all together now and they will come for me, for murder. The DNA will link the two incidents. Now do you see?"

Amanda held Viv tight in silence, stroked her hair. The two of them stood there saying nothing, resisting nothing.

"All these years you've held this in." Amanda released her hold and asked, "And that's when you ran away?"

"What else could I do? No-one was going to believe me."

"And that's all the homeless time? It all makes sense."

Amanda's gut wrenched with pity, with sympathy, with longing, but something in her kept her steady; she could not afford to lose her centre. Even for Viv. Amanda was remembering back to her talk with Geoff Armitage and what he had told her. He had assured her that Viv had been a victim most probably, just a runaway, not in the frame for Reg Dawson, but that it was her friend Paula they would be looking for if the green gloves and mobile ever came to light again.

"And what about Paula?"

"What about her?"

"Did you tell her? Did you call her, that night? She was your friend."

"I was going to. You know, Amanda, this is a really bad film script." And for some reason, Viv could not stop laughing at this thought. She was almost hysterical at her own recall, for the first time allowing herself to know exactly what she had gone through and what she had suppressed in order to survive. It was too much. She kept laughing until she could laugh no more. "Is this even really happening?" Tears rolled down her face.

Amanda refilled their glasses as Viv picked up the thread again.

"You are not going to believe this, I couldn't believe it either at first, but the following day I had arranged to meet up with Paula and tell her, get her to help – she always used to have a plan, money, whatever... And I waited for her at a hotel in town. She said she'd be there, but she must have got everything muddled. I was in a big wing chair in the reception, waiting, and I saw her come in, but before I could go over to her, she was going towards the lift."

"What?"

"In that moment, I knew everything. My father was there, wasn't he? The bottom really fell out of my world. There was no-one at all I could trust, and that's never changed. I watched the numbers of that lift. Third floor... that's not a dining room, is it? She was fifteen! She was my friend! Could he, could they, betray me more? That's when I flipped, panicked, ran away and however bad it was after that, it wasn't as bad as those two days."

With her cool head, Amanda was weighing up the risks of the gloves being found again against whether or not any of Viv's DNA had been taken from Reg and, if so, whether it had been lost. *It is possible that no connection would be made after all*, was what she was thinking. She should check with Geoff before they made another move, but that meant she had to come clean too. What if finding Geoff and getting him to think about it all again had stirred it up to the point that it would hang Viv out to dry?

"Darling, please don't hate me for this, but I have something to tell you too."

After she had downloaded about her visit to Viv's parents, to the police, to Geoff, she concluded with, "I had to know who you were. I thought I could help you bring back your memory."

"Oh no." Viv moved away. Was there no-one she could trust? "You shouldn't have done that, gone behind my back – don't you see that that has happened to me all my life?"

"But think about it, if so much evidence was lost, could not your DNA be lost too? Might they still be wanting Paula for this? Geoff, the police officer, told me you were not in the frame, that it was Paula they would look for if she came back to England."

"What? Why?"

"The gloves. The mobile."

Viv was lost in thought. Paula's gloves might have had Reg's blood on them. And what about the rape? If they had thought it was an attack and not rape, might they not have taken DNA from those parts of him? That was crucial. If the link was made, clearly self-defence was a possibility? The risk is if they examined the gloves for her DNA, but really, would they? Besides, if they did that, they would find Paula's DNA too as she was the one who had worn them more. Would that prove anything more than that friends lent each other clothes?

"So, the police have the gloves?"

"I'm not sure. I have to find out."

Viv's mind was racing. If they did have the gloves and they were known to be Paula's, and Reg's blood was there, should she intervene to save Paula? Or, as she recalled seeing Paula with her father, do nothing? She concluded that she owed her nothing; fate would decide this one.

CHAPTER 8

Amanda returned to London, leaving Viv with one of her credit cards and firmly told her to get another phone. And, she had added as an afterthought, move hotels every day. That way, the twenty-four-hour passport check could be held at bay. There was only Linny who knew where Viv was, and he lived in a nerdily detached IT world and would never think of doing anything to betray the connection. Amanda smiled as she thought of him. Besides, Amanda had known him since university and what she had always loved about him was his shiny innocence. Life was a giant toy to him. It was fine.

Back in her flat in London, her first call was to Geoff. She could hear he was getting to like being in the swim of things again. Like old times.

"Hello, Amanda."

He kicked the sitting room door shut as he took the call. This time and attention to the old case was beginning to rile his wife.

"I'm sorry to bother you," Amanda began, "what I'm hoping is that I didn't stir things up too much when I came to see you."

"No, no, of course not."

This didn't sound like the reason for her call; he waited for more. He thought she would be pleased that he was actively thinking about the case she had brought into his life again, but perhaps not.

"But I did look at the case again, talking about it made me question the detail. I asked my old junior at the time to see what he could do to rescue the evidence, and also have a look at the father's laptop which we had taken at the time."

Amanda's heart went to her boots, but she kept her tone neutral.

"Oh, and what have you found?" She tensed herself against hearing what he had to say, regretting having stirred all this up.

Amanda could hear Geoff's wife calling, "Geoff, can you help me in with the shopping?"

He chose on this occasion to ignore the Tuesday plea and continued.

"Very interesting. All the evidence did come back from forensics in the end, plus their report, but because we were manpower short and because it had taken so much time, it all got put to one side, filed. Cold case."

Amanda wasn't sure she wanted to ask what the report had said. The crunch question was whether there was any DNA or blood that could be connected to Viv's taken at Basingstoke.

Geoff went on without Amanda's intervention. "Truth is, without further work on it, we have blood matches with Reg, but nothing yet to connect either Paula or Evie," (Amanda had not told Geoff that Evie had become Viv and felt, mistakenly, that this was oddly a layer of protection for Viv) "with his murder yet. There was obviously some sort of attack but because we haven't got anything we can match with anything taken from them, we can't go forward. Unless, of course, Evie is found or the Force finds some money to go to the States! Besides, if he did rape her, we haven't got a worthwhile case against him, because he's dead."

Amanda heard Geoff's generous laugh and shivered.

"Of course. I understand."

"The father is the question mark over all this, though, his name just keeps cropping up. First the domestic violence that went unattended to, then there was the fact that he was a character witness for Reg Dawson when his dubious activities were discovered. But listen to this: we had a look at his computer, and the hard drive answers a lot of questions. He was a member of the Masons and so was Reg, who was clearly half involved with some sort of dubious sex ring activity. The father was a magistrate, a school governor, all-round good guy. But he had money invested in Reg's garage, that much was clear, so he is compromised to say the least, but we don't know how much. Reg kept trying to draw him into their circle, but he was having none of it. He was terrified – and rightly so. Oh, and the other thing that emerged is that he was a benefactor of the local nursing home, where his mother lived. And he visited her every week until she died. So, dodgy, but in the eyes of the world, not all bad. Question is, why didn't we take it further with him then?"

Amanda had no idea how to answer this without either encouraging or accusing Geoff.

"OK then, so can you keep me updated with anything further you find?"

It was only when the call ended that Geoff questioned Amanda's degree of interest, wondered why, if she was only looking for Evie, she was so interested in the murder case. For Amanda's part, she had not settled in her own mind quite how much danger Viv was still in, and what action Viv should take. It was possible, just possible, that nothing would link her, but the likelihood of material from Reg's fingernails being part of the forensic report was very high, and that meant that time was running out for Viv. She didn't feel she could ask too specific questions about Reg; it would have given away her reason for talking to Geoff, given away that she indeed knew where his Evie Riley was. Viv had been right to run, but mistaken in the belief that this would in the end solve her problem. What should she tell her?

She emailed Viv, *Tell me your new number.*

It was two days of checking her phone before Amanda received Viv's new number. She called her at once, excusing herself from the office meeting to do so. Eyebrows were raised; this was not usual for the punctilious Amanda. She took the call outside in the street, keeping her voice low.

"Viv, Viv…"

"Hi."

"How are you?"

"I can't go through all this… I can't… I've made my decision…"

"No, wait. Wait." And Amanda explained about the evidence being found, and of the possibility that the DNA would be a match and that she would be arrested and charged, but possibly only as a rape victim. She was at pains to point out that they were pretty certain that whoever attacked Reg did it because they were his victim. "The way he was found, and in those circumstances, they are not talking about a voluntary lovers' tryst. So, what I'm saying is your plea could be self-defence."

Amanda waited in silence for Viv's reaction to this.

"I can't, I can't. I'm sorry."

"Wait, Viv. Is there someone I can call for you? Someone legal before the proverbial hits the fan?"

Viv had never heard Amanda use colloquialisms like this.

"I don't know..."

The defeated tone in Viv's voice was what most alarmed Amanda. This was new.

"Wait, just wait, I'll come back to Paris, we will make a plan."

*

Viv walked each day, much as she had done all those years ago in London. Along the Seine, through the Latin quarter, through the rich arrondissements. She felt like an automaton, with no idea of where to go or what to do. She wondered how the enjoyment of the years building up V. J. Wheeler had disappeared so fast. How could they just evaporate like this? She caught sight of herself in the smart, glass shopfronts, but quickly turned away. She was a fraud. Was Amanda right, should she face the music? Surely that would mean going to prison for a very long time. The very thought was surreal but was a real prospect. It was as she was imagining the whole legal process that Arun came to mind. Would he, could he, help her? Give her advice?

She returned to her hotel late in the evening, taking with her two bottles of red wine. In the end she had not changed hotels but kept the door locked. It was just too much. The night porter had begun his shift; there was a quick *bonsoir*, and she had passed him on her way to the stairs and climbed up to her room on the second floor again. She drew the curtains, leaving the room in darkness. There was a small table and chair, the wine and glass placed on it. Viv needed to think. Alone. There was a church nearby; she could hear the mellow clock bell on the hour. Except for that there was no noise. She wanted to numb herself out with the wine. What she was facing was overwhelming. She was panicking. There was nothing she could do now; the net was closing as surely as a hangman's noose. She turned on the small side light. Flashes of when she was a young child came to her mind. And as she saw their house, the sense of her mother came back so strongly. She had turned back that last morning and her mother had never looked so forlorn, so beaten, as she stood there waving in her shapeless grey cardigan and untidy hair. Viv had always been angry that she would not stand up for herself, would not go to the police with her. Now, though, she only felt she wanted to wrap her up in a big soft rug and protect her from her father. She moved to the window, but it was night now and Viv was engulfed in a fleeting moment of self-pity. What options truly had she got now? *I could, I imagine, create another identity*, she thought, *but they would be looking for me in France, as my passport would be tracked. Where would I go anyway? And I could no longer write, I couldn't start over again.* She could try America, but then again, if she stayed, the formalities and the paperwork that presented themselves to Viv in the darkness of that room just seemed a mountain too far.

Had she come to the end? She put her head in her hands. God she was tired. All that effort to escape; perhaps it would have been better to stay. Could she now, though, face prison? And that wasn't the worst of it. There would be a trial, it would be reported because of the V. J. Wheeler name. Her parents would emerge from whatever shadows they had been living in. *I would just be Evie Riley again. Facing my parents. Facing the world. Total shame. My home gone, my name gone, my career gone.* Would Amanda wait for her? Unlikely. Viv had by now finished one bottle and her anger at the unfairness of it all surfaced – after all, she hadn't asked to be attacked like that. It had been bad enough living with her father's violent temper, the assaults when he lashed out, but she had not asked for Reg's rape. Burying her head in her hands once more, she was surprised to feel them wet from her tears. She never cried! But now that she had begun, nothing stopped the tears.

She stood up, somewhat unsteadily. Her eyelids were like lead, she had to lie down. Taking the rest of the wine with her, she lay down on the bed cover and slipped into oblivion.

CHAPTER 9

"Look at this, Sarge."

It was the younger policeman who had taken Viv through the blood and urine offers, taken her prints.

"Look at this, we've only got a match."

"Match for what?"

"Only murder."

This got his superior's attention, and he came over to look at the screen. Sure enough, there it was.

"Don't you remember her? That difficult one. Bolshie, she was. Over the limit, speeding. Maybe she knew more than she was letting on, and that's why she kept digging her heels in."

Yes, the sarge did remember her and the adrenalin coursed through him. This didn't happen every day. Viv's DNA, her blood sample, proved a one hundred per cent match for material taken from the scene of a murder of one Reg Dawson.

"Right, arrest warrant. Search warrant, double quick. We don't want to lose this now we've got her, and don't forget she must have known that we would be coming for her. Get on to it. Check passports. Check her address too."

*

In the morning, Viv woke, taking some time to realise where she was. When she did, the despair came back and dropped like a boulder inside her, dragging her down and down; she was drowning. But half an hour later, something that Amanda had said floated into her foggy brain. She had suggested contacting legal help. She remembered Arun again. Arun, he would be 'legal help', wouldn't he? Could she trust him?

So, at the same time as a warrant was put out for her arrest, Viv reinserted the new Sim card and called Arun. *His work would be done for the day, maybe,* she thought, *he might even be in the club, her club.*

"Arun?"

"Yes, this is Arun speaking." He didn't recognise Viv's heavy voice.

"It's V. J."

Viv never called Arun. Their friendship, such as it was, was based around sharing the club and meeting now and then.

"I didn't recognise your voice."

She made an effort to lighten the tone, quipped, cleared her voice and pressed her temple to stop the pounding headache.

"I need to talk to you. I need a favour."

"I'm listening."

"I need some legal advice. Can we talk soon?"

Viv felt her energy returning somewhat at the thought of action.

"Of course. Say, lunchtime, late, about three? Tomorrow? I should be done for the day by then. The club?"

"Perfect."

All Viv needed was to get back into the country without raising the red flag. But how? Walking to the bathroom, she drank two glasses of water in an effort to sober up, clear her mouth and throat; she needed to think straight. If Arun gave her bad news, she would then have to decide her future, and quickly. But for now, it felt positive that she could lay out her case to him. He was young enough still and early on enough in his career to be eager, and Viv knew he liked her.

The more she thought of it, the more she felt uplifted. She needed coffee now and, putting her hat on, she struggled out and down the street to a café where she sat in the too bright sun, nursing a precious black coffee. After the second one, her mind was functioning a bit better.

She went inside to the back of the café to the toilettes and caught sight of herself in the mirror. Quite awful; she looked into one eye, then the other. It was a small space, just two loos, both occupied. Viv tried the handle of the one to her right.

"*Pardon!*" came through the door.

Viv turned from the mirror and collided with the woman coming out of the one on the left.

"*Pardon!*" she apologised.

"*Non, non. Pardon.*"

The woman was in a hurry now; she pushed past Viv in the cramped space and exited the loo. Viv saw in a flash that on the sill of the small space the woman had just left lay a credit card and a passport. It was too obvious, too unreal. Surely it was fate actually helping her. A sign! Another sign. She had to believe that and snatched them before the woman could realise they were missing, paid for her coffee in cash and walked at speed back towards her hotel, taking the stairs two at a time.

What was she doing? A young man hurrying down collided with her, swore at her. Her heart was beating fast. Amanda had joked that she was a criminal, hadn't she? She opened the passport photo page and a middle-aged woman no-one would remember especially looked out at her. They weren't that different except Viv's hair was shorter. That wouldn't matter. There was no time to feel bad about this, her need was so extreme. But she had to be quick before the passport was reported and cancelled. Using her new Sim card, she booked the next flight to London for Madame Brodeur – Camille Brodeur.

And she texted Amanda.

Coming back.

*

As Viv came through City Airport on her midday flight home, the only reason she stood out somewhat from the other passengers on the small plane was that she was plainly not a businessman. Wearing her hat and Puffa jacket, she walked behind groups of people, never looking up at camera height. All the same, at passport control, even though the checking was somewhat cursory, she held her breath and tossed up whether to brave the manual check or leave it to fate with the automatic recognition stall. She had arranged her hair to look like Madame Brodeur's but other than that she could not do much. Placing the passport face down, she assumed the confidence she would have had a week before. A red cross lit up. She swallowed hard and placed the passport the other way up and held her breath. She removed her hat, and the green light came up, then the Perspex shutters opened! She was sweating now as she made her way to public transport without pausing for anything else.

There were no street cameras along her road. She let herself into her flat and for the first time in a week, Viv felt her body give way as she rested against the closed front door. She was home.

It was an illusion of safety, a reprieve of sorts, she knew that, but all the same, it was an overwhelming feeling; relief didn't come close to describing it. She was about to leave straightaway for the club to see Arun, but so much had happened since she had last been there. She paused. How much had been in the papers, on television? Was it still her club? Was it wise to go? She shivered at the thought of being disbarred, but it wasn't that thought that made her pause, it was the thought of not *feeling* welcome anymore. She wasn't thinking straight, she knew that. Meeting Arun, she reflected, she would now be placing her fate in someone else's hands. But there would be no point in talking to him and getting his advice if she did not lay out every single card she had – or almost every single card she had. It was time for as much honesty as she could afford. As she set out to walk to the club for her meeting with Arun, she toyed with turning back and every step she took seemed like a debate, but in the end she arrived at the small, recessed, black door of the club in Arts Street.

In a second or two of getting there, she could see that in her short absence she had indeed become a news item, and one that appeared not on the front page of the broadsheets, but a few pages in.

"Afternoon, Maurice!" Viv greeted the doorman in what she hoped was her usual voice, but he looked away. She could tell as he replied that he had heard something. How much and what, was the question. Walking on into the main room with the table of papers, she was making for her favourite chair only to see that it had been taken. She walked over to Lloyd, about to order a drink. She half smiled. He greeted her but there was an awkwardness about him. She tried an order, nonetheless.

"Coming up." But he turned away from the bar as he said it.

Heads turned, no-one spoke; it was difficult to discern in the members' nods or half-smiles whether she still belonged here. Some members had clearly read about her, others hadn't, but, of course, it had been a talking point. Should she have agreed to meet Arun elsewhere? Jerry – she couldn't remember his other name, but he had worked for the BBC for years – stood and, gathering his belongings, headed for the door at the same time as reaching for his mobile in his pocket. No, this couldn't be happening! Betrayed here? By another member? She wasn't about to stay around to make sure she was right. She silently cursed herself for trusting what she had considered to be a haven of friends in the club, and without hesitation, she turned, leaving her drink on the table, and walked out into the daylight. She reached for her phone and called Arun once she was outside.

"Arun, it's Viv. I can't meet you in the club, I don't know what I was thinking."

"V. J., I quite understand. But we should meet."

And he suggested meeting at his flat for the sake of privacy. The gratitude Viv felt at that suggestion was something she wished to hold back for the time being and so answered with brevity.

"Yes, that's a good idea. Send your address through. In an hour?"

Arun lived in the Barbican and Viv felt as though she was walking through a moonscape – it was so concrete and so full of odd shapes and so unpeopled. She guessed that everyone here had lives elsewhere during the day and that it might be different in the evening. Still, it was hard to imagine any warmth here. Finding Arun's flat through the maze, she rang the doorbell and went up to the first floor.

"Come in, come in."

Arun is every inch the barrister, thought Viv, and although they were friends of a sort, a professional consultation was what was on the table. He was still formally dressed even though he was at home. Arun had, of course, the advantage over Viv in that he had heard the news; he was unsure, though, how much Viv knew.

"So, bring me up to date, V. J. What do you need from me?"

There was a decanter of water and two glasses on the table. Viv disliked intensely being the supplicant but at that moment she had no alternative. All the same, she paced as she explained.

"I, I, well, just over a week ago, I was speeding, got caught – bit too much whiskey!" Viv tried a smile.

Arun knew that this could not be the full extent of the problem. Viv could handle that, surely, it was a hands-up job and deal with the punishment. You couldn't argue your plea in that sort of case, and if indeed that was what Viv wanted to talk about, that would be his advice. But he had seen the news item, and he had seen it in the newspapers, so he waited.

"Water?"

He poured two glasses while Viv regained her nerve. Viv got up and walked to the window.

"This is difficult, Arun, very difficult."

"What happened at the police station?"

Checking the time with a quick glance at his watch, he decided to nudge towards the problem. Viv's mind flashed back to that vile little room where she had in effect been a prisoner and she shuddered at the memory.

"The usual tests, fingerprints, that sort of thing."

She couldn't look him in the eye.

"It takes, I understand, about two weeks for any further communication. About two weeks for…"

"A match?"

Time was getting on and Arun wanted to at least have the facts before him.

Viv looked up. "You know then?"

Arun nodded. "It was on the news and in the papers."

"Exactly what?" Viv bridled, feeling wrong-footed.

"The police wish to question you in connection with an attack and murder in Reston."

Viv's legs buckled. She sat down abruptly.

"Yes. Exactly so."

"So, tell me all you know. I can't give you any worthwhile advice without all the facts."

To her surprise, Viv felt overwhelming relief at being able to talk to Arun like this; she hadn't expected it. In that moment, she longed to lay her soul bare, confess everything. Absolutely everything. Covering her face with her hands, she took the deepest breath and steadied herself; she would tell Arun as much as she safely could. She looked again at him as she began. His face was so kind it was distracting.

"I ran away from home years ago and assumed a different name."

She had wanted to say 'a pen name' to give it a better gloss but she stayed with 'a different name'.

"I had no memory of *why* exactly." She leant over the table. "You have to believe me when I say this. And it was only when I was arrested for speeding that the half glimpses of the past formulated in a memory that I knew for certain had been real. It shook me. It's hard for me to admit this, but it's true."

"And the murder, who was that? Did you know anything about that?"

"Yes. But again, not until recently. Yes, I know everything about that. He was a foul man, Reg Dawson, and he attacked me one night at a bus stop as I was going home after the cinema, and he raped me out in the street where everyone could have seen – only, no-one, so far as I know, did. The first and last man," she glanced at Arun, held up her hand to him, "no offence. And I felt my hand curl round a concrete stone, and I brought it down on his head."

"And that was when you killed him?"

Viv nodded. "And I left him. I was frightened he would come after me. I looked back at him; I didn't know for sure he was dead. I'm glad I shamed him, leaving his flies open… he deserved that."

Arun, for the time being, ignored that last comment.

"So, could you have hit him *while* he was raping you?"

Viv was irritated, why the detail at this stage?

"Or are you sure it was *after* he had raped you?"

She thought for a moment.

"He had slumped for a moment. It was then."

"I don't wish to hear that he slumped. You are saying that it was while he was raping you?"

There was only the slightest hesitation before Viv looked away as she spoke.

"Yes. During. I was fighting him off."

"And did he scratch you at all?"

Viv tried to remember. "Yes, he did, but he didn't draw blood."

"And did you leave any incriminating evidence at the scene?"

Despite the circumstances, Viv was rather impressed with this professional Arun. She thought again for a moment, and the green gloves and the bus pass came to mind.

"I lost them that night, but I don't know where. It might have been at the bus stop; it might have been when I walked home after that."

Arun was thinking, assessing what he had just heard.

"Do I have a way out of this, Arun?"

"Well, it's not clear cut, whichever way you look at it. It will boil down to the efficiency of forensics if there were no eyewitnesses. And, as yet, we do not know what the police gained at the original scene, nor how much of a match they produced after they arrested you."

"Next step?"

Viv felt a slight return of her authority, as though she was the one with choices, but Arun was quick to dispel this.

"The bad news, I'm afraid, V. J., is that it is not yours to take, unless you want to flee!"

As soon as he'd said this, he realised that was not only in poor taste but could also be seen as giving wrong professional advice.

"Believe me, Arun, I've given that some thought but coming to see you is evidence that I'm not taking that path." Part of Viv kept in reserve. "Yet."

"You will have to wait until your hearing for the speeding, and they will notify you of this in good time, or, more likely, you will be hearing from them because their match is conclusive."

"Your opinion is?"

Arun leant back in his leather chair. "I don't want to have to tell a friend this, I truly don't, but I think the second option is most likely."

"They don't yet know I'm back in the country, Arun. They know I left for Paris. I'm not sure I can face this, go through all this, I could still—"

"No, no, don't tell me your plans. I must not know them. All I can advise you is when they speak to you, it is likely that the charge will be murder but – and there is a big but – you will have a very strong self-defence plea. A murder victim left with his flies open… well, you did yourself a huge favour doing that."

Despite herself, Viv allowed herself a small smile and a quiet, "Yes. Can you advise me the process?" She studied his face. "Would you defend me?"

Hearing herself ask the last question was literally astonishing to her. She held her breath. She was trusting Arun with her life.

"If you don't disappear, if you stay, or, even better, hand yourself in, then I'm confident you have a case, and I'd be honoured."

Viv was touched at this last remark. 'Honoured'.

"As Evie Riley?"

"Especially so."

Viv felt tears of relief at sharing the fears, the burden, but it was more than that. She looked at him and, in that instant, wished she was different. She hid her face in her hands and as she came back to the here and now, he smiled and held out his hand to her.

"Thank you, Arun."

In another life. In another life.

CHAPTER 10

That evening at six o'clock, Rosemary turned the television on for the news; there was something oddly comforting about topping up the anxiety level she always carried with her. Somewhere in the back of her mind was always the hope that she would hear that her Evie had been found. That friend of hers coming to the house had stirred up her feelings. Had Rosemary thought about it rationally, which her depression didn't allow, she would have known that her daughter, just plain Evie Riley, would never be on the news. Although she still talked to Evie as she dusted and cleaned her room, it was far more likely, she concluded, that she would never hear her name spoken by anyone else again.

Foreign and parliamentary news dominated, and then, "Police are searching for the missing author V. J. Wheeler in connection with a murder committed fourteen years ago in Reston."

Rosemary was on the edge of her chair, straining for every word; it was the word 'Reston' that woke Rosemary up.

"They are making it clear that they only wish to interview V. J. Wheeler to eliminate her from their enquiries."

That was it, that was all the item said. *How odd there was no picture of this author; you would think that would help to find her, whoever she is. Reston, though, that has to be that garage man. What was his name?* Forgetting that somewhere she still had the cuttings from that time, she decided to ask Douglas when he was back; he'd remember. He didn't get back till eight that evening and Rosemary ate her omelette alone in front of the television. She liked omelettes, as they were light on the digestion. So, between the early news item and Douglas returning, more memories returned to Rosemary, in particular the fact that her husband and this man were somehow connected. She suspected the Masons; she had never liked them, never knew what they were up to. Nor did anyone else, that was the problem with them!

Douglas never talked about Evie, wouldn't let Rosemary bring her name up either. He said it had been her choice to go, we had to respect it, get on with our lives the best we could. But it wasn't like that for Rosemary; she was her mother and every day, every waking morning, she thought about her missing daughter and wondered if she could have done anything to stop her leaving. It was partly because Rosemary didn't know why she had left that doubled the pain.

Douglas had never mended his violence, his vile temper, and Rosemary had to pick and choose her times to bring up tricky subjects. There had been times in those rages that she had feared for her life, sometimes that moment had hovered then receded, but the memory of his face, of those moments, never had. On reflection, she thought that the garage man might be one of the tricky subjects too, given how Douglas had been at the time. So, instead, later that evening when Douglas wanted to see the late news, Rosemary sat with him, hoping that he would see the item she had seen and say something. She wouldn't need to bring up the subject herself this way. She watched his face closely, waiting for the name

Reston to come up, but when it did, he was inscrutable, not a flicker, not a twitch.

"Reston, Douglas. What do you think?"

He got up and went to bed. "I don't think anything."

Left alone with the repeat of the earlier bulletins playing, Rosemary's mind went to the duvet she had stripped from Evie's bed that last morning, with the dried blood on it. Before she went up to bed herself, she checked at the far back of the cupboard under the sink where she had secreted it all these years. Yes, there it was. The blood was dried and brown, but the faint smell was still there after all these years. It was a loaded gun, and one, she hoped, that would help her daughter one day. She was sure that it had been important to save it like this and prayed that she would know the right moment to bring it out. The only problem was that she was making assumptions; she didn't know what had happened. Hunches, that's all. She knew from what she had heard that night when Evie had come home late and wet that something had happened. Something had definitely happened, but she couldn't ask Evie that night or the next morning. Douglas was angry, hovering, and she didn't want to make matters worse. She knew that Evie had brought the blood home with her but was it her blood, or from an attacker? If it was an attacker, who was he? And why had Douglas been out that evening too? Had it been Douglas who attacked her? She knew, to her cost, that he had the temper for it. Only coming home an hour before her daughter, his jacket wet? Sitting there in the dark sitting room, the television the only sound, Rosemary decided it was time for her to find out. She didn't know how yet, but she had to find out exactly whose blood that was.

CHAPTER 11

It was now six o'clock. As Viv walked home from the station, her thoughts crystallised, and her heart felt lighter than it had in some while. She knew what she had to do. She called Amanda. It went to answerphone.

"Amanda, I'm back now. Home. If you are free tonight, please come round; it will be the feast of the damned, one to savour." Just before she clicked off, she added, "Even if you're not free – come. Please. It's important."

When Amanda received the message, she wasn't entirely sure how to interpret it. She had had time to consider all that had gone on in the past week, and the risks to her and the film if she became more involved.

Viv passed by her favourite shop on the walk home and, despite the hour, there was still fresh fish on offer.

"What's left, Eddie?"

"For you, V. J., anything!" He ran through the list of fish – red mullet, hake, bream – and then he paused. "Got lobster too?"

"No choice in that – it'll be lobster."

He lifted up a small one. "One or two?"

"Two."

She would remain positive. Eddie ran to vegetables and popped in some samphire free. *How can today feel so good*, Viv wondered, *when tomorrow is the gallows?* At least it was her decision and no-one else's.

When she had had her first success with *Riots Inc.*, Nancy Kane had congratulated her and given her a fine Bollinger. This she had never drunk, thinking that one day a suitable moment would come, or a suitable occasion she could celebrate with others. Only, it had never really worked out like that; for all the time she had lived in this flat, she had never had anyone over the threshold except for Don, who had built the concrete balcony. Her home had been too precious, too much of a sanctuary, and something had always stopped her. But tonight would be different.

She set about her process using the best of everything – her best glasses, the Bollinger on ice, her best and unused plates. And then, knowing that the meal would not take long to cook, she placed the mayonnaise on the table and ran a hot bath. Again, there was so much unused and saved-up luxury which she had never permitted herself to use – the lavender oil, the candles. If anyone who knew her could see her now, they would be amazed; this was not the Viv of the sharp tongue, the fedora and the on-tap rebuttals of intimacy. But here it was, the last night of the condemned. Tomorrow, she would go to the police station and turn herself in; she would not, under any circumstances, wait for the knock on the door. She would be master of her fate. She had expected to feel sad, frightened even, but as she lay there in the hot bath, she savoured every minute and felt only gratitude for the years she had claimed for herself.

And she felt only sorrow for Reg. No guilt. He had deserved it, after all. She had had no choice. The warm water relaxed her. The only choice she had had, she conceded, was that she could have stopped at one blow, enough to stun him unconscious; she hadn't needed to go on. Had it been survival? Or something else? Had the blows she had rained down on him been for all the other times she had taken the violence, sucked it in and coped without complaining? She ducked under the water, holding her breath.

Am I a murderer?

She repeated the word 'murderer' until it sank in. It made her 'other'; it made her a 'criminal'; it was something she could never erase. She remembered trying to kill ants when she was a child as they were overrunning the kitchen – had that been so very different? Had that already made her a killer? She remembered Reg as she had met him at his garage and shuddered. But it was when she remembered that above the garage was where his wife and children lived that she wavered. She had wrecked their lives too, she had taken away her husband, their father. But what to do? She would figure that out… For now, she had to save herself as best she could. She sat up in the bath, smoothing out her wet hair.

"I couldn't have done anything else."

She thought of her father. She thought of her mother. She thought of Paula. What was it in her that made people so easily betray her? And what of Amanda? Would she stay with her? With that thought, she shuddered, reached for the giant bath towel and buried her face in it.

By seven, Viv was in the kitchen, dressed in a white man's shirt, fresh out of the packet, and her usual gear. It felt decisive. She checked her phone to see if Amanda had replied; the feast of celebration would continue with or without her. Etta James was keeping pace with her – 'All I Could Do Was Cry'. Viv hummed as she popped the lobster in and put the samphire in a small saucepan and looked through the window to the river, her river. Perhaps her prison would overlook the river? Some forlorn hope, but even so, miracles could still happen. It was as she brought out the first lobster that the doorbell rang. She pulled the samphire off and checked the video monitor – it was Amanda. She took a deep breath to steady herself.

They stood looking at each other on the threshold for a while, before embracing, knowing what the moment was.

"Come in, come in, come in."

Viv could hear Etta had moved on to 'Fool That I Am'.

"I'm sorry I didn't call back but there was so much on that I had first to deal with. How are you?"

They had moved into the main living area.

"Wait right there!" And Viv reappeared with the champagne on ice, two glasses. "Here's to happy lives, good fortune – and gratitude!"

Amanda sipped. "I didn't expect you to be back, or be so upbeat – what's going on? Did you get advice? Did you hear anything more from the police? Is it over?"

Amanda realised that she had not called Geoff again for an update, she had been so busy.

"I did, and I have not. My toast is 'to tomorrow!'. I shall go to them; they shall not come for me."

Amanda now understood; she took it all in and drained her glass. Her feelings were in turmoil.

"There is absolutely no point – and indeed *that* is a crime in itself – not to drain the Bollinger!"

It was a sweet complicity, mutual denial. They drank in silence, knowing how much weight this evening had. They knew too how much had indeed been unspoken during their time together, how much resistance to acknowledging what had been growing between them. Amanda was sure that she had never yet felt like this about another person. Viv was it for her. And now she may never see her again.

Amanda leant over the table. "You do know I'll be there for you, don't you?"

Viv looked intently at Amanda. Did she mean it? And what exactly did 'be there for you' mean? She reached for the Bollinger and refilled their glasses. Amanda held her gently by the wrist.

"You do believe me, don't you?"

Viv exhaled and slumped back. "I'm sorry. It was ungracious of me… it's just…"

"I know… trust."

Viv nodded. "Would you come to the magistrate's court? It feels overwhelming, and if I could see a friendly face, you know."

"Of course."

Viv was high on resolution. At last she felt no longer the victim and acknowledged that in all the wonderful V. J. Wheeler years – and they had been wonderful – there had been a paranoid element lurking somewhere. Now all was out in the open and the process of the next part of her life would shortly begin, she felt giddy with excitement. The last thing she had expected to feel. The writer of that letter held nothing over her anymore, but still she was going to find him.

The lobster, the samphire, the mayonnaise, the candles, the champagne were all so fitting. It was a feast.

Amanda reached across the table again. "I don't want to spoil this wonderful mood, darling, I want the best for you… for us."

Viv held up a finger to her lips. "Shh then."

"…But we have said so little of meaning to each other. You must know how I feel about you?"

Viv's reluctance had dissipated at long last; there was no downside now, nothing to fear.

"I know."

"Well then?"

"But how will you – we – cope if I go to prison? You have your own life. What will happen?"

There was a long pause before Amanda answered, "I will wait for you." She reached across the table. "I promise."

Amanda held up her little finger to link with Viv. "Promises."

Viv rose to take the plates out, avoiding the offer.

"Here…"

Viv sat down again, trying to erase the memory that gesture had brought up. That had been Paula's line – 'pinkie promise'. They linked and silently vowed to each other that this night would last beyond tonight.

"I love you."

Hearing her own words out loud for the first time dissolved all resistance to trust, to love. She had never said those words to anyone.

Viv stood, held out her hand for Amanda, and she led her to her bedroom, which had panoramic glass sliding doors as did the sitting room. The view was of the darkening water, the lights coming on here and there. Viv undid her own shirt and invited Amanda to lie down with her. Amanda, roles reversed, came into the crook of Viv's arm and the remembered phrase from school came to Viv: 'the peace which passeth all understanding'.

She kissed Amanda's hair. Amanda turned to her and kissed her gently until their lips met and the kiss was so deep it was as though it could last through the coming years. For both of them, the sweetest night of their lives. It carried the promise of a future, but one that might be postponed. Tonight, though, was theirs.

CHAPTER 12

Viv woke before Amanda and turned her head to look at her sleeping. Her blonde hair had fallen across her cheek and Viv tenderly pushed it back. The light, at first a soft glow and then strong as the sun broke through the cloud, came at an angle. She followed the shaft of light, dust particles dancing, thinking, perhaps for the first time, how extraordinary it was that light never of itself chose not to bend, it cut straight through or became blocked.

She ran mentally through her bag of essentials for the day ahead, and with that quickly done, she focussed on what she would wear to survive a day of ritualised humiliation.

Viv kissed the top of Amanda's head and breathed in deep the special scent of it. She knew it would have to last; she knew in that moment, though, that it would not, whatever they had promised to each other last night. She took such a deep breath that she involuntarily juddered. Amanda stirred and moved her arm further across Viv. She felt Amanda's hand tighten around her and Viv softened and turned to hold Amanda one last time. Last night, they hadn't discussed at length what Viv was about to do, but both of them knew and both knew also that beyond today, neither of them could determine what their time together would truly mean. Amanda looked up sleepily to Viv and kissed her, not lightly, not passionately, in place of words.

Viv leant over to the side table. "I got you this."

Amanda registered surprise and murmured, "You shouldn't."

"Shh, open it."

It was a small box with a bracelet inside that Viv had found in Paris. Amanda picked it out and saw there was a small heart attached, and a message which read *Please*.

Amanda encircled Viv.

"I will. Of course I will."

Viv had never wanted to believe something as strongly as she did in that moment.

She ran mentally through her bag of essentials. The hat was important; it had been with her on all momentous days and others not so momentous; it was the link between Evie and Viv; she would wear the fedora. It seemed less important to figure out the trousers and top since they were all black. She hated herself for this thought, but she knew black would last longer than a light colour in a police cell. The squalor ahead of her was something she had thought she had left behind her, and she had hoped never to return, but here she was.

Footwear was vital for so many reasons. It was practical, it had to endure, but it also had to dictate her tread today and for many days – she was sure of that. Glancing over to her wardrobe, the door ajar, she could see the Doc Martens she had kept more for sentimental reasons than anything. They had seen her through the worst of what life had thrown at her; they had seen her through days of keeping them on, all weathers, walking for miles to find somewhere to sleep that night. They were seasoned, scuffed – she would polish them for today.

It was Viv who left the bed first, and as she stood under the shower, she tried to imprint on her memory every second of the night, every second of every drop of this shower as the water played on her skin.

Within ten minutes, Viv had dressed and waited for Amanda to follow suit. She began almost to bark instructions as to where to find her computer, the code, her phone, her car, her keys; she knew all this she might not be returning to, perhaps for a long time.

"Please, please don't do that."

"What?"

"Be this… person… Not yet."

They embraced and the contact served as permission to once again separate. Viv could not afford to carry her vulnerability further. Last night was last night.

"I have to. I have to be quick now."

Any delay would be painful, make her re-evaluate, even falter, and she would not do that. Any delay would mean losing control of her plan and that she would not do; she would go to the police, not the other way round.

As Amanda left with Viv's keys in her hand, she held the door open and turned away, refusing to watch Amanda's disappearing form.

Her nearest station was oddly further out of London. Sitting on the DLR, she marvelled at the airiness of the train, the lightness of the journey; not so many people went this way for work, it was the other way round. Four other people travelled to the scaffold with her, a West Indian mother with her two-year-old boy. The whole five stops he fought to get off her lap; she hauled him back at first with words then a slap on the legs.

"Sit still!"

He appeared to fall in line but caught Viv's eye with a wicked smile which seemed to say, "I've got this."

An old woman was opposite, washed through with tiredness, the colour gone from her hair, her face, her skin, loose and sagging, heading fast back to the earth from whence she came. And two Eastern European girls talking fast, laughing, excited. Viv wondered about them but came to no conclusion as the station name at first flashed by the window then stopped slow enough for her to read and be sure that this was it. Passing by the front of the train, none of them, she reflected, had found it odd there had been no driver; it seemed ironic, putting yourself in the hands of fate. Was it a good omen that she had arrived in one piece? She had no luggage, other than a small bag. Everything would end up in a grey plastic tray in any case; she had decided to travel light. Indeed, in an odd way, now that the road was narrow, the course clear, she felt lighter than she had for a long time, and she strode out.

Police stations were now something of a rarity, and the paradox of the dual need for felons to be captured and at the same time preventing the ease of surrender was not lost on Viv. Red-brick Victorian police stations with their hanging blue lanterns were almost worthy of National Heritage status. Some, she knew, had adapted to having glass fronts, automatic doors. Most had surrendered the deeds for necessary cash now that the government had ceded responsibility for citizens' safety to the status of a lottery. Some had become cafés; some had been converted into 'luxury' flats with glass balconies.

Any which way, it meant that the citizen and the police now mostly connected through the internet with a drop-down choice of options for reporting a crime. Either that or a flashing police car. It bred extreme positions and reduced the concept of cooperation.

As she walked, she was conscious of every step. How delightful with the DLR rather than the underground not to have to climb up into the light, how delightful the air did not choke her with diesel particles, how delightful at this moment to feel upbeat.

She walked on and was about to leave the curly Thames to her right, but she was compelled to say goodbye as though to a friend and took the pathway away from the main road. The tide was going out, a fast flow, as though in a hurry. The sun had disappeared, and she shivered, drawing her greatcoat further around her, collar up. The river would at least be there when she got out; the river would not desert her. She passed a hairdresser, an Italian café, and turned right. *How quaint, how apt*, she thought, *it is a cul de sac*.

Once she found the station, there was security in the form of impermeable glass with a little round vent with petal-shaped holes. She had to bend, sort of sideways, to get level with this. She had always considered herself of average height, perhaps shorter, but whoever had designed this would have had other views.

"Yes?"

Was this neutral or bored?

"May I see someone? In regard to a crime?"

"That's what we do here."

Without a smile, that statement lacked irony.

"In private."

"Fill this in." She shoved a form in the till under the glass. Viv looked down at it. She had steeled herself for a dramatic high point, this was admin.

"No."

She pushed it back and rang the bell marked 'press for attention' and did not let it go. The girl behind the glass frantically gestured but could do nothing to stop this.

"Wait here!" She disappeared out the back.

"Exactly."

Viv was not about to be someone's victim.

A policeman, his rank not clear, but presumably junior and the only one left manning the fort, was Viv's assessment.

"I wish to talk with you about a crime. In private. Not through Perspex."

He pressed a release button; the Perspex relaxed and opened. Viv walked through to the back of the small station, down a corridor and to a room so empty it was hard to take in. Still painted in 1950s colours, half dark green, half discoloured cream. The officer took one chair, scraping it on the hard floor, gestured to the other, not looking at Viv. He leant sideways and flipped on the recorder.

"Interview beginning," he glanced up at the clock, "eleven-fifteen. Detainee Viv Wheeler… and DI Jackson in the room. Address…"

The need for so much admin irritated Viv but she took a deep breath and chose to humour the officer and completed all the information he needed, but reverted to her own, Evie Riley's, date of birth.

"Now may we get on to what I came here for?"

"Attitude is never a good thing."

"I was stopped on the M3 near Basingstoke for speeding, over the limit. Taken to Basingstoke."

"When was this?"

She gave the date and details.

"This will go to the magistrate's court, then either the Crown Court or the county court depending."

"On what?"

"Whether you are up for reckless or dangerous driving. Reckless is Crown Court. Jury." The officer's boredom was palpable. "It'll all be on the record, no need to come down here, it's out of our hands."

"That wasn't why. That was merely to give you the

background. When I was arrested, my DNA and fingerprints and so on were taken."

The officer actually shrugged at this point. "All procedure."

He broke off from tapping the table to reach out for the phone, but paused when he heard Viv say, "Which will lead to linking me to a crime of fourteen years ago, and I wish to pre-empt this and hand myself in."

The officer decided, taking in Viv's appearance and her hoity manner, that he had a nutcase, a timewaster on his hands and, more to the point, someone who thought they were better than the police. He'd met her type before. Nonetheless, he was obliged for the paperwork to ask which crime that would be.

"It was a rape and a killing. In Reston, Middlesex. In 2003."

"Interview suspended. Wait here."

CHAPTER 13

Viv looked up at the camera recording her in the officer's absence. Except for the table and two chairs, the clock on the wall and the recorder, the room was barren. She struggled to breathe. She sat on her hands and forced herself to stay motionless; this was training for prison. She could do it. She could do it. The officer returned, this time with a frisson of energy. He had verified Viv's information on the main computer upstairs. He switched the recorder back on.

"Interview resumed. I need to caution you that, from now on, if this interview should come to a charge, anything you say will be taken into account. Anything you may need to later rely on in court may be used in evidence against you."

Viv could see that he had a printout of the Reston cold case.

"This was of one Reginald Dawson?"

Viv nodded.

"For the tape. Yes or no?"

"Yes."

"And the forensic evidence from the scene has matched up with your driving charge. Although the forensic at the scene is under the name of Evie Riley. What have you to say to that?"

There was a tinge of triumph in his voice.

"For the time being, all you need to know is that I was Evie Riley. I am now Viv Wheeler."

The officer pressed a buzzer and a minute later, after Viv and he had sat in total silence, another officer entered the room. Despite the change of name, which he would need time to look into, the officer had no alternative but to go ahead with procedure. DNA didn't lie.

"Evie Riley, I am arresting you for the murder of Reginald Dawson. Do you have anything to say which might later be relied on in court?"

"At this stage, I will say nothing. I will wait for my solicitor before I say anything more. But I am innocent of murder. Now it's down to you."

The officer frowned and was about to challenge this switch of command. It irked him. Instead, he stood up and turned to his colleague, towering over Viv.

"I am authorising your detention. Do you understand?"

"Of course. Lead the way." She stopped herself from adding 'o thou great Jehovah'. A step too far in the circumstances.

She followed the two officers down the concrete steps at the back of the building to the downstairs holding cell. Her nerve held, she had prepared herself for this, but all the same, her heart fell at the sight of the thin, blue, plastic sponge mattress, the lack of adornment or windows, the hanging light bulb. Viv was about to turn round when she heard the door shut and lock.

"How long will I be... here?"

The words died.

Too late. The smell was something she would have to get used to. There was, as far as she could see, no ventilation to let the evidence of the past users of this cell to depart. The smell of disinfectant overrode anything else. There was no clock. Just a high up horizontal slit of a window. After pacing around, she sat on the single bed. The soft sponge bedding sank under her weight. Viv felt panic choke her; it was as though the amount of air was finite. Wasn't this a form of torture? Wasn't this against some EU ruling or whatever? She wished she had looked into all that, but there had been enough to think about. The first opportunity of access to a computer, she would check this out. It was inhuman. The internal dialogue continued for how long Viv didn't know. She lay down on the mattress and studied the marks on the ceiling. She couldn't hear anything either. Would no-one hear her if she called? No panic button either. What about water?

How long had elapsed she couldn't tell as counting seconds, minutes, for any longer than half an hour would have sent her mental, she knew that. There was meditation and there was meditation. She jumped at the sudden noise; the grille was shoved roughly aside. She stood, could make out a face, someone checking she was still alive.

"Hey, hey…!"

But the grille had gone back. Like a switch, the hunger came on her. She would die if they gave her no food. Was she being melodramatic? She stood, paced about the cell, measured the length and breadth; hearing her own footfall emboldened her. She marched to the door, fist-banged on it until the grille clicked sideways again.

"I need food."

It clicked back but not before she heard him say, as he turned away, "Later."

Keeping her ear to the door, she heard laughter. She had to get on top of this, on top of herself. She had endured worse, after all; this was ridiculous. At least she had a bed. She slowed her thoughts and tried to focus on the explanation that she would give the magistrate's court the next day. But as Viv endured the rest of that day and the night and part of the next morning, she had no idea of whether it was day or night, a thought more disconcerting than expecting to be attacked while she slept. Supper of sorts had eventually been left for her. She had to eat and forced herself to overcome her revulsion of the smell of cabbage and the flatness of the pizza. She must have dozed off as she jumped at the sound of the grille being shot sideways.

"Stand away from the door."

Hardly necessary if you could actually see me, was Viv's thought. She felt filthy already but stood to see the officer holding out handcuffs for her to be linked to him. Her mind shot back to that night when she had fled. *How ironic*, she thought, *to go through all that I have just to be here*. The officer was overweight, his nylon shirt bulging at the waist, his dark, greasy hair pulled back into a stub of a ponytail.

"Sleep?"

Viv supposed this was his attempt to break the ice.

"No."

He took her into a canteen of sorts at the back of the station where he ordered two teas and toast. Still with the handcuffs linking him to Viv, he managed to get the tray back to the bench and table without spilling them. Viv had never contemplated this close a union with anyone, and certainly not with an overweight man whose idea of what a cop looked like had come to life by watching American films.

"You're up this morning. Leave in half an hour."

The van that took Viv and her new friend to the magistrate's court was one that she had seen on news footage, always with the photographers leaping to flash the camera at the darkened windows. The seats were either side. There was nothing to say, and so the journey of nearly an hour went by in silence. Viv had an image of being passed from one airlock to another as, after the van journey, she was placed in yet another holding cell at the back of the building until her case came up. The cuffs were off at least for now. She almost didn't mind what the outcome was as long as she could be free on bail, with time to figure out if she had a life left at all. She knew Arun would make that happen.

The door opened, the cuffs were back on, and she was walked across the courtyard to the magistrate's court itself. She filed in and they stood behind the reinforced glass wall, separating them from the court. She sat on one of the plastic chairs. She looked around, to the back of the court where relatives sat.

The first person she saw was Arun; he looked up and gestured a hello, bobbing his head in acknowledgement. Viv felt a surge of love for him in that moment. She smiled and tried to raise her hand, but the handcuffs pulled it down. To her right was the bench and the three arbiters; in front of her was Arun and beyond him, the CPS.

The usher was on the far side shuffling papers. The barrister to the court read out her name and the charge.

"Murder of one Reginald Dawson, second degree. There are lesser charges, too, My Lady, but for today we should consider only the murder charge."

As the crown prosecutor read out the charge, Viv heard the baldness of the facts and felt the unfairness of it all. Bile rose into her mouth. She stood as though to move and speak to Arun.

"Sit down."

The wind went out of her. She was no longer V. J. Wheeler, but just a prisoner, the accused. She drank the water in the little polystyrene cup next to her and looked over towards the visitors' benches at the back. She scanned the faces for Amanda. Must be caught in traffic. Amanda might not know the exact time – how could she? It was Arun's turn and the familiar sight of him brought a lump to Viv's throat. How could she have imagined where they would end up when they had first met in the club, he then slightly in thrall to the great V. J.?

"My Lady, this is the charge only and I would point out that there is no evidence at all that my client committed murder. My client was, however, raped. She defended herself and she escaped further suffering as a result of these acts. Which brings me to the question of bail, My Lady."

The CPS, in his spivvy, shiny suit with a double hack, popped up, anxious not to give Arun more time.

"Bail should not be granted to the accused as she is an escape risk."

Here he alluded to the flight to Paris. Viv knew she could not have done anything else at that point but could now see that it would be the major obstacle to her freedom until trial.

"My Lady, my client will surrender her passport, and lodge her own bail surety of £100,000."

The CPS stood up again, a cocky little shit enjoying his audience.

"Didn't stop her last time, did it?"

"Court rise!"

And the three magistrates trooped out like elves in the forest to consider their determination.

Viv checked the visitors' rows once more. No Amanda. *Yet*, she told herself.

During the break, the atmosphere quickly relaxed with the CPS bantering with police at the back of the court. Arun moved to the glass, beckoning her to the voice slit.

"Can you increase the bail amount?"

Viv nodded.

The elves returned and the middle one began leaning into her microphone.

"We have."

"My lady," this was Arun, "my client can increase her bail money to £500,000."

"Thank you. We have considered all the facts, and we have decided that with the Crown Court date set for six months' time, the accused should be remanded in custody until that date. The amount of bail offered is immaterial in this case."

Viv held up her hand. "What?"

Arun dropped his head, turned to look at Viv, mouthing, "I'm sorry. I'll come and see you."

As Viv was led out towards the back door again, she checked one last time to see if Amanda had arrived just at the last minute. She was, this time though, relieved that Amanda would not see this humiliation. It was, she told herself, a good thing.

CHAPTER 14

She couldn't get her head around what was happening. Straight from the dock to the waiting van. There were four other prisoners, all handcuffed, all sitting on the side of the van. *A bit like an aircraft carrier*, was Viv's thought. All women, of course. *Are we such a dangerous species? Really?* As she looked along at their faces, it seemed they were more like victims, miserable and trapped, but not dangerous. The woman at the end, the oldest by far, had the lined face and sunken mouth of a smoker; she sat clenching and unclenching her hands, not talking to anyone, her thoughts far away. Perhaps, despite her age, this was her first time. Or was it, in fact, a familiar trip, all the more fearful for knowing what was ahead? Next to her was a girl who looked little more than a teenager, scuffed trainers, tracksuit, ponytail, rings on nearly each finger and bitten nails. The other two knew each other, so either they knew each other in the real world, or else they had been arrested together. Viv thought the latter; conspiracy against the world seemed to link their body language.

"Do you know where we are going?" she asked quietly.

"No talking!"

"Belton," the girl whispered under her breath.

There were no windows to see out of, just blacked-out windows high above. The driver, two guards, one in the front and one with them. Viv could smell petrol as though it had been spilled when filling up. She thought of her car, and for a fleeting second, she remembered the freedom of driving. She shivered, sat upright, looked down at her handcuffs. She relaxed slightly at the memory of having handed over her keys and valuable information to Amanda, who would take care of it for her, but as the van made its journey along the M4, she remembered how she had scanned the fast emptying court and not seen her. She had been so certain Amanda would have come. If only she could just hold her one last time, explain more; they had had so little time. Viv shut her eyes. The van braked enough to jolt her out of this moment. The journey seemed so long that Viv had no sense of where they were, or when they would reach the prison. She rubbed her brow with her sleeve, her sweaty hands on her trousers. They stopped. No-one was speaking. Viv heard the driver's door slam again and the sound of him walking away. Soon he was back, and Viv could see through the high-up window that a gate had been lifted and they were driving through. Brakes on, engine cut, doors open. The back van doors were unlocked, held for a moment, then fully opened and the light flooded in. Viv was stiff but got up and stepped down from the prison van.

"Riley!"

The van had stopped yards from the back entrance, little risk of escape here. The routine of being led by the wrist, waiting for every door to open and be locked again before the next one opened had already become familiar.

She was made to wait for processing in a bleak room with red plastic chairs around the sides. There were three other women in the mouldy, airless room. They were all sitting at the far end, together, but Viv chose to sit alone. She could feel their eyes on her, suspicious and judging. She glanced at her wrist, massaged the space where her watch had been. Five minutes later, she looked again. The habit of needing to know what time everything was happening, how long she would wait, kept pressing on her, but she was quick to realise that this would have to stop. Her will would have to go if she were to survive in here. She longed for privacy, even to cry one day, not now, perhaps, but one day. She struggled for breath. A woman officer, well built, in her forties, came in with a clipboard. Viv could see from her taut, shiny skin she had not washed the soap off her face; that was what happened when you didn't see yourself as a person anymore. Probably not even in a bathroom mirror. She checked down the list.

"Vernon, Fisher, Mgusi, Riley?"

What were they meant to say? The names were read out again.

"And this time, tell me you are here! Reply!"

Viv managed a reluctant and barely audible answer. "Yes."

"Riley, you come with me."

Viv followed the woman officer into the room at the far end.

On the Formica counter there was a tray with a pillow, a duvet, a sheet, pyjamas, a toilet roll and a bar of soap. Next to this was a grey, wool tracksuit. Next to that was another tray that Viv had to put her valuables in, only there were none, as she had taken care to leave them at home.

"Rings? Piercings?"

"No."

The officer ticked off her list anyway.

"Name, address."

It was all falling away; she thought of the tombstone where V. J. had been born.

All the processing was done, and she was shown back into the larger part of the room to wait until the others too had been processed. Viv, out of habit, now glanced down at her bare wrist and rubbed it absent-mindedly. She pulled down her sleeve. Slowly, slowly, control was being taken away.

At the press of a bell, a second officer appeared.

"Riley, come with me."

Viv hadn't been called Riley for years.

"Wheel…" she began; she was still Wheeler.

Clutching the bedding and clothing pile, she followed the officer down the corridor and out into the central courtyard from where she could see there were five different wings. A Wing, that was the one they went into. A Wing, for the murderers. Viv's heart sank; even she knew from her brief knowledge that this was the most secure wing, the one for violent offenders, and fear flooded her from head to foot. She straightened her back, raised her head. Would they attack her? Would she get help? Would they be locked into their cells? For the first time, she thought that might be a good thing. The locking and unlocking of doors, the key on the warder's chain, all went on until they were inside, and Viv could feel the agitation, the instability in the air, before she saw anything. It felt like anything could happen in here. Shrill voices. She kept her head down as she walked behind the warder.

Viv felt overwhelming relief that it was a single room, just her. The bed had a dip in it, was already covered in a coarse, grey, wool blanket, but she had, she remembered, slept in worse.

"Put your bedding down there."

She did.

"And get changed into those."

Viv did as she was told. The warder waited, registering nothing, and took away the clothes she had worn into court.

"You'll get these back at the end."

The end, the end, when's that? thought Viv.

"Canteen is at the end of this block. Supper at six. Lock-in at eight."

She was about to leave.

"Wait! I'm sorry… can I make a phone call?"

"There'll be time for that."

"No, no, now, I need to now. Someone was meant to be in court and they…"

The warder's voice was blank, weary; she had heard it all a million times before and walked out of the room.

She could still hear voices, strained to hear whether they were angry, excitable or threatening. She tensed. Was something going to break out? It seemed that the others' curiosity about the new inmate would wait as no-one came and Viv stayed sitting on the bed until she smelled food. She wished she had a jumper or a scarf; she was shivering. Why hadn't Amanda been there? There were only two explanations, really, she knew that. She had entrusted Amanda with her computer, her mobile, her flat, everything really – herself, too, she had entrusted to Amanda that last night. She wished she had kept something of Amanda's to remind her, but of what? A late blackbird flew past her window.

She took a deep breath, then another. She wanted that reminder of feeling safe; she had felt safe with Amanda.

She could hear feet, people passing her door on the way to the food. After a while, it eased off. Viv cautiously peered out and followed the pathway down to the canteen. She had no appetite, but thought she could perhaps smuggle something back if she was hungry in the night, an apple maybe. She remembered her first day at school aged five; she had been terrified then too, had held back. Looking around her, keeping as low a profile as she could, she joined the queue, avoiding eye contact, and helped herself to something that looked like beef mince and rice. She collected the spoon from the tray – no knives and no sharp forks, only plastic ones. Ugh!

The desire to be back safe in her flat gripped her stomach so tight it was as though the thought would manifest, like a time machine, a teleporter – and this would all have been a bad dream. She found a place on the long benches and set about trying to eat something if she could. She tried to eat, she retched.

"First day?"

Viv nodded.

"Gets better."

"No it don't!"

There was laughter. Viv managed a smile. Too early to ask for names, but she studied the girl's face. Teeth missing, dark under the eyes, she looked already old but was probably her own age.

"How do you make phone calls?" She almost whispered this to her neighbour.

A shrug was the only answer forthcoming.

Somehow, Viv got through the meal, and it was time to leave.

She heard behind her, "Stuck-up cow!"

She kept walking, didn't turn round.

"Stuck-up, cow!"

Viv quickened her pace; her room already had the feeling of sanctuary, and she was keen to get there, but lock-in wasn't until eight. Would she be attacked before then, bullied even? Would they follow her in? She would be ready if someone came into her room. She wasn't up to a fight yet though, she knew that. There was a television in her room; she had no books. She switched it on. *EastEnders*, oh God. She turned it up loud. She flicked through the channels, hardly noticing what was on, left it playing just for company to drown out everything and lay back on her unmade bed.

She could hear the warder knocking on each door. The rattle of the chain on her key, a clank as it fell back after each lock turn. It was eight o'clock. Viv's was suddenly locked – she ran over to the door, about to call out. Instead she slumped against it, fell down to the floor, all energy drained, and just heard the receding footfall of the warder. It was useless, this is what would happen every night now. The light was almost gone. She flipped the slatted blinds down. There was a small fly trapped in the light fitting somewhere. Buzzing. She wouldn't sleep, she couldn't. She was exhausted, her nerves alert.

She spent that first night wide awake, trying to marshal her thoughts and block them out.

There were no birds, but she heard a fox. At first she thought it was a human baby, then recalled the foxes she had heard at home. She curled up tight in a ball just as she had that first night at boarding school. What lay ahead?

She could hear screaming coming out of a room down the other end. It went on and on, it never stopped the whole night. This was like being back in Reston, trying to work out from the sounds around her, people's voices, what was happening, what was about to happen.

She could do with a drink. She really could.

CHAPTER 15

She needed to process what had taken place, laid back on the rough grey wool of the bed. But it was to Amanda that her thoughts drifted. She retrieved the small photo she had of her and Amanda in New York. She had hidden it in her bra. There they were. It was another world, their two faces smiling, open, and the sea wind blowing their hair about. Manhattan skyline in the background.

Speaking to Amanda's face in the photo, she whispered, "Don't say you love me if you are going to abandon me."

Viv kissed the photo and replaced it with care. It was all she had but in the silence since, she had begun to doubt that picture. *Photos can lie*, she told herself.

There was a row down the corridor. Viv turned and blocked out the noise; she needed to think. That night, Amanda had held her hands in hers and promised, absolutely promised, that she would wait for her. She curled up tight in a ball, her knees up to her chest. How long could she go on thinking that?

She dislodged the photo again from its hiding place. *Is this photo a giant, ghastly lie after all? Am I the fool?*

*

It was the following week, the Tuesday, when she saw her name up on the visiting board, next to it, *A. Rosbury*. She stopped dead in her tracks, bumped into Tracy.

"Watch out!"

"Sorry, sorry."

So, she was coming, Amanda had not deserted her. And it was Rosberg, not Rosbury. Viv was there five minutes early. Her heart was beating out of her mouth, her hands were sweating. She chose a table and chairs in the far corner; no-one wanted those, but it was a good place for Viv as she could watch the door and would see Amanda before Amanda saw her. And then, with the clock showing seven minutes past two, she imagined the slender, beautiful blonde. Viv anticipated the familiar perfume. She smoothed her own hair in the vain attempt of making it look presentable. Amanda asked Evans where Viv was, Evans pointed, Amanda smiled and made her way over. Viv couldn't work out her mood. Did she want to be here? Or would she rather be a million miles elsewhere?

"Hello."

Amanda looked so straight and square at Viv, held her gaze searching for the answers to questions she had not yet asked.

"Hi." Viv felt like a teenager, awkward, almost shy.

"How are things in here? How are you?"

Viv looked away, the answer would only describe and widen the gap between their two worlds. Amanda reached for her hand.

"No touching!"

"Sorry."

"Really though, Viv, please, how are you? I have not been able to sleep thinking of you here, in this place."

Recovering her composure, Viv went for the unvarnished truth in one unbroken sentence.

"It is a living nightmare. I think I will wake up and find it was a bad dream. I am alone, I have to see it through. I am counting the days to the trial, and then it will be over. I looked for you in the court."

Amanda's face registered surprise.

"Don't *you* think so? Don't you think it is a strong case? Don't you think Arun will get me out of here?"

A slight pause. "Of course."

Viv leant across. "I have to get out. I have to."

Amanda changed the subject. "What are the… others… like?"

Viv shrugged.

In the outside world they had talked easily, but here was different.

"So, how is the film going?"

Amanda talked at length about the production, the locations, the problems, the other people.

"Would you rather not talk about this? It must be difficult."

"No, yes, I do, it reminds me that I have – had – another life."

"And you will again. You will again."

"I have another five months here before the trial. Will you visit again? You don't have to…"

"Of course I will. But what shall I bring you next time?"

Viv brightened at the thought of another visit. "I'm sorry, this place changes you, this can't have been much fun for you." Viv pulled out the photo of them both on the island ferry. "Remember this?"

"I don't need a photo to remember that day. But just keep it with you."

And with that, she was gone, leaving once the bell went. No contact, just a wave much like waving a tot off to nursery. A little wave.

As Amanda had made it once to the prison, Viv, in her need to see her, had already made this to be a weekly, possibly monthly, commitment. Amanda had not let her down, after all. So it was that Viv was handed a letter a month later; she knew it was Amanda's writing. At once wanting to devour it, savour it, she was filled with dread that it would contain the last thing she wanted to read, and once read, she would not be able to forget it.

My dear darling Viv,
 It was, I was going to say, good to see you but, and I have debated whether to write you this letter, it was not good. I cannot bear thinking of you in that God-awful prison, everything metal, cold and hard. I dread to think of your cell, your bed. I like to remember you in your wonderful big soft bed looking out on to the river.

Tears came easily now. Viv held the letter, unable to go on. She knew what was coming. And what Amanda was saying was, of course, all true.

So, my darling, we have to keep in touch and hope that when you are back in the world, our world, we will still connect. So, what I shall do is write to you every now and then, tell you news, and I would love for you to do the same. Will you?
 With all my love, Amanda xx

CHAPTER 16

It was five-thirty in the morning by the wall clock. Not a sound, not anywhere. Then an early blackbird began, and another. Soon it was six-thirty. Viv needed to call Amanda today, she really did. She heard the far door at the end of the wing unlock, a voice, then two, then laughter, then each door unlocking one by one, and the footsteps got nearer. She heard her door being unlocked. Lights went on. She stretched, rose, and opened the blinds. Rain ran down the pane in rivulets.

"Oh."

What had she hoped for? A view? Some hope? It was just a yard and wet outbuildings.

Breakfast, she knew, was at eight. She should shower; perhaps that would help her feel better. The central light bulb went. Breakfast was the same routine as before, out of the little hatch, just a choice of cereals and toast, coffee which tasted like nothing resembling coffee. Viv carried it back on a tray, hoping to find an easy space.

Something had happened in the night. No-one was talking, but Viv had heard the outbreak of banging on the doors, of yelling. She wasn't about to ask, not this early in the game, she'd get to know soon enough if she needed to.

She asked her neighbour, a woman of about forty, hair greying, waist going.

"What's happening today?"

"You'll be put to work. Gardens or kitchen?"

"Do I have a choice?"

There was laughter; Viv decided to join in. Safer. For now. It was getting chilly, autumn was drawing in, she would prefer kitchen.

The officer with the clipboard called out, "Riley!"

Viv raised her hand, old habits returning as though she had never lived a successful life as V. J. Wheeler.

"Follow me."

As they walked, Evans, the officer, told her, "You're on gardening."

"Can I make a phone call today? Sometime today?"

Evans caught the desperation in Viv's voice and turned to look at her.

"After the garden, come and find me. I'll show you where."

With that, she indicated where Viv was to go, who she was to talk to in the garden.

"You're to rake the beds clean and tidy, weeding, take the stones out. If you need anything, ask them."

She indicated two women on the far side of the garden, already stuck into their tasks. It was cold, and the icy air hit her as she went outside. Viv walked over to the courtyard where she was led to a small grassy area on the far side. Hardly a garden, but that was what it was called. Potatoes just showing through on one end, grass, and some dead remainders of autumn flowers. She took the rake from the shed, and leaning on it, took stock. The ground was stony, the earth a poor, light colour. Would anything grow here?

She saw Evans had stayed to watch.

"The grass!"

Viv moved to the grassy area and repeated the raking, making sure any small stones ended up at one side. *The grass looked like a child's hair just brushed,* she thought. She remembered her mother doing her hair before school. It was cold, but she kept moving. *What this garden needs is a good compost.* She thought that she might ask if she could take the waste out for them. Would it look odd? Draw attention?

As she passed Evans on the way back in two hours later, she asked her if that would be a good idea.

"Why go changing things?"

"But is it OK to ask?"

Evans shrugged. "Follow me, I'll show you where to phone."

With dismay, Viv could see that the phone on the wall, although partly out of sight round the corner, would be in full earshot of anyone who cared to listen. She knew Amanda's number by heart. She dialled and waited, willing for the phone to be picked up. She glanced at the wall clock; it was just gone two, perhaps she was still at lunch? Then a worse thought: of course Amanda would not recognise the number she had called from. Perhaps... But just as she was elaborating the options, she heard Amanda's voice.

"Hello?"

For a second, Viv hesitated.

"Hi, Amanda, it's me."

She waited.

"Oh darling, I am *so* glad you called." Viv could hear Amanda excusing herself to those she was with. "I'm taking this outside, hold on."

Viv waited, knowing that her time would be restricted.

"I am *so* glad you called. How are you?"

Viv glanced around. "Oh you know, you know." She

remembered the letter from Amanda but went on. "I need to see you. Can you call and check visiting times?"

Viv could see Evans winding up the time with her hands.

"I have to go... please come soon."

*

The next time Viv was on gardening, she chose a spot out of sight, behind a small laurel bush, and began to build her pile of possible compost from what the kitchens had given her. Any worms she found in the earth she would carry over to the rotting vegetables.

It took three months for any change to happen, but by the time the cold months gave way to warm, late spring, she had the beginnings of some healthy compost to rake into the barren soil. There was a robin who seemed to live there, or at least came and settled to watch her work whenever she came out. Viv stood watching him, his little head acute to every noise, his breathing not visible.

"Hello."

His head turned, he stared for a second and flew off. She watched him go.

"I'm calling you Terry and I will see you tomorrow."

She liked the solitude. At least here she was free of having to calculate every interaction. She had found a wheelbarrow to transport the compost, but it needed oiling. She managed to find some oil in the small tool shed and applied it liberally to the front wheel.

"There, that's better."

She stood back, hand on hip, admiring her work, pleased that she had created something that worked here. The air and the light were beginning to feel like spring and soon she would be planting the vegetables once they arrived on the order. She took a deep breath, but instead of feeling calm, she realised that the smell of the oil had brought back the memory of Reg's garage.

Back in her room after supper soon became Viv's favourite time. *Odd, she thought, this had been the time she had dreaded most on her first day.* The conversation that had begun in her head continued in these hours as though unbroken, providing a catharsis, and she began to remember people, events, facts. She had had a blank about the key events until now, but that was beginning to change; she began to recall more and more.

She thought most about Reston and what had been her home for sixteen years. She didn't think of it as home, it had never been what she would call a home – sixteen years of just trying to figure out how best to survive.

*

Three days later, at breakfast.
"Riley!"
She turned, stood.
"Visitor today."
"Who is it?"
Her face brightened; surely Amanda was here. But the screw had already turned and gone. Visiting was at two, she knew that much. She was ushered in a quarter of an hour early. There were six others already there, all on separate tables. All with two chairs, one taken, one empty. Glancing at the clock every two minutes, she saw it was five past two. She raised her hand. The warder came over.
"Do you know who my visitor is?"
"Wait your turn."
And just minutes after that, Viv saw Arun's familiar face

enter and look around for her. It was with mixed feelings that Viv stood and held out her hand. Where was Amanda? She looked at his serious face as he walked towards her, his briefcase in his hand. He had done his best out there in the court, he had, but all the same, here she was in jail for six months with the sword of Damocles hanging over her.

"Arun!"

"No touching!"

They sat at the Formica table.

"How are you, V. J.?"

It felt good to be called V. J. again.

"Jury's out!" She tried to rally her old spirit.

"I know, I know."

"You've seen these places before, haven't you?"

"I have indeed. But, forgive me, we will not have long, and I have to talk to you about how we should best prepare for your trial. This is most important."

Viv felt a slight embarrassment at her surroundings.

"I'm sorry."

Her plastic chair scraped on the concrete floor.

"No need, no need."

Arun was quick to dispel this awkward moment and keen to focus on what he would have to do at the trial. She leant forward across the table.

"I have here the notes I made when you came to my flat."

Viv nodded. That already seemed a lifetime ago.

"I need to know though, now, V. J., that I have every bit of information in order to defend you when the trial starts. So tell me please *all* the detail leading up to the attack. Hold nothing back."

"How far back do you want to go?"

"Please?" Arun was surprised. "Had this been going on for some time? Had Mr Dawson threatened you before?"

"Yes. I probably need to tell you about him – stop me if it is not relevant – but it might be."

And Viv recalled in detail the day of the bike repair and how she had kneed him in the balls when he had pinned her to the garage wall. It was the same man, after all.

"Thing is, Arun, I thought violence was normal, that was what it was always like at home." She needed Arun to understand this. "I had – have – a violent father."

"Did you report him?"

Viv brushed this aside. "No-one outside ever saw this, we never thought we would be believed."

"We?"

"My mother and me. I think. His anger was never foreseeable, that was the terrifying thing. It just erupted out of nowhere. We were all in fear of him, just dealt with it in different ways."

"And was he physically violent?"

Viv held out her left arm, pulled up the sleeve. Where he had broken her arm, she had had a tattoo done. *Never forget.*

"And I haven't, I mustn't. My mother too."

"I see."

But does he? wondered Viv. *Does he see?* Viv could picture Arun at home, his doting parents, order and respect at every turn in a comfortable suburban home. Probably Hindu. Wembley or somewhere in Hertfordshire. Soft carpet and the smells of long, slow cooking.

"At this first stage, it would not be relevant; indeed, it might harm the defence to introduce the nature of your father. It might be seen that you were ready to inflict violence yourself. But it is important, I know."

Viv turned again to the door, but it was closed, no-one else had come in.

"Would you excuse me for a moment, Arun?"

Viv held up her hand. The screw came over.

"If I have another visitor, can you please tell her to wait for me?"

"No-one for you, Riley."

And the warder returned to her standing position by the wall.

"Now, as to the present?" Arun looked up at Viv to check she was OK with this leap. "I have seen all the police reports, and they indicate a lot of uncertainty, ambiguity. They suggest that there were two, perhaps three, blows. The evidence they have is forensic – the green gloves and the two mobile telephones – not, as far as we know, any eyewitnesses. These items suggest that your friend Paula was with you."

Viv averted her eyes.

"The evidence confirms a sexual attack, but not necessarily rape, although the ensuing violence would seem to indicate that. Your defence rests on ambiguity. It will be my job to paint a true picture of this man. The charge is of murder, but of that there is not clear evidence either; it could have been self-defence." He looked intently at Viv as he said this. "And it could have been murder, and it could have been joint enterprise. It all rests, V. J., on what order events happened in. And who was there that night. So please, tell me again, of that night."

Arun was intent as any bird listening for a worm. Viv sat upright, her hands in her lap.

"It was an unprovoked, silent attack out of nowhere. I was – we were – waiting for a bus. I can assure you that it was rape." Hearing herself say the word out loud, she paused, leaning forward. "It was *rape*, Arun. I know we are talking about murder, but it feels as though this act is being sidelined just as part of a defence. I just feel… as though it ought to have had its own court case. I'm sorry, I'm not making sense."

"No, no, please. Indeed you are. And you are correct. Wholly correct. But it is the timeline and the fact that he is dead that forces our response to be primarily about the murder."

"I defended myself as best I could. I found a lump of concrete, it had stones in it, reinforced concrete… and I used that to hit him on the head."

"This is where the police evidence is not clear. Were you standing, or were you on the ground? As the damage to Mr Dawson's skull was in one part only, it is not clear whether there was more than one blow, although three blows are a possibility. This is critical, V. J., critical as to whether the jury sees you as a victim, or a perpetrator. Was it self-defence, or was it attack? Was he already unconscious after the first blow or – and think carefully – were all the blows necessary to fend him off you? Were you defending yourself? That is all this hangs on."

Viv tried to weigh up how to deal with this. She knew it was pivotal. She knew too that the first blow of three had been while she was lying flat back on the ground, and probably only knocked him out, and the second one too. The third, however, had been from a half-standing position while Reg was already unconscious. Judging from what Arun had just said, forensics could not prove what had happened that night. The field was open. Who could prove at this stage whether it had been her or Paula who carried out the successive blows that actually killed him? And during or after the attack. No-one saw. If what Arun had told her was reliable, then she could see a way forward.

Without blinking, she told him, "I defended myself, Arun. Anyone would have done the same, if they had been there, and they had felt the concrete in the palm of their hand. I had to get away. Paula was with me… you need to talk to her."

Arun hesitated, cleared his throat.

"I will ask you a question, a devil's advocate." He allowed himself another slight smile at this. "If, as you say, your friend Paula was with you, how could he attack you? Would Reg not have thought it a risky strategy in the circumstances? After all, she could have raised the alarm for you."

Viv had not considered this.

"Arun, this was a drunk, an irrational person. He saw only me."

"So where was Paula? After the attack?"

It was a light bulb moment for Viv, a way out. She didn't need to elaborate. It felt like a sort of truth as she told Arun that.

"She just stood there, stared at me, then ran."

Arun changed tack. "So, we are clear then, are we not, V. J., that you were on the ground when you made the blows to the head?"

Viv felt in that moment that she had been fighting for her survival her entire life; she slumped back in the plastic seat, closed her eyes, head back – what was one more effort? He was throwing the lifeline to her, and she had to take it.

Making herself upright again in the chair, she replied, "Correct, Arun." Despite herself, she couldn't resist elaborating. "You have to understand the degree of shock I was in." Her face betrayed nothing of her thoughts.

There was a long silence. The lunch trolley with its metal containers and smell of cabbage clanked past the interview room on its way back to the kitchens.

"Were there, in fact, three blows?"

It was important, Viv was considering, to admit to the three blows just in case there was forensic that Arun did not know about. She nodded.

"I only remember two blows. If there was a third it must have been someone else. I just can't remember clearly."

"I see."

Arun could not look at Viv at this point. He held his breath.

Viv could see Paula's face clearly, it was a face she had loved, but Paula had looked straight through her that night at the Trafalgar. Now, it was her turn to cut her loose.

Arun ventured, "Paula?"

"It's possible. I don't remember."

"And the mobile phones? Of you and your friend Paula? How did both your phones come to be at the scene of the crime?"

"Paula was with me at the bus stop. She saw the attack."

"And lastly, the gloves. The police investigated and found that these, although covered with Mr Dawson's blood, were in fact belonging to Paula. It was not possible, apparently, to discern any DNA, your DNA, on the gloves as there was a problem with the forensic laboratory at the time."

Arun had been busy taking notes all this time in an A4, lined, ring binder pad, with the inscribed fountain pen his proud parents had given him when he was called to the bar. When he finished, he looked up and smiled at Viv.

"Well, do we have a case, Arun?"

"This is a clear self-defence plea to causing damage to Mr Dawson. But the evidence could possibly point to Paula having killed Mr Dawson. If there were three blows, it is most likely that the third killed him. There is sufficient doubt to give me a degree of hope."

"What will happen to her?"

"I – the police, too, initially – have made investigations and it seems that soon after this incident, the family, whether by choice or coincidence, emigrated to the United States. Again, this could be presented as connected to that night."

"Have you found her?"

Viv knew that Paula would have a very different story to tell that would challenge hers, but the forensic was definitely on her side. It had created doubt. It would be her word against Paula's.

"It is very sad, and I am sorry to tell you that your friend Paula met with an accident, a car accident, and she is no longer—"

"What?!"

"It is true. I am so sorry to tell you this. Are you alright, V. J.? You have become very pale."

Viv leant forward on the plastic table, her chin in her hands.

"It's fine, Arun. It's fine."

"Well, I will prepare the case, based on this evidence. I will do everything in my powers, V. J., to gain your freedom." He looked around. "It is not right that you are here."

"Thank you, Arun."

He held out his hand to say goodbye.

"No contact!"

Viv watched Arun leave. It had felt like old times to have an intelligent conversation again and with the news of Paula, it felt too that she was regaining an inch of power. She stayed at the table; perhaps Amanda would arrive late. Perhaps she had not notified the guards in time.

"Riley!"

Viv turned.

"Time to go!"

CHAPTER 17

The six months in Belton was almost at an end. Viv began keeping everything shipshape, ready to leave at any time. She would not be coming back, she was certain of that. Arun had visited three more times. They had gone over and over everything, and he assured her that he felt cautiously optimistic for a good outcome. Freedom. She could almost smell it.

"Cautious?" Viv had probed.

"Yes, indeed. One must never assume any outcome. Much depends on which judge we get."

It was on his last visit that he informed her it would be Judge Crawthorne.

"Good? Bad?" she quizzed him, searched his face, hoping for reassurance.

"Not entirely good, I'm sorry to say. But please be assured I intend a good outcome. Still."

He put his hand on her arm; the guards appeared not to see.

She watched Arun leave for the last time before the trial. He, at least, would not let her down. She would be free. She was sure of it. She would be not guilty of murder. How could any jury feel there was no doubt? It all came down to who wielded the third blow on Reg Dawson's head. Everything else could be argued away.

She caught sight of herself in the small mirror in her room. Her skin was pallid after six months in prison; her hair had grown longer than she liked.

"Well, V. J., have we pulled it off?"

She pictured herself making a statement to the waiting reporters. Or, perhaps, would Arun do that for her? Head held high. She hardly slept the night before the trial; up early, everything ready, packed by the door and she was first in to breakfast, collecting her food from the hatch as she had done for half a year.

"You're up yourself this morning!" This was Kelly, always wary, always checking. "What's up with you?"

"'Er trial." Christine said this dully, not looking up from her breakfast.

"Oh."

If Viv had expected a 'good luck' from anyone, she was mistaken. No-one wanted better for anyone else. A trial could mean freedom, and what did they have? Years more of not seeing their kids, battling through.

She climbed the steps from the cells to the court with the officer. She gasped. Suddenly she had risen to court level and saw everyone looking at her, even the judge. She stood handcuffed and waited behind the reinforced glass. Viv had steeled herself for this moment, but the theatre of it all, the silence, the way all faces of the jury turned to inspect her, she hadn't been ready for that. As the judge intoned, instructing order for the case, she looked at the jury's faces to see if she could read their intentions. But it was all too mixed – young, old, male, female, black, white – except for one, a woman in a pink cardigan, too old for pink, with rimless glasses and a pained expression already on her face. Then she turned to the visitors' gallery and saw her father. She gasped. What was he doing here?

The court was airless, no windows. The neon light flickered.

PROSECUTION CASE:

The prosecution barrister rose, theatrically paused, looked around the court room, before stating his simple case.

"Evie Riley... or is it Vivienne Wheeler?" The barrister paused for effect, looked over at the jury. "Had committed murder on the night of the incident. She had been alone, although you will hear an allegation that her friend Paula's gloves and mobile are evidence that she was at the crime scene too. You will hear pleas of self-defence, but Evie Riley's actions far exceeded any defence I have come across in my long career," another pause for effect, "as the deceased had been rendered unconscious with the first blow, enabling Evie Riley to flee – if she had *chosen* to. Bear in mind, members of the jury, Your Lordship, that two more blows were inflicted. How could they be classed as self-defence in the face of his inertia? Cut and dried."

He flicked out his gown behind him before sitting down with a flourish.

DEFENCE CASE:

"I agree with my learned friend's assertion that this case is simple."

Viv gripped the guardrail.

"It is the case of a young girl of sixteen, an innocent virgin of unblemished record, if I may say, who is enjoying a night at the cinema with her very best friend. Innocence personified. And it is the case that my client's friend was expecting her friend's father to collect them safely in his car. And if he had done as he had said, we would not be here in court today. But he did not.

"My client was… let down. And so my client, innocent of any wrongdoing, made her way on a dark, rainy night to catch the bus home with her friend for company. What else could she have done? She had to escape the wrath of her father – but you will hear more of that later. It was as she waited for the bus, as many of you members of the jury will have done, that she was the subject of an unwarranted, unprovoked assault. The attacker took her by surprise, assaulted her – you can imagine her terror – and the worst of all fates for a young girl, he raped her."

Here Arun looked over at Viv, whose impassive face gave nothing away. For the trial, she had dressed as he had advised in a white shirt and navy-blue jumper, black trousers.

"It was while she was on the pavement, on her back, that she struggled against her attacker. He was a big man, and it was impossible. Until her hand found a lump of concrete to hit him with in order to enable her to escape. She hit him and rendered him unconscious. It was a simple case of self-defence. You will be wondering at this stage why her friend could not have helped her? My client was in trauma, and it was only as she stood up and away from the attacker that she saw her friend pick up the concrete and, from a standing position, hit the attacker once more. And then flee the scene. Only that blow can be considered an attack. My client only acted in self-defence."

Viv looked across at the jury, and then down at the exhibits table, all with little cards, A, B, C, etc. Her phone, Paula's phone, the green gloves, the bus pass.

PROSECUTION WITNESSES:

A nod, hardly discernible from the prosecuting barrister, and a call from the usher went to the outside hall. Moments later,

Creech, now deputy commissioner, entered. Geoff, sitting in the gallery, shifted his position, sat up straighter, alert to the interrogation which would follow.

Barrister:

"Deputy Commissioner Creech, may I take you back to 2003, the night of the murder," (slight stress on murder, no mention of the rape), "of one Reginald Dawson. Can you tell us why your police search involved the garage of the deceased?"

Creech:

"Indeed. Once the victim had been identified—"

Arun:

"Objection! My client in the dock is the victim here. Mr Dawson is the deceased."

Judge:

"Allowed."

Creech:

"We searched both his home and the garage to see if any background information, or artefacts, could throw light on the events of the night."

Barrister:

"And did you find the video recording, Exhibit A? Please tell the jury what this video contains."

Creech:

"This was not found at the garage but at the home of the defendant's father. In his car, there was a black box of sorts provided by the insurer. While the engine of the car is running, the video records. Once the engine is turned off, it ceases to record. This recording showed the attack by Mr Dawson on the defendant."

Barrister:

"And was anyone else present at the scene?"

Creech:

"No."

Barrister:
"Thank you."
The judge looked over, with a question on his face, to Arun.
"I do, My Lord. I wish to cross-examine Deputy Commissioner Creech."
Creech's face was held expressionless by his professionalism.
Arun:
"Deputy Commissioner Creech. Am I right in believing that the video was not the only artefact found? We have not talked about the scene of the crime at which," (and here Arun looked over to the exhibits table) "I believe a pair of green leather gloves with a distinctive pattern," (Arun waited for the usher to hold them up to the jury) "as well as a bus pass were found?"
Creech:
"You are correct."
Arun:
"And did you ascertain to whom they belonged?"
Even with her life at stake, Viv could appreciate the fine use of grammar and allowed herself the smallest of smiles.
Creech:
"The gloves belonged to the defendant's friend, Paula Johnson."
Arun:
"So, it is possible, is it not, that Paula dropped her gloves while she was at the bus stop that night."
Creech:
"It is possible if she had been there. We believe she was not."
Judge:
"Facts, please, not opinions! Members of the jury, please disregard that last sentence. Carry on."

Arun:
"And now we come to the mobile phones, one belonging to the defendant and one to Paula Johnson. Where did the satellite signals place them at the time of the attack?"

Creech:
"They were both established to be together at the bus stop."

Arun could not resist. With a flourish, he turned to the jury, a beam of triumph on his face.

"They were both present at the bus stop. Thank you, that is all."

Viv wasn't ready for what came next. The police had had a late call from Rosemary. She wished to testify on her daughter's behalf that she believed she had been brutally attacked that night, and she feared her husband had hurt her. Her daughter was innocent. This was her moment; she would clear her daughter as his victim, and she would see that his violence to them both came to light. She had waited a long time for this. She had evidence that she had kept all these years – the blood-stained duvet. She had intended, of course, to be called for the defence, but instead she was called by the CPS, who kept their views to themselves and decided that Rosemary would bolster their case, but for a different reason.

PROSECUTION WITNESS:

"Call Rosemary Riley to the stand!"

The usher brought the slight figure of Rosemary Riley to court.

Viv watched in shock. For the prosecution? Wasn't it enough that her mother had remained silent? Was she now going to crucify her in open court? Viv leant forward, prayed that Arun was ready for this. Rosemary was dressed neatly in a grey suit, but Viv noted the make-up; this was new.

"And I believe you have evidence of your daughter's… involvement… that night?"

"Yes, I do." She pointed at the duvet from Viv's bed that night. "It has blood all over it. She was attacked that night, she was raped, she is innocent. None of it is her fault."

She looked up at Viv, searching her face, pleading for what, Viv was not sure.

"And," here the prosecutor pointed to the exhibit and Viv felt violated all over again, "the blood on this duvet, as you rightly say, Mrs Riley, is that of your daughter and of Mr Dawson, but of no-one else. What is your opinion of that?"

Here Rosemary faltered. "No, that can't be right, my husband was there, I know it. He was involved somehow, he and Reg were friends, my husband was there. His blood must be on it."

"And how do you know this?"

"He told me years after that he had seen everything – and he did nothing to stop it. He told me that he had been on the way home from delivering papers to a colleague and had taken the short cut and was about to join the main road from the unlit side lane when he saw Reg and Evie. He saw Reg attack my daughter. I don't believe he did nothing." As Rosemary uttered this last sentence, she stood tall, perhaps for the first time in years. "He is guilty, I know he is."

"And did your husband say if anyone else – Paula, perhaps – was present at the scene?"

"He didn't say, and I didn't ask him. But he was there, he did this too."

This was all badly backfiring. Arun, unprepared for this, rose, called for a recess.

Viv's palms sweated.

"Sit down, Mr Seth. I think this is a good time to adjourn for lunch. All rise for recess. We meet again at two o'clock."

Arun managed a few minutes with Viv, during which time he was quick to comfort her with the fact her father would be taking the stand again after lunch and he would cross-examine him as to his involvement that night and his connection with Reg, and why he seemed to be defending Paula.

Viv was led back to the cells. Before long, Arun joined her for an urgent conference.

"Arun, did you know this was going to happen?"

"No, and for this I need to seek time with the judge in chambers. I can't stay now."

While Arun made his way to the judge's chambers, he was assembling the case he would put to the judge.

Douglas, as a magistrate himself, had no wish to enter the witness stand for either side, but once the police had found the video, he had no choice. The fact that he had witnessed events that night, he could no longer deny. His exit from the gallery was blocked; he needed to get out, he needed a drink.

"Excuse me, excuse me... mind."

And he was out, stumbling towards the main exit. Crossing over the Strand and down a side road, he found the Wig and Pen.

"Double brandy, please!"

He barged in front of a woman trying to order. Taking the drink to a corner seat, he needed to collect his thoughts, be ready when the CPS called him. He was playing out in his mind how it would go in the afternoon, but in truth he had so little room to manoeuvre. The only question was would he be willing to perjure himself if push came to shove? He thought of getting a ploughman's, but it was too much work to get through the crowds again; besides, it felt too much of a challenge for a churning stomach. His association with Reg, which he had always hoped to keep from seeing the light of day, would be revealed, as well as Reg's attempt to blackmail him. Reg had had his shady side. Douglas was not primarily involved, but Reg had made sure he would have a friendly magistrate on his side; he had implicated him by taking a photograph and had kept this in his back pocket against a rainy day. No, no, this could not come to light. What it came down to was Douglas's own reputation and life, or his daughter's fate. He downed the rest of the brandy, left the pub and decided on a walk to clear his mind. Up to the Strand again, and down to the mad tourist zone of Trafalgar Square; it was chaos. People walking in front of cars, cars hooting. Someone called out his name; it distracted him, and he looked right when he should have looked left. The car braked suddenly but not in time. Douglas was knocked unconscious and spent the afternoon in A & E, not Court No. 1.

Arun's petition to the judge came to nothing in the end. Rosemary had confused matters, but at least today it could not now be made worse by the appearance of her husband. Instead, Arun took up the cudgels.

"My Lord, the defendant's father stated that no-one, especially not Paula, was present that night at the bus stop. If he had been here, my questions to him would have been, 'And why are you protecting Paula?' To which he would have replied, 'I am not,' to which I would have brought forward Exhibit C."

The usher held up the photo Viv had taken that night of Douglas and Paula kissing passionately outside the Hotel Trafalgar. The phone had recorded the date.

"I would then have rephrased my question as, 'Are you protecting Paula because of your intimate association with a minor?'."

Arun checked along the jury's faces to see if he had gone too far.

"Thank you, that is all."

CHAPTER 18

The case continued, back and forth, this witness and that, over two days. When it came to the judge summing up, Viv strained to read the faces of the jury.

"And so, members of the jury, you have to decide whether you believe the defendant's mother that her daughter was the victim of a vicious and unsolicited attack – in which her own father was involved – and whose only 'crime' was that she fought for her life. Or whether you believe the evidence of the father, submitted from hospital through his solicitor, that the defendant was alone at the scene and used violence beyond the needs of self-defence, and that he was witness to it. Or whether you believe the defendant that she was with her friend, Paula, and that it was Paula who delivered the fatal blows."

When Arun came to see Viv during the jury's deliberation, he did nothing to lift her mood.

"It could go either way."

"No shit, Sherlock. I'm sorry, Arun, didn't mean to say that. Tense." She patted her jacket out of habit. "I need a smoke."

She stood and paced up and down, then sat again, looking straight at Arun.

"It's not going to work, is it?"

Arun wanted more than anything to see this fierce survivor survive. He wanted, too, to put that feather in his cap that said his career was prospering. But the shadow of doubt was too heavy for him to dissemble in this moment. The most he could hope for, if things went badly, was to plead mitigation and this would possibly reduce the sentence.

"V. J., whether it is one day or four years from now, I will buy you that whiskey in the club." He had tears in his eyes as he said that.

Viv looked away. Time to go.

"Court rise!"

Viv stayed standing as the jury reassembled. None of them looked in her direction. That didn't look good.

"Members of the jury, have you deliberated on your verdict?"

The foreman stood, paper in hand.

"We have."

"Have you found the defendant guilty of murder?"

There was a sharp intake of breath. Viv heard her own gasp, her legs buckled, as he replied, "We have."

"And what is your verdict?"

"Guilty."

Viv's free hand went to her head.

Arun shot to his feet. "My Lord, we plead—"

"Court rise!"

All strength went from Viv's legs; she couldn't stand, looked behind her for a seat. The warders weren't in the mood for a delay and yanked her now handcuffed wrist and led her unsteadily downstairs and out to the van. Viv was alone this time, except for the officer. No-one was riding back to the prison with her. It was a huge black cavern, the windows so high and dark.

Groundhog Day.

*

While Viv had been on her way out to the west of London, Arun had sought out the judge in chambers and made the speech of his life. The turn of events had taken him by surprise in so far as he felt his own insides torn out at the verdict. He was losing a sister, and that could not happen. The jury had got it wrong; Viv was the victim here. Why had the police never tried to trace Paula? He found oratory at a new level as he pleaded with the judge to be lenient in his sentencing, given the mitigation and ambiguity of the case. The judge took all this in. He had seen it often, but never quite so movingly.

"Please, My Lord. You will have heard the situation, the aggravation, the need for self-defence. I plead with you to be merciful when sentencing. This is not murder, premeditated murder, by my client, but self-defence."

There was a pause once Arun had finished.

"Very well, Mr Seth, you will await my verdict."

"My Lord."

Viv was back in court two days later for sentencing.

The judge never took his eyes off Viv as he spoke.

"The jury have returned a verdict of murder, and I am bound by that, but in the light of the circumstances of the case and the defence plea for mitigation, I sentence you to the minimum imprisonment of four years."

A pause. Not waiting for any reaction, the judge rose and left the court.

Arun spun round, met Viv's gaze. He tried to smile.

Viv looked at his earnest face. It was a surreal moment. They had had a different relationship in her previous life, and now she was dependent upon his help. An uncomfortable feeling, however much she trusted Arun. She had lied to him, and it had failed. Her mother had tried, and it had backfired.

This wasn't over. Of that she was sure. She needed time to steady herself. Surely with deductions for being held already for six months, for good behaviour, she could be out in three years.

The court cleared rather like a classroom at the end of term and soon it was just a room. The guard led her by the wrist again, downstairs and out to the waiting van again. But as she was led off, she caught Arun's voice.

"Remember, I will not abandon you. You have my word."

The van door opened, Viv climbed up and in and sat still handcuffed on the side seat next to the officer. Viv felt she would be sick; the fear rising up in her was so great at this moment. She could hear the engine running. She had literally no choice in anything in her life at this moment. Her head was full of pins and needles of panic; she felt faint.

"I'm going to be sick."

There was no reply; the guard was used to this. He just sat there staring. Two drivers in the front. It was dark. How would she cope with being locked up? *I can't do this.* She remembered the day of driving over the limit, saw it all so clearly. If only... but it was too late.

She needed Amanda's calming voice, but Amanda had not been at the trial either. Amanda would be able to tell her how to get through this. Perhaps now that the sentencing was real, she would make contact again, perhaps even visit.

Viv could hear cars hooting, the driver of the van slamming on his brakes. Viv shot forward, held only by the handcuff. All her life she had coped by knowing ultimately she could run. Now she could not. Literally, she could not. The van smelled of old vomit. She needed some water. So many things ran through her mind; Reston, her mother at the trial. It had been a shock to see her mother like that, she needed to think. Four years locked in behind walls; she would be thirty-four when she came out. Why hadn't Amanda been at the trial? Why? She thought of that last night with Amanda. Well, perhaps she was right never to have risked such vulnerability before. More angry hooting.

"Where are we?"

Viv had no idea of the time, or when they would arrive. No reply.

"Where are we?"

Something of her old spirit, just for a moment, appeared again. He could answer her that surely.

She had never felt so deep a tiredness, not even on the streets.

The engine was turned off; no-one was speaking. Viv heard the driver's door slam, heard him walking away. Soon he was back, and Viv could see through the high up window that a gate barrier had been lifted and they were driving through. The back van doors were unlocked and held for a moment, then fully opened and the light flooded in. Viv was stiff but got out with her jailer and walked into the back of the building to the familiar process area. There were three other women in the mouldy room. They were all sitting at the far end, together. She could feel their eyes on her. She glanced at her wrist, massaged where the cuffs had been.

CHAPTER 19

Viv had somehow expected to go back to her old room but was now in one at the far end in a different section. There was a knock at the door. Viv shot up from the bed, startled out of her thoughts. She opened it just slightly.

"Yes?"

"What's up then?"

The two of them, Viv and Kelly, the old hand, stood there.

"Nothing's up."

"Yeah it is, you haven't said nuffing to no-one."

"Oh."

Viv recalled the stuck-up cow comment; she didn't want that again. She didn't need to make enemies in a place where she could not escape.

"What happened then? In court?"

"Nothing. It's over. Four years. What are *you* in for?" Viv could have bitten her tongue out.

"You don't ask no-one that."

"Apologies." She could see that her vocabulary was all wrong. "Sorry. It's difficult."

Now, here was common ground and Kelly found a way in.

"Always is."

Viv bit back the question as to whether this was Kelly's first or tenth time in this prison. She found it hard to comprehend that anyone would risk coming back more than once.

"You on gardening then?"

"Yes." Viv's face relaxed. "Yes. It's cold, but at least outside. How do you cope with not getting out of the building? I feel like breaking through walls."

Kelly laughed. "You get used to it. Yeah, you do."

She kept glancing up and down the corridor as though expecting someone. Kelly's pallor told a story, been in here too long. Was it drugs? Viv was not about to ask any more direct questions; besides, she did not want to let down her guard despite the attraction of having some allies in here.

As though the first question was still in the air, Viv ventured, "You get to think in here, don't you?"

Kelly shrugged.

And a thought came to Viv. She was a writer, for God's sake, prison couldn't change that. A surge of energy shot through her. A writer makes use of everything, don't they? She needed pen and paper.

"Can you get computer access here?"

Kelly shrugged. It hadn't been a requirement for her, getting clean was hard enough. It had been heroin that had landed her here, and she needed to get rid, and this was oddly her chance. But the prison's idea of getting clean was short and violent, cold turkey 'clucking'. Kelly wasn't clean, she just didn't have the drugs.

"I'll ask."

*

Viv learnt to watch and wait, sum up the different warders. The women were tougher than the men, mostly. There was

Solomon; she liked his rhythm, not fast, but even. He was a big guy; he was never out of his depth. Watching him walk down the corridor, she knew that she'd find a way to get alongside him. She needed to write and for that she needed a computer, and for that she needed Solomon.

The system of earning privileges was against Viv; she hadn't been here long enough. She'd picked up just by listening as to what could land her in getting deprived of privileges – sleeping in, messy bed, not doing allotted duties and so on. She'd been careful, and so far had not infringed. It was nearly six months since the prison door had slammed shut behind her and it had become her home. She was learning the ropes, never dropping her guard, playing the game. If there was a computer, it wasn't clear where that would be. Perhaps in another wing. Viv's heart sank; she was still in the high-security category. She would find a way. Solomon would help her.

"Hey, Solomon?"

He looked over. "It's Officer to you." He wasn't smiling.

"Can I ask you something?"

Nothing.

"Are there any computers in here?"

"Not for the likes of you. Just the office."

"Oh."

"What you want it for?"

Viv shrugged and looked him directly in the eyes. "I'm a writer, I miss writing."

Solomon saw the paper and pens that Arun had given Viv.

"You can write with those."

"It's not the same, it's not enough."

Viv looked away, waited for Solomon's response. Viv began to move back into her room. She heard Solomon walk away, but then his steps retraced.

"What do you want to write? All letters get checked, you know that."

"It's not a letter, Officer. It's a book."

Solomon was intrigued. This didn't happen often in his life, meeting a writer.

"You written one before?"

"Several."

"You can't get internet."

"I don't want internet; I want to write my book. I would thank you on the first page."

Solomon straightened up at least a couple of inches. This was new. He was flattered.

"I'll ask. That's all. I'll ask."

Solomon's asking brought results exactly one week later.

"You can have two hours each day in the workroom."

The workroom was where trusted prisoners did courses, rehabilitated. Viv was silently ecstatic.

"Thank you, Solomon. I'll keep my word to you."

"Three till five each day, and that's all." Solomon was not about to be tapped for more. "That's all."

"Thank you isn't enough, Solomon."

"How grateful?" He half smiled. For a second he misread Viv, hesitated, smiled.

Viv looked away; she would find a way of thanking him, but not that, please, God, not that.

*

Viv's allotted two hours gave rise to questions, some bullying on the wing, but she began to write the book she had held inside her since she was fifteen. All of it. This book was writing itself and seeing on the page the truth of what she had survived. What she had silenced in order to survive began to change her. She brushed her hair each morning now, ready for work. There was a glow, a purpose about her. It took her a whole year of two hours to write her book. She knew the title before she wrote it. *The Final Sentence*. And, indeed, her last sentence shocked even her, but it was as though the words just came through her; they were barely her choice to write.

*

Oddly, there was no church on Sunday. Not that she was a churchgoer but somehow she had thought there would be at least a Bible room; and besides, it could have provided a punctuation mark in the week. But then again, they would have had to cater for the mixed population. Friday night and the Sabbath for the Jews, Sunday for Christians and five times a day for the Muslims. Viv realised with an odd degree of pride that she had, after six months, become institutionalised, obeying timekeeping, rules, avoiding trouble. That was new for her – perhaps it was a good thing. She couldn't tell. No drink, no cigarettes. As much as she longed to be out, to be V. J. Wheeler in the outside world, test the water, she could see the advantage of so much empty time. The memories were flooding back in a way that made sense to her. She knew she was remembering the facts clearly. She no longer doubted herself and a new energy was developing, and she wanted justice, revenge.

Time for lunch. The food was foul, but again, survival meant you stopped complaining; perhaps even that was good for her. What once she would have rejected, she now ate. Pressed boiled cabbage. She thought of Hugo, of Boodles.

"What's the smile for, Riley?"

This was Solomon. Viv looked up. He was a beauty, was Solomon.

"Oh you know, just remembering stuff."

"Well, don't do too much of that in here, it can play with your mind."

"I want it to, Solomon. I want it to. It's time."

"How's it going?"

"You'll have to read it one day."

*

The evil warder Christine walked down the corridor, and as she neared Viv's room, she shouted out, "Visitor, Riley!"

"When? Who?"

Viv did not leave her room to call out. There was something that Christine hated about Viv.

"You'll be told."

Kelly put her head round the door. "Don't worry about her, bitch. Visiting is over there today – B Wing."

Kelly was proving a friend, but even so…

So it was that Viv was sitting at the Formica table once more, staring at the door. Who would it be? And there at the door, slightly hesitant, was Arun. He looked around for Viv. Viv got up, about to go to him.

"Sit, Riley."

She caught Arun's eye, waved.

"Arun." She reached out a hand.

"Riley. No touching."

"V. J. V. J."

Still the formal and the courteous. Viv, at that moment, wished that she was straight, studying his face, familiar, and so unchanged. So dependable. His shirt was laundered, not home-washed, his nails filed and clean. There was a slight hint of cologne.

Viv managed a wry smile.

"Don't ask me how I am, just don't."

"No, no, of course not."

Arun handed Viv a small package that had been checked and approved with a stamped mark. Viv looked – this was Christmas! She began to undo the paper bag. Inside were two A4, lined, ring binder books, and six of her favourite pens. She held them close and breathed them in. Had he known that she was writing again? She looked up and there was a softness in his eyes. Did she like them?

"Arun, you have no idea just how much they are the totally right thing to bring. Fuck fruit cake!"

A slight wince of shock at the language, but they shared the joke.

"Yes, indeed."

"Did anything happen after the trial that I should know about? Never hear anything worth hearing in here!"

"Ah yes. Your mother came to see me. She was distraught at the thought that she had made matters worse for you. She wished me to say to you that it had been her intention to clear your name."

"You mean blame my father!"

"Well, yes, that is clear also. She asked me to pass on good wishes and to say if you wish her to visit, she will. She is not sure whether it would be welcome."

Viv shook her head. "I don't think so, Arun. Too soon. I need to figure out every piece of this puzzle."

"Ah."

The bell rang; Viv felt her heart constrict. Arun was a true friend. How long before she would see him again? She could not, would not, ask.

"Keep as well as you can. Remember, one day, you will be free."

"And I will buy you a whiskey!" was Viv's rejoinder.

"Indeed."

Viv watched his neat vanishing form on the other side of the room with a pang of loss.

CHAPTER 20

Viv had been writing for two hours in Arun's notebook, hadn't noticed the time. She got undressed, shivered, and got under the blankets.

What was clear to her as she remembered all those previously elusive events was that she had not killed Reg in self-defence; she had killed him out of rage, out of fear. She could never admit this to Arun now. Arun believed she had been a total victim; it was with shame that she realised how she had played this useful card at trial. But it was also a realisation that her whole life had been so far about trying to survive.

It was visiting day again tomorrow. Viv checked the board to reassure herself that no-one would be visiting. She liked it that way now. Simpler. She had rebuffed her mother, she knew that. There was no way her father would visit, not after the trial, and even if he did, for whatever twisted motives, Viv could not handle that. Not yet. It would have to be on her terms or not at all. Half nervous she would see his name there, she ran her finger down the sheet. She caught her breath. Amanda Rosberg. Amanda was coming today. Her heart beat faster. Why now? After all this time?

Viv checked her own reflection, going near to check for lines, for changes, her hair. She would have to do her best. And then a sudden thought came: was something wrong with Amanda? So many conflicting questions.

"Slow down, slow down, slow down."

"Slow down, yourself!"

Viv spun round. Kelly stood in the doorway, laughing at her.

"What's up with you? Got any visits?" Kelly persisted.

"Looks like I have."

"Girlfriend? Boyfriend?"

"Work friend."

Kelly wandered off, leaving Viv to her own thoughts again. Sitting at the end of the long table at lunch, trying not to heave at the smell of long-kept warm fish, she looked to see who else was there. New face at the end; she had hair shaved at both sides, longer on the top, and a tattoo on the right side of her head. Seconds later, Viv looked again – did she know her? Something familiar. Characters changed every day.

With lunch over, it was time to focus on the visits. Amanda would be here soon. Viv could tell her about the computer, that would be good news. It felt like the worlds could be joined up again, writer and film-maker.

It was two-thirty. By three, she would see Amanda again. She forced herself to breathe.

"Riley." This was Evans. "You're off the list, get back to gardening."

"What do you mean 'off the list'?"

"Visit cancelled."

"But why?"

"This isn't a hotel, it's a prison. No reasons given."

Viv walked after Evans, but Evans never turned, just

walked faster. Viv walked slowly back to her room, sat on the edge of the bed, her head in her hands.

"I said gardening." This was Evans again.

Without saying anything, Viv rose and made her way out and round to the central garden, picked out the hoe from the tools and edged a line on the grass so deep and sharp it would have withstood any storm. There were days when she wondered whether she should be using this prison time to be an altogether higher being. To forgive, move on. But she couldn't, she wasn't that much of a higher being and certainly she couldn't sustain it; the revenge days kept butting their jagged way in. She just hoped that one day she would wake up and know what the right way was.

One night after supper, she lay back on her bed, hands behind her head. She could hear her clock ticking, sounds from down the corridor. It wouldn't always be like this; one day she would be back at home, free.

The door opened and in walked the girl Viv had seen at lunch that day.

"Thought it was you."

Viv waited; what did she want?

"You've changed, haven't ya?"

Viv stood and looked again at the girl. Without her pink hair, Viv hadn't been able to place her, but now she could.

"Hi. I know who you are now."

She was about to say, "What are you doing here?" but saved herself in time.

"It's good to see someone I know – I knew... helps."

"Yeah."

To break the ice, Viv offered that she would probably be out in just under three years, not four – she seemed to be asking for a similar confidence.

"Short one this time."

"How long did you stay in the squat… after I left?"

"Not long. Moved around. You know." Pink caught sight of two of Viv's books on the windowsill. "Any good?"

Viv laughed. "They're mine. I mean, I wrote them."

Pink moved closer to study them. "So you went on then? After the God-botherer?"

With a shrug, she turned and left.

CHAPTER 21

Viv pictured her flat. She remembered, too, her last night there, the one she had shared with Amanda. The closeness they had shared that night seemed unbreakable, the leaving the next morning unbearable.

"Will you wait for me? Visit me? If I have to go to… prison?" she had said.

"Of course."

Viv had held Amanda away to look her in the eyes.

"Yes, but will you? Really?"

She hadn't seen Amanda in so long – no texts, no emails, nothing. Not there at the magistrate's hearing, Amanda had fallen at the first fence, but still Viv had made excuses. Then prison for six months, and then the trial. Once she had begun her sentence, she understood when Amanda wrote explaining how difficult it was, but it hadn't stopped the ache. She tried and failed to remember what she had looked like. She still had her photo, but it hardly seemed real now. Viv had emailed. She had even managed to get time on the hall phone to call her but only got her answerphone. At first she had kept it light, as though she were equivocal, but now, nearing the end of her sentence, she penned a long, clear, and detailed email, a request.

Dear Amanda...
Really? But what else could she do?
My dear Amanda...
But was she anymore? Anyway.
My dear Amanda, I am being released soon on [...] It is a lot to ask (Really?) *but it would mean more than I can say if you could meet me at the main door and I could make my way out to the world again not completely alone.*

That couldn't be clearer in all honesty, could it?

She was about to ask Amanda to reply but stopped, as it chipped away too much at her dignity. It was obvious it needed an answer; she would not beg. All the same, that last month it played on her mind. Amanda, she reasoned, was cool; she might feel she didn't need to confirm. She would be there. Of course she would be there.

And then, with under a month to go, she had received a handwritten letter telling Viv that she would be there to meet her on her release. It was a promise; she would be there. What had prompted this change of heart?

PART III

CHAPTER 1

The day was here. Viv leant over the basin to check herself in the face-sized mirror, turning this way and that to see every line, every blemish. There was nothing she could do to change how she would look to the outside world after more than three years behind bars.

She smoothed her now baggy grey trousers. She tried to arrange her hair, but it was no good, she no longer looked like V. J.

"Well, here I am." It was almost under her breath.

She hadn't slept but had showered at six o'clock, was up and dressed. She checked the time every five minutes. It was quarter past ten and suddenly she heard her name called. She stood, waiting, listening for more. No. She had imagined it. She slumped back on to her stripped bed with its folded blankets. She knew she would be called, just not exactly when. They had said midday was her release time. There would be a processing of sorts for getting out as much as getting in, she expected that, and another warder had rattled through her options of trains and buses, but Viv hadn't taken it in.

She sat bolt upright as a thought came to her.

Amanda! Would she know the time? Would anyone have told her?

She glanced up at the clock, it was still only ten past eleven. She was dressed for the first time in the clothes that she had come in – grey trousers, T-shirt and jacket. They felt odd, like someone else's. Her belongings, such as they were, were in the holdall she had brought in with her; her luminous clock which had helped her through many sleepless nights, her radio, her hairbrush, her books, her zip file. She pulled a face; there wasn't much to show for her occupation of Room 36.

Bile rose at the back of her throat. What would it be like when she left? For a mad moment, she wanted them to say, "No, you're not going, we made a mistake, you're staying." Or else let her go that minute. She sat with her head in her hands. Was her flat still there? Would Amanda be there to meet her? Lloyd? Would he still be there? And she prayed silently that Amanda had not deserted her after all, that what they had shared had meant the same to her. There would be catching up to do, some adjustment, of course, but surely, please God, they still had that something that they had had before.

She had gone for breakfast as any other day with all the other inmates, except this morning had been different. Expectation, jealousy, longing, all these hung in the air around her.

Viv had smelled it as she walked in; she was going, and they were not. Viv had made friends here; not many, one or two. She thought of Pink and Kelly, and she felt the illogical injustice of leaving them behind bars, or at least behind the perimeter fence that passed for bars in the prison. She was torn, felt bad for them, but not bad enough she would risk her own freedom. They would soon forget all about her anyway, she told herself. That was life. Leaving the queue with her porridge and coffee, she had looked for a space, but no-one was moving up for her, not today.

They had stopped talking as she passed them; she would be soon gone. The defences with which Viv had got through prison this far sprang to her aid. She was not about to show that she had noticed; she would walk evenly to the back of the room until she found a space. She chose, after breakfast, not to go in for long goodbyes, make promises she knew she would ditch once she smelled the open air. Her heart began to race at the thought. Never had she felt more feral. She returned instead to her room and there she chose to stay until the door opened and the woman screw she hated most, Evans, barked, putting her head round the door.

"Riley. Time to go."

She jumped up, not making eye contact with Evans, and left her cell without looking back. It felt like a gallows walk, not a celebration moment. Only one hand reached out and patted her on the back as she walked down the long corridor.

"You go, Viv."

That was Kelly. Viv turned at the sound of her voice, held up her hand in acknowledgement. Kelly had always been generous.

The walk took her down her own wing, across to the main building and there through a series of doors locked and unlocked by the key hanging down from the screw's chain, until she found herself in the outer lobby. The air was colder, coming through the main outer door. She remembered seeing the space shuttle Columbia astronauts waiting before they got on their transport to the shuttle. *Keep breathing, keep breathing, nothing must go wrong.* She hoped her fate would be better than theirs. The window to the left lifted up a fraction and she was handed her wallet, an envelope with £50 written on it, her mobile phone, small Sobranie cigars she had had to leave, and her lighter. The last door was unlocked and the air rushed in. It made her gasp; it was so huge, so sweet. The grass in front had just been mown.

She only just heard the screw saying, "And don't come back."

"I'll do what I can." Viv muttered this under her breath.

It's what she probably says to all leavers, thought Viv, *what is she hoping for, new recruits? Or out of a job?* What did it matter? In a moment she would be free. She had focussed so intently on the passage from prison to freedom that she had not thought what she would do next. The door locked behind her; the air was cold. She looked back just for a moment, but no-one was watching her go or waving her goodbye.

It was a wide open expanse that met her eyes; wide pathway, even wider grassy expanse either side. She was certain that Amanda would be there to meet her. She scanned the entire grounds – where was she? Viv turned back, knocked on the glass window of that last office. She beckoned for them to open the door; she should have asked if there had been a message for her from Amanda. Anything. The woman in the office waved her away, like a dog, and turned away. She was not about to reopen the door for what was now an ex-prisoner.

CHAPTER 2

With a sudden realisation that Amanda couldn't have been told the time of release, her spirits lifted. She would call. She took out the mobile she had been handed back, grateful to see that it had been fully charged, and scrolled for Amanda's number. She called, but a second later, she called again but it went to answerphone.

She moved along the building until she was out of sight of the main entrance, with its high up cameras, and rested against the red-brick wall, beating her fists in frustration. She would be fine. She repeated this like a mantra; she would be fine. She would wait for Amanda. She took out a cigar. Three left. And then that would be it, she promised herself. After all, she had given up drinking in there, so why not? She lit one. It was half past twelve. She walked away from the building, but she would give it a bit more time. She wandered over to the playground on the wide grass area. There were no children at this time of day, and she sat on the far swing, pushing herself gently, the rhythm soothing her. How could she just adjust to freedom in a moment? She felt perspiration on her forehead despite the cold day, wiped it away with the back of her hand.

Steady now, it wasn't *Shawshank*. She smiled at her own joke. She inhaled deeply, stubbed the cigar out, lit another. How long had she been there? One of the officers, walking by and seeing her, called out, "You OK? Waiting for someone?"

Viv was about to answer – yes, no, which was it? Her voice choked and smiled, waving her away. It had been over two hours. It was gone two-thirty. *One last time*, she told herself, *one last time, like a throw of the dice.* She called Amanda, but again it went to answer. Amanda's voice sent shivers down Viv's spine. She was about to speak, but the futility of doing so stopped her. Amanda was abroad, at a meeting… all these things were possible, Viv had to allow this. She would make her own way back.

She stared at the long drive; some off-duty warders smoking and checking their phones by the shop, occasionally looking in her direction but not bothered. She regretted now that she hadn't listened as to whether there were trains or buses. She kept walking down the long drive until she found the main road. It all felt so jarring; the traffic was loud, large cars rushed by her so close. She caught her breath and looked for somewhere to sit and found the bus shelter with its red lean-on seat.

She would wait here. But looking down at the shiny, red plastic, she made the connection with that first bus stop night. It was what had brought her to this place, and she heard the sound of her own laughter.

"Can I help you?" an old gentleman, who clearly thought laughing on your own at a bus stop was not a good sign, asked. He looked genuinely concerned.

Viv looked at him and his kind face and thought how different he was from vile, dead Reg. This one was sweet. White hair, what was left of it, and a stoop. Life was overlaying the past.

"No. No. I'm fine."

He smiled and carried on. Viv got out her phone and called a local taxi firm. She couldn't get used to the noise, the smell of the traffic, it all hurtled by so fast. It wasn't long before he drove up in a slightly beat-up old Maxi. Paula's father had had one and that night, he had not come as he had said he might. Viv felt that life was smiling on her at last. At least, she hoped it was and it wasn't a sour joke from the Almighty.

"Where to?"

She had no idea at all in that moment. She realised how deeply she had been relying on Amanda's reassuring presence. She would have taken charge, known what to do, and Viv, as yet, had not got her sea legs in the outside world. And then the old defiance rose up; this would not defeat her, this would be a good day.

"The Ritz, Piccadilly, please."

He turned. "That is a very long way, young lady, very expensive."

"I have it, please don't worry."

And indeed she had. The royalties from her books had continued to roll in while she had been inside. Her books had sold particularly well in the States, the largest English-speaking market, but also not done badly in translation. How odd to think of a Japanese girl having read her book now funding her trip to freedom. Warmth suffused Viv as she sat back, lowered herself in the seat as though to hide from view. The car smelt of cigarettes. He braked too suddenly. Her arm shot out to the back of his seat. She peered through the gap. Would he manage to stop at the pedestrian crossing? Would the woman get knocked down? The cars overtook so close, she shielded herself by moving to the middle of the back seats. Every now and then, the taxi driver kept checking.

"Are you sure, young lady?"

Viv held up her credit card in the driving mirror to reassure him. She could see the funny side of it. What *did* she look like? Her hair she had managed to keep short, but to say it wasn't a good cut was understating it. She had a lot to do to get back into life, *her* life. Realising what her appearance might say about her prompted Viv to book a room at the hotel online before she got there, that way she wouldn't get turned down because of her appearance. They could not say no, however many eyebrows got raised.

She looked out of the window, trying to get her bearings. Of course, when she had come here it had been in a van with blacked-out windows. Just roads, the odd park, office buildings – then a sign to Kempton Racecourse. Later a golf club. Then her heart leapt at the sight of the river as they crossed Richmond Bridge. She sat forward and peered over towards the moored boats, the terraces that probably looked better in summer. The parks and golf clubs began to look a bit more prosperous until suburbs gave way to city as they crossed majestic Hammersmith Bridge. Beautiful riverside pubs, hanging baskets, people going for drinks – ah, at last, the buzz. Then it was on through Knightsbridge to Piccadilly.

It had all taken just over an hour and a half. The driver pulled into Arlington Street. She got out on the pavement side and paid by card. *He might have an old car, but he has certainly caught up with the payment system*, was Viv's thought, and the next was that life was playing into her hands. She walked up to the side entrance of the hotel; she just wanted to get safely in. It had all tired her out in a way she had not expected, the energy had gone from her bones. She was about to enter when she noticed the boy just by the entrance. So, life had not changed that much in the time she had been locked away! The stained sleeping bag, the scrappy pillow stopped her in her tracks for a second. She saw that the boy was not that old under the fear and exhaustion, perhaps nineteen. Someone's son. Just as she had been someone's daughter. She bent down to talk to him.

"Hi."

He turned, looked at her blankly, but did not answer. She saw his near-empty pot. Not for the first time, Viv thought that it was the rich who did not give; he had chosen the wrong pitch.

"Hi, how's it going?"

Again he did not answer, looked down at the pavement.

"Are you hungry?"

At this, he looked up again.

"There's a café over there, shall we get something?"

At this, he looked up, his eyes like a hopeful puppy, his face smudgy with dirt and tiredness. With a pang, Viv recognised in that split second that he was grateful not to be alone and that Viv was offering a reprieve from that. In that second, she recognised too her own need not to be alone. It wasn't a greasy spoon, certainly, this was Piccadilly, but all the same, it was a place to have something hot. They walked up the side street to Piccadilly without talking. She glanced at him, remembering how easy it was to forget how to talk when for most of your day you didn't. As they were about to cross the busy road, she took his hand, but he shook free. Thank God there was a middle island by the lights. She had surprised herself, grabbing his hand; was that for her or for him?

They walked along and into the café, found a window seat and settled on the diner, black, plastic seats. The café was warm, busy and smelt of bakery. Realising that Viv actually meant her offer, the boy made the most of the opportunity and ordered sandwiches, coffee, cake. *More than he has had in a while*, thought Viv. He kept his eyes down, but surreptitiously glanced up at her now and then. More to keep him company than anything, Viv too ordered coffee which actually smelled of coffee, unlike this morning's offering, which had come out of a large industrial tin of powder. And to her delight, they had an almond croissant. Her mouth watered at the mere thought of it. The first in all this time. So both of them scoffed in secret delight. She was glad to be sharing this moment with someone, if not Amanda, then someone.

"That was good!" Viv leant back, savouring the tastes.

The boy looked up in surprise, a question on his face.

Viv leant forward. "We aren't that different, you and me. I just got out of prison, and I used to be where you are."

He couldn't process that much information, a blank look again on his face. He kept eating. She took stock of him and could see that it was hunger that gnawed at his bones, not drink or drugs, mercifully and amazingly.

"So, what's your name?"

"Ian." He carried on eating.

How suburban, how ordinary. Was life still throwing her past up? Was this the plan?

"Well, Ian, what's next?"

He shrugged. The food was making him tired; he yawned. But it wasn't long before Viv got his story out of him. Her shadow was tugging at her new life, not letting her go so fast. His story was of a stepfather who had chucked him out. He told Viv that his mother had not stopped him. "He's old enough" were the last words he heard her say.

"But I'm not, I wasn't, I can't…" And, almost as if in slow motion, Viv saw tears begin to form and she reached out her hand to stop him going further, but it was too late. In the comparative safety of being with Viv, the boy let go and began to sob, his eyes closed. For a full minute she watched him cry, then moved a paper napkin over the table towards him. She leant forward and almost whispered that she was going to the loo, and not to leave, she would be back. After that, the mood had changed. He had recovered somewhat, was brittle and defensive again.

"When I said we weren't so different, what I meant was I survived two years living on the streets, dodging around, looking over my shoulder, never feeling safe. Like you."

She had meant it to be encouraging, but instead it sounded patronising. She was, she reflected in that second, proud that she had survived, but she had not meant to create a distance between them. Acutely, too, she felt the need for human connection but was not about to let her guard down. Instead, she wrote down a whole list of organisations, places, people who might help and told him to try and get a council flat.

"There aren't none anymore."

"Please." She pushed the envelope with the £50 across to him. "Use this for food and go and see this man."

It was the vicar of St Anne's. Or had been all those years ago.

"I have to go now."

She put her hand over his; he drew it away. He opened the envelope and peered inside, looked up at her, unsure what to do with it. A fiver in the bucket was a good day, but this, he began counting, this was much more. Viv could see the disbelief on his face; she smiled.

"It's yours."

She stood, she needed to find her own new base, but paused at the question from the boy.

"What's yer name?"

Viv paused. "I'm not sure exactly anymore – sorry."

The last time she had said sorry was a very long time ago. It sounded familiar and strange, like an old language. And without looking back, she crossed the road a little more confidently than before and entered the Ritz, checked in and breathed in the air that the people who do not have to worry breathed.

CHAPTER 3

Viv checked in and read the consternation in the clerk's face as he looked her up and down. Knowing he could not actually stop her booking in, she chuckled to herself at the ludicrous situation.

All she carried was the small bag with her belongings, including the zip file of the novel she had written in prison. She had sent this to Hugo, and Hugo and Nancy had found a publisher without delay or much editing. They had loved it – fiction again! *In a way,* thought Viv, *all dressed up as fiction, but no-one is left out of this. The Final Sentence.* They weren't to know it was more fact than fiction. This book had felt necessary to complete the circle of events that had landed her in prison. She needed justice, that need still gnawed at her. *I'm just not a good enough person to let it go,* she thought as she trod on the deep pile carpet towards her room.

The porter waited at the door.

"Thank you."

He hesitated, a question on his face, then left, closing the door quietly behind him.

"Wow!"

She took it all in. This morning she had been in a prison, in a room where she could touch both sides with her arms out, all surfaces wipeable, jailers with chains and keys, windows with tiny gaps for speaking. Now, she could walk twelve paces before she reached the window. The refined rumble of traffic came through the double glazing and elegant net curtains. She was exhausted. The bed would have held a family. As she fell back on it, she breathed in the smell of beautiful laundry and remembered Amanda and their night together before she had given herself up to the arms of correction. Where was Amanda? It had been so long. Viv's instinct told her that however much Amanda had loved her, Amanda's need to keep herself safe, and her work safe, superseded that. Something had broken and she could not tell whether it could ever be mended or whether it was what she wanted anymore. All the same, she would have to contact her at some point as she had Viv's keys.

As yet her plan was not clear, but she knew that the book was a beginning. She liked to think so, and that was part of it, but it was also for her. She had to own that. In time she would come to see that through all this jungle of thoughts. Her main goal was to stop this man, her father, and all the men like him, from hurting any more women. She had to see to that. And there was really only one way. She had to out him. She had gone over and over it all so many times. Her father had played such a huge, hidden part in getting her to here, and he had got away with it. He had seen it all happen that night at the bus stop, and he had not tried to stop it or save her.

As for Paula, that betrayal still burned in her. The impossibility of ever trusting anyone again that closely after Paula was what hurt. She had let Amanda in, trusted her but she too, probably, had betrayed her.

She thought of Arun and all that he had done for her. Arun, bless him, saw her as the innocent victim. If only.

Viv thought too of her beautiful home on the river. The excitement to see it was intense, immediate. She stood and took stock of herself for the second time that day but this time in the long mirror on the wardrobe, beautiful French rococo, and it brought a lump to her throat. *I look so ordinary*, was her first thought. *Just average – height, weight, hair, clothes, all so very, very ordinary.* Evie Riley from Reston. Where was V. J.? Had she survived? In prison, Viv had grown a shell but lost her edge. But thankfully not her memory of London; Fortnum's was nearly next door, and it had a barber's! She had once slept in the doorway there.

As she wandered down and into the store, Viv tried to hide how deep her pleasure of good oak floors, mirrors that shone, leather wing chairs was as she booked a cut.

"This is a barber's, madam." He had meant it helpfully.

"I know." She smiled. "This will be perfect."

The soft towel round her neck, the unguents, the care, not just the elegant cut – very short but with shape, panache – was bringing Viv back to life, back to V. J. Wheeler, not Evie Riley. She studied herself, every inch of her face in the mirror as he cut and snipped; she *was* still V. J.

She then toured the clothes floors but was irritated with what she saw. It reminded her of that night in Piccadilly, first alone in London, when she had seen those oh so correct women in floral dresses and navy blazers. She decided to see what the men's fashion had to offer, and with ease and delight and joy she bought and wore out of the store well-cut navy trousers with turn ups, the whitest of white fitted shirts and a dull brocade waistcoat.

"Hmm… this is more like it!"

For tonight, her royalties would certainly cover this embrace from life that said she still had a place in it. She decided not to eat alone in full public gaze, it was too soon to be in that sort of dining room, and instead smuggled in a hotchpotch of delicious foods she had missed – smoked salmon, yogurt, dark chocolates – and ate them in her room that evening, savouring each and every taste.

She had left one message telling Amanda that she would need to collect her keys. She must know by now that she had been released. She decided on a text to prepare Amanda for her call. Three false starts, then Viv settled on breezy as the right tone.

Hi, Amanda, I'm out in the free world. I will call you in an hour. Can I collect my flat keys tomorrow?

Yes, that was OK, neutral enough, and she clicked send. On reflection though, she realised how fearful that minimalism was. Well, that was how it was, and she needed to get into her home. Had Amanda looked after it? Had she been there or just held the keys? Was Amanda even in England? It was early evening. Was she perhaps at some star-studded reception and not got her text? All mad thoughts, like a teenager before a date. Viv called before the hour was up. She needed to get this over and done with, know one way or another how things stood between them.

"Amanda? It's Viv."

Amanda, having received the text from early that morning, answered but with a nanosecond pause.

"How wonderful, Viv. I'm so glad for you... that it's all over... How are you?"

Amanda could have been anyone in that moment. So polished, so smooth. Viv struggled to hear the woman she had known. She noticed in that split second that she had wanted so much more.

"Fine. All good. I need to collect my keys." And then, after another second's thought at how ungracious this sounded, "Thank you for holding them. Could we meet tomorrow?"

"Sure, sure. We should do that."

And they arranged to meet at noon in Battersea, not far from Amanda's office, for lunch.

CHAPTER 4

The restaurant was Italian, small but with an outside space in front of it, in the old square at Battersea. Viv strode up to it, gave Amanda's name and chose her table outside where conversation could be less overheard by the next table.

"Well, if you like…" The waiter obviously had another table in mind.

"This will do fine."

Viv straightened the cutlery, marvelled at the shininess of the knives and forks. She ordered a glass of wine. She smoothed her hair. Then she saw Amanda walk into view. She took a drink of water. Amanda had not changed, still groomed to an inch of her life. Still pale grey silk, Nordic blonde. *Does she ever perspire?* was Viv's thought as Amanda caught her eye. In that moment, they could have been anyone, two strangers, colleagues, anything but lovers.

No, certainly not lovers.

Amanda reached across the table.

"Viv, I'm so glad – you should have told me you were coming out of prison, I would have come to meet you."

Somehow Viv doubted this.

"I left a message for you…" There was a pause.

Amanda chose white wine. Viv raised her glass in salutation but just as she had the drink to her lips, Amanda paused and placed it on the table.

"I would have visited but, you know, the film has taken up so much time; in fact, you were lucky to catch me in London, we have been on location—"

Viv held up her hand. "Stop. Just stop. It's fine."

As Amanda read the menu, Viv glanced over. It felt like spying, prying; her hair was well cut, soft, her nails manicured. The same perfume. The waiter came and looked expectantly at one and then the other.

"Oh, I haven't quite decided, sorry."

They ordered, but in truth, Viv was out of the habit of eating good food; it was too rich after the diet in prison and last night's splurge was distinct in her memory.

"How is the film going?"

"Very, very well, you will be pleased with the result. We had problems at the beginning with funding falling through, and then with the delay, the lead cancelled, but all this is normal." She looked at Viv. "I can't wait for you to see it."

It's helpful, thought Viv, to have this life raft, called the film, in between them. At least they had that in common. She still loved Amanda's voice; it was soothing. And her hands, long, thin fingers, so beautiful. But try as she might, in the gaps of the conversation, Viv could not remember how it had felt when Amanda had held her. She just could not.

"I have a favour to ask."

"Oh?"

"I remember you had a techy friend who could trace things?"

"Linny?"

"Yes, Linny."

"What is it?"

Viv softened at the concern in Amanda's voice.

"I had an anonymous letter and then an anonymous email before I went to prison and I hoped that whoever it was would just go away, but I need to know who it was. Could he trace it for me?"

Amanda relaxed. "Yes, yes, of course. I wasn't sure what you were going to ask!" Then a pause. "Is this still your father?"

Viv stopped in her tracks; she had forgotten she had confided all this in Paris.

"Yes. Yes. I think it is."

Amanda lent over the table and lightly held Viv's forearm. "May I give you some advice? Feel free to ignore it."

Viv nodded.

"Don't fool around in the shadows anymore, it isn't you, it isn't the girl I fell in love with. Even if you find out it was your father behind all this, what are you going to do? Have a quiet night in and get depressed? Or take it to him?"

Viv sat back and took in every inch of her erstwhile lover's face. She was right.

"Thank you. Thank you. That was the shot in the arm I needed. Can we talk another time about this?"

Amanda nodded.

"Did you bring my keys? Is the flat alright?"

Amanda opened her large document bag and retrieved the keys, placed them on the table.

"Oh oh… that is so good, did you go and check – is it OK? And my computer, is it there, or do you have it?"

"Everything is there. I'm sure it is all fine."

"You haven't checked?"

Viv had trusted her to guard what was precious to her, and Viv had understood that Amanda knew that. But hearing Amanda's words now, Viv knew that the promise of that night had not been kept alive.

With her lunch not finished, she scraped her chair back she said, "It's a long way. I have to go now. I have to go. Thank you for keeping them. I'll pay the bill on the way out."

Avoiding the need to choose between a hug, a kiss, a handshake, she left Amanda sitting there, trying probably to make sense of all the gaps in their conversation. It was indeed a trek, one train after another, and after nearly two hours she felt that she had seen what London looked and smelled like. It was overcrowded, dirty, noisy and alien. Her senses were overloaded, she needed peace. All the same, she was full of excitement, anticipation as she walked down the road where she had bought the lobster for that dinner, past the newspaper shop and yes – there it was. She had never bothered with an alarm, but suddenly she wondered if that had been overconfident. Was everything still there?

The key turned easily, the door needed a push to unstick, mail was knee deep on the mat, and the smell of the unlived-in home hit her hard. Picking up handfuls of post, she glanced at the dates of the postmarks. With more relief than she was willing to acknowledge yet, she saw that although it looked like a mountain, Amanda had indeed been keeping a now-and-then eye on the place. She went over to the window and walked the sliding doors open; the river air, the boats, suffused the rooms. Her tension dropped a level. Like an animal, she visited every room, anxiously checking everything, patting the sofa, the bed, running the taps, until there was nothing more to do. She fell back on the leather sofa. Music would be good. The strains of Etta James connected Viv back to the home she loved. Kicking off her boots, lying back with her eyes closed, Viv took a deep breath and let out a sigh. Her wallet dropped on the floor and, picking it up, Viv saw still hidden inside was the note from her mother, written during the trial.

She recalled how she had looked at the trial. So neat and tidy, but there had been something more about her, almost a jauntiness now that she was free of abuse. She recalled her mother's request, through Arun, to come and visit her in prison, and how she had refused point-blank. She had somewhat startled the kind family boy with that, but then she thought he didn't come from a family like hers.

"No." She said this out loud and surprised herself. "No, I don't need to justify myself."

She had left the glass doors open and the air was changing, afternoon to early evening chill. She shivered and went over to slide them shut. A riverboat was passing, and she could hear the laughter, the voices. She wrapped her arms tight around her.

"I'm lonely, that's what."

Turning the music up, she busied herself with unpacking, checking the fridge and realising too late that she had forgotten to buy any food. She grimaced. Something about her mother was still bothering her.

CHAPTER 5

Viv reached for a glass from the dusty top shelf, but it dropped and shattered. She found the dustpan and brush and spent a long time brushing every shard of glass, every speck of dirt from the floor. As she tipped the mess all into the pedal bin, it came to her. It was all broken, all of it. Her family, such as it was, was as broken as that beautiful crystal glass. At one time, the hopes of all concerned must have been as beautiful as that glass but look what happened.

"I can no more put that back together, even if I wanted to, than that glass."

The music ended; she returned to the sitting room and pressed play again. Again she pictured, or tried to picture, her mother, who had never intentionally hurt her and who had, indeed, in her own muddled way, tried to save her. She herself had been drowning with no way back to the beach. Viv slapped her thigh, wanting to break the mood.

"Enough, enough of this melancholy!"

And with that, she Googled the Chinese takeway that she had fantasised about many a night in Belton. Her spirits rose in expectation of her order arriving – it felt like a sort of celebration. She turned on the television with no idea anymore of what was on. And the clear thought came to her: she and her mother needed to bear witness to the end of this horrible saga. Together.

*

Viv's initial thinking was that it would be easier to meet in a café somehow. Easier to meet on neutral territory. On one of Arun's visits, he had given her a message from her mother, the one where she had offered to come and visit her in prison. His sweet face had looked hopeful; a possible rapprochement; he could arrange it.

"Not yet, Arun, no," she had said.

"I understand."

Sometimes he was like a kind dog, you could feel cruel so easily around him.

"In the future?"

She nodded, holding out a bone to him, and his face had brightened.

"I will tell her."

And they had talked about other things until it had been time for him to leave.

Each day in the trial, Viv had glanced up at the public gallery and she became used to seeing her mother from that distance. She had been intrigued by seeing her dignified, slight figure in a grey suit, a sort of 1950s buttoned and collared jacket suit, a brooch. She had changed. But too much time had passed, Viv thought, for them to say an easy hello.

One night on her prison bed, she had left the blinds of her cell with the slats open and lay back thinking what had become of her mother. Why had she never been able to make Viv feel safe? Why couldn't she have stood up to Douglas? She had clearly burned her boats now, though, bringing the duvet evidence to court. She must have known by doing that that her marriage would have been over. Viv shuddered at the thought of her father. Nothing much would touch him, nothing much ever had. He had got away with everything. For now, anyway.

It was dark; the sky and river became one shape with only the lights of buildings to distract from it. She walked out on to the balcony and searched for stars, but it was cloudy and none were yet showing.

Going through the saved emails from before she went to prison, she found her mother's messages.

"Poor Mum."

Laying the phone face down, she felt genuine empathy for the first time probably in her life. She had a second thought: she had no idea where her mother lived anymore, or whether this was still her phone number.

Arun, poor Arun. He would know.

"You wish to contact your mother?"

"I do, Arun, it is time."

He supplied Viv with her mother's address and new phone number. She was oddly shocked to realise that her mother had a whole new life now of which she knew nothing. She had changed her name back to her maiden name; she was now Rosemary Goode. Would they be strangers? Had too much time gone by? Was this a mistake, an indulgence? She looked at the address she had written down. Brighton. She was no longer used to nipping in the car or hopping on the train, for that matter. Distances seemed more daunting than before. Brighton.

She had emailed, they had exchanged a willingness to meet. The language on both sides had been stilted, not formal but self-conscious, cautious. It had been a 'you first' type of exchange. It had been Rosemary who had suggested the seafront café. She often called in there for a cup of tea, she said. So it was on a grey, sleety, collar-up April afternoon that they had agreed to meet. Viv glanced at her watch; it was five to three. She looked around the café; not many there on a day like this. One or two people just passing some time before the rain stopped; an old man in the corner looked like he came here every day for hours, never moving, one cup of tea. She could perhaps just ask how her mother had been? Ask her what she was up to now? In leaving, Viv had found her power, but had it been at the cost of her mother? And then, a new thought: what would her mother think of her daughter being a murderer? Is that why she had changed her name?

Viv would wait to order; they would order together, that would be a good beginning. If she ordered first, it might look as though she was wanting to leave early, pay separately. No, she would wait. A couple ran in, glad to escape the cold, and sat in the far corner. The old man with thin legs sat with a look of resignation on his face. Viv looked out of the rain-spattered window; the sky was grey, not much wind, and the waves were not huge. They only broke with surf as they hit the stones. Dog walkers went by. She looked at her watch again – three o'clock. Perhaps her mother would not come. She rubbed away the window condensation and peered left and right. Neither of them would be the same as when they had last seen each other, she realised with a jolt, her head spinning. Apart from the trial, the last time she had seen her mother had been the morning she left for school and never returned. Her mother had waved her goodbye, a long grey cardigan wrapped tightly round her.

Viv dropped her phone on the hard, stone, mosaic floor, bent down to pick it up and, as she did so, she saw Rosemary pushing through the heavy glass door. Viv stood and smiled.

Her mother smiled. Viv gestured to the chair. Her mother's beige raincoat was spattered with rain, her black high-heeled shoes not made for walking. Rosemary sat down opposite, placing her bag on the chair next to her.

"Yes, yes…"

Her mother was glad of direction. She undid her headscarf as she sat down. Her hair had gone completely white, Viv saw with a shock.

"Terrible weather."

"Yes, terrible."

The waitress had been patient, but now strode over, anxious to make at least a small sale today. She had the paper pad and biro in her hand.

"Yes?"

"How about tea?" This was to her mother.

"Yes, yes…"

The waitress scribbled. "Anything to eat?"

Viv shook her head. "Not yet."

The pause before the waitress turned said it all; she had no time for small orders. Viv noticed her mother's nails were now manicured, slightly varnished. Was that a colour? No, no colour.

"Did you come from London?"

Her mother made it sound like a journey from Mars, but Viv curbed her tongue at the thought.

"Yes, yes, not bad. Straight down. On the train."

Viv had decided not to change her car, certainly not yet, she wasn't sure what sort of person she was anymore, what sort of life she would have now. Too early to buy another car.

"Good service."

"At least you are free on the train!" Her mother bit her lip, put her hand to her mouth. "I'm sorry, I didn't mean…"

Viv laughed; it broke the ice at least.

"How long?" Her mother's face was anxious, lined with concern.

"...Have I been out? Call a spade a spade, please!"

Her mother peered at Viv, a mother remembering her baby. A concerned look came over her face.

"What was... What I mean is... are you alright?"

Viv was unsure where the marker for 'alright' was any more, but she could see that the question was meant kindly. She nodded.

"You?"

"Well, I... you know... I've bought a house, not far from here."

Viv's mother's face changed as she spoke of her new home; the lines of care softened, and her eyes lit up.

"I'm glad. I mean, I'm glad you no longer have to endure the..."

"Yes."

Rosemary was anxious not to spell out the words describing the past. It was all about the future now.

"I'm sorry, you know, I'm sorry for all..."

Viv looked away. She wanted to say it was alright, but as she heard her mother frame those words, she realised they didn't come close to dealing with the damage of the past. The waves were still breaking on the shingle. She needed fresh air.

It was her mother's turn to look away. *So, we are both alone now*, thought Viv. Her mother no longer a wife or, indeed, really a mother, and she not much of a daughter and no longer a lover. Viv resisted thinking of Amanda; it was too painful, too unresolved.

"So, would you like cake then?" Viv offered.

Her mother brightened at the thought; it was a treat to have cake.

Viv looked over to the waitress who had been standing, leaning back to the counter.

"Hi."

The waitress pushed herself up to standing and came over.

"Yes?"

"We would like two slices of chocolate cake, please, and more tea."

As the waitress left, Viv asked her mother, "That was the right order for you, wasn't it?"

"Yes, it was. It really was… I wanted to ask, what made you want to see me after… all these years? And after all that has happened?"

Viv was relieved her mother had asked the question.

"I thought I knew why. I thought that we had to draw a line under everything together somehow." Viv reached for her mother's hand then looked her square in the face. "But if I'm being brutally honest, I'm not sure I can yet."

"I'm sorry."

"Me too. I wish everything had been different. I wish you had stopped my father that day taking me to board, I wish you had stopped him attacking me. I'm sorry… it's just that it's not over for me."

"I wish I had been different for you too."

"How much did you know about my father and his violence towards me? Did you know that he did that?"

Viv had not meant to be saying this. Her mother looked down at her tea, pushed the cake away.

"I didn't know. But in a way, I must have."

"That's brave to say that."

Energy drained out of Rosemary and she leant back in her seat, her eyes closed.

"I've been dreading that question for ten years. Does that make me a coward?"

"A coward wouldn't have come to meet me today."

Rosemary's eyes widened as she looked at her daughter.

"That is generous of you, Evie. Not a day has gone by that I haven't relived what I could have done to protect you. I didn't... and I could have—"

"No," Viv interrupted her mother. "No, I don't think you could have, he was too much for both of us."

"I'm sorry I left that morning without letting you know... but I had to."

Her mother was silent.

"You do understand that now, don't you?"

Her mother nodded, pain still etched on her face.

"It was difficult for me," her mother wiped her mouth with the paper napkin, "to hear all, all the details at the trial."

"I couldn't help that. But I am sorry that you did."

"I wanted to visit you in prison."

"I know. I couldn't."

They sat in silence for a while. When the tea and cake were finished, it would soon be time to go.

"Penny for them?" Rosemary's voice was gentle. It wasn't a rebuke, but the question brought Viv back to the present. "You were miles away."

Viv decided to tell her the truth. "What I was thinking about was my father. Douglas."

Rosemary didn't take sugar but stirred her tea over and over.

"Your father?"

"When did you last see him?"

"I... er... I... well, at the, your, trial. But, of course, you know how that went." She managed a wry laugh.

"You were brave."

"Foolish more like. Why couldn't I just have found out the truth before properly?"

"It did the job."

"What job?"

"You, your freedom. Without that, would you just have gone on living with him?"

The faintest shrug, but Viv could see that mention of Douglas had brought back memories, stirred up feelings in her mother. She couldn't help it; she had to settle the past once and for all.

"I'm sorry, I didn't want to—"

"It's fine."

"It's still not fine with me, it's not finished. Do you have a contact for him?"

"Oh, Evie, don't go stirring up trouble for yourself."

At this, Viv erupted with laughter. It broke the mood.

"As opposed to what? Being raped, killing someone and going to prison? What sort of trouble do you have in mind?"

Rosemary looked younger as she laughed. There was a connection between them for a moment.

"I know it was difficult when you were at home." Rosemary could not look at Viv as she said this.

"Did you? Did you really?"

"I know what you're thinking, I've thought the same, why didn't I stop him? I couldn't, I simply couldn't."

The rage, the injustice, the impotence all came to the surface hearing her mother say this. *Yes, she could*, Viv was thinking, *yes, she could*.

"If there was one thing I could undo, it would be that."

"It was that that framed my whole life. I wanted a father who loved me, not one that I had to walk on eggshells for, not one where I had to duck out of his way."

"I know, I know. I am so very sorry."

"One that had a right to exist," she added under her breath.

This last Viv said softly, almost to herself, under her breath. Viv looked across at her mother, saw the skin beginning to sag, the lines of disappointment around the mouth, and the nearest Viv could come to forgiveness was acceptance that Rosemary had been a different person then and she had lived in terror herself.

The weather had not let up; it was still windy and threatening and the waves held that gunmetal grey as their white tips crashed over, destroying them each time. Viv watched the rhythm of these waves, crashing with predictability, with energy. It was calming.

"Well? Do you have a contact for him?"

"Please don't. Promise me you won't. No good will come of it."

"I can't promise you that."

Rosemary gave way and scribbled out a phone number and an email for Douglas.

"There."

The look she gave her daughter was like someone sending out the messenger in the face of crossfire.

Once Viv had put the paper in her wallet, an energy surged into her. Of course, this was the missing bit. She leant back on the plastic chair. *I've wanted to kill him, make him suffer, humiliate him, all that for years, probably most of my life, but what I need to do is talk to him, look him in the eyes – and ask him, why? Give him that chance. Why did he do that to me?*

"Promise me you'll take care."

Before she could stop herself, she answered, "Bit late for that, don't you think?"

"You know what I mean."

"I know what I need to do, absolutely it's the missing piece. I have to set myself free from all of this, everything, everyone."

Rosemary looked away.

"I'm sorry, Mum, it's not personal, it's survival. I need to start again."

"Don't go and see him, please don't. He will hurt you, I know he will."

Her mother had not changed that much.

"I haven't decided yet what I will do about many things, including him. In fact, the only clear decision—"

The waitress interrupted, "More tea?"

"No, no thanks. The bill."

"...The only clear decision I have made since I came out was to have this talk."

"Thank you, Evie, and I'm sorry."

"No more of that, there's no point, both of us took the only choices we were capable of."

The waves had gathered even more power and were breaking further up the steeply banked stone beach. There was a rhythm to it, a waiting for the next crash, then the pull back of the sea.

Walking along the seafront afterwards until Viv had to cut north for the station, they stopped. Rosemary moved towards Viv about to embrace her. Viv held out her hand.

"Well, this is me. Thank you for coming." Viv pointed up towards the station.

"Yes, yes..."

The two women, who had been through so much, shook hands, left in different directions.

CHAPTER 6

On the train home, it wasn't so packed that Viv couldn't find a seat. She settled into a corner so she could take in the places they passed but keep an eye out for the inspector. It still felt odd to be deciding what to do each day, to be able to travel freely through miles of countryside, towns and villages. The hours of the day for Viv were still twelve for lunch, six for supper, and eight was lock in. Viv glanced at the time; five o'clock. Her phone pinged; she dug around in her trousers pocket to retrieve it. A message from Hugo.

"Oh!" Her face brightened.

Welcome back from the other side!

How typical of Hugo, still uncomfortable with messy intimacy.

As you know, your book came out (as well!) and we should talk about the future. I've booked at an Italian restaurant just off Queen Square. Can you make one o'clock tomorrow?

Her step was light as she reached her flat. Having plans set for the next day buoyed Viv up.

*

Arriving at La Trattoria the next day, she wove her way through the plastic vines and Chianti bottles hanging from the ceiling until she saw Hugo at the far end. *Same place, same menu, same Hugo,* thought Viv. He hadn't changed. Not really. A few grey hairs at the side, that was all, but it suited him. She saw a frown come over his face as he watched her approaching.

"Hugo." She held out her hand.

He stood. They smiled awkwardly, then both sat. Hugo reached for the menu.

"So, how is life? I mean, now?"

"I know what you mean, Hugo – shall we get it out of the way? I went to prison, and now I'm out. There, not too difficult, was it?"

She heard her own aggression, and seeing Hugo's expression change, she remembered that she still needed an agent if her life were to continue well and held her hand up for a high five.

"Amends!"

He held up his hand. "Granted. Glad to see you've lost none of your acerbic edge."

"Ouch."

The waiter appeared. "What would you like to drink?" Hugo asked Viv, unsure of his footing.

"Tonic."

Hugo affected shock but Viv was not about to offer any explanation. He leant back in the raffia seated chair, played with his signet ring.

"So, tell me." Then, leaning forward, lowering his voice and looking around, he asked what he really wanted to know. "What *was* it like inside? Really?"

Viv didn't answer straightaway. Hugo was such an old gossip.

"Well, your notoriety, if I may call it that, played into our hands. Good print run, moderately good initial sales, not all bad."

"Only you, Hugo. Only you could come up with that as the first statement of the day."

Giving their order to the waiter was a welcome distraction. Viv noticed the waiter's apron where he had wiped his tomato hands across it. Not Boodles anymore then.

"I liked the cover. Great title, don't you think? *The Final Sentence*."

"Depends what it means."

Hugo took his time drinking the claret.

Viv thought, *if he continues with that, it'll soon show on his face, but for now, he is still quite elegant, even youthfully slim.* Hugo pushed a royalties sheet towards her. Viv took her time studying it. The book had not been out long, but the sales were not as good as she had hoped, not as good as her previous books.

"So, what are you thinking?"

"Well, while the publicity was good, you might have lost a few fans. That's what it looks like.

"We need a rebranding."

Hugo brightened at this thought. The restaurant was filling up, the noise gathering.

"So, what would a 'rebranding' entail?" Viv suggested.

Hugo leant towards Viv. "The publicity of your case might have helped sales here – there was a lot of coverage, a lot of sympathy… you must have seen?"

Memories of Belton and how different their lives had been during that time swam back to Viv.

"*The Times* was not delivered to my cell. Foreign sales? Is it out in America?"

"Not yet… I was coming to that. In the States, we wanted to wait until you were out. We would have to take a different tack. They like a revisionist, a penitent, a born again."

He didn't dare look up at this point. Hugo was about to order more claret but paused. He was drinking more than he used to; he was thinking how different it was between them now, almost awkward.

"You should know that if America is to go ahead, we will need better sales here. Americans are… shall we say… different? A bit more judgmental. So I – we – wanted to wait and talk to you about giving the book a proper boost here first, now that you… can boost it… personally. How do you feel about that?"

Hugo was talking more than Viv remembered. Was he nervous?

"What are you suggesting then?"

"We need a launch party. The right people coming, good visuals, good coverage, even…" he looked cautiously up at Viv, "even an interview?"

"Ah, yes." She lifted her glass. "Let's drink to no more running!"

"Indeed, but you'll have to do the penitent thing! Think you can manage that?"

"Who would fund publicity in America?"

"The American publisher, if sales pick up here."

"Well, that's promising."

The waiter brought the main course, fussed around the wine bottle held in a white napkin. The pair of them remained silent, grateful for the interruption.

"It all comes back to the launch, or relaunch, here. We decided to wait till you were back… with us… and we could discuss it further. How does that sound? It's not usual practice once a book is out but in this case…"

"It's not usual practice to be held as a guest of Her Majesty."

"Yes. Exactly."

"Hugo, why do I get the impression you are embarrassed about a party? There's something you aren't telling me."

"Never, Wheeler. Never embarrassed."

"Reluctant then?" Viv was backing him into a corner.

Hugo took his time eating, and a penny dropped for Viv.

"Ah... I get it. It's on me, isn't it? I'll be footing this bill."

"We aren't a welcome-home institution. I'm sorry, that wasn't meant to come out like that." He reached across the table. "I'm sorry."

Viv straightened out a ruck in the tablecloth, moved her glass as she began.

"If I funded it, would I have to plan it too?"

"Look," he leant towards Viv, "if it's too much, if you don't want to do it, that's fine. Take your time thinking about it. Sales are OK. No-one's going to die. But we need to keep you up there."

Hugo tried a weak smile, half a question on his face. He left the remainder of his salmon, leant back in his chair and studied the face of this woman with whom he felt such conflicting emotions, always had done.

"You're a mystery, Wheeler, always have been."

Viv laughed.

"Shall we talk dates?"

CHAPTER 7

Viv began the walk from the restaurant and over Blackfriars Bridge towards home. She had expected it to be uplifting seeing Hugo again and getting back into her old life, but, leaning over the bridge watching the gulls landing on a moored boat, pecking for scraps, she felt depressed.

At least in prison it had only been about day-to-day survival. Not this complicated. Did she really want to put herself in the ring again, get the publicity that she had shrunk from at the trial? Was she ready for that?

Walking always helped though, and as she relaxed, she began to argue with herself. *What if I turned this around, and totally owned it? No more excuses, no more hiding. What is the worst that could happen? There aren't any more secrets to come out.*

And then, in sight of her flat, she had a blinding revelation! The party could even suit her own purposes. Two birds with one stone!

*

Towards lunchtime the next day, she made her way to the club. It was time to test the water. Taking out her mobile, she found Arun in contacts and called.

"Hi, Arun!"

"V. J., where are you?"

"I'm calling because I'm out!"

"That is, indeed, good news. I promised you, did I not? That we would celebrate."

A pause.

"V. J., V., J., are you still there? I can hear traffic… are you anywhere near our club? If so, I will meet you there in half an hour?"

'Our club'. Viv took a deep breath before answering.

"I can think of nothing better, Arun."

Her stride quickened and a smile played on her face.

But as she neared the club, the reality of rebuff loomed as a possibility. Out of the corner of her eye she saw Colin Meadman, who had been one of the cast of characters always at the club's main table. They had never particularly spoken but each knew who the other was. She looked up just as he was looking over at her, then he looked away.

"Huh!"

She was almost at the entrance to the club alleyway but walked on past the entrance and walked back along the main road instead. She wasn't ready. This was like the last time. *I can't go in, I can't.* She reached for her phone to call Arun, but as she did so, she almost bumped into an old man she remembered from the club.

He stood slightly back, raised his hat.

"V. J., welcome back!"

It was old Ivan Metcalfe.

"Metcalfe!"

"I heard about your… troubles. Never let bad notices get to you, soldier on, that's my motto!"

"Thank you." Viv's voice had a catch in it.

"Are you headed to the club?"

"Well, I…"

He strode on, assuming she would do likewise, and they fell into step. Metcalfe entered first, Viv following.

Maurice was still the doorman. She'd been right about him.

"Morning, Maurice!"

"Good morning!"

He'd never greeted her so formally and had turned away to check on some papers before the greeting was out. She chose not to indulge it but strode in over the huge, worn, old floor stones and into the dingier bar. Metcalfe went to his usual seat at the main table with the newspapers.

"Lloyd!" She strode up to him. "Am I glad to see you!"

Even Lloyd looked around before saying, "Good morning, V. J., nice to see you. Usual?"

It was on the tip of her tongue to say yes, but she shook her head.

"No, Lloyd, nothing's usual anymore. A tonic with ice and lemon."

As she turned to see which chairs were free, Arun walked over to her. She hadn't seen him there and he shook her hand in full view of the members.

"Good morning, V. J."

Even theatrical.

He held it there until he was sure that they had been seen. He was no stranger to the depths of injustice, and it wasn't just his profession that had given him this sense. His grandparents had been caught up in partition and their stories of persecution and fleeing to India from what became Pakistan had mythologised in their family. Protection, defence, justice, flowed through his veins. Viv covered his hand with hers and met his eyes. *Such steady eyes*, she thought.

"Better surroundings!" She was nervous.

"Indeed, but now we shall look to the future. The past has gone."

She turned back to Lloyd. "Whatever Arun orders is on me."

They sat in full view of the members, but out of earshot, and Arun's first question was as to her welfare. He could never quite, even in their intimate connection, drop the formality he had been brought up with. So correct, so polite.

"I'm out, Arun. I'm out. I have to get used to that. I'm not sure," and here she cast an eye round the club, "how much damage I have sustained. Not yet."

Two members chose to leave; two talked quietly behind their hands.

"You look a little pale, V. J., you need the fresh air of freedom."

"I want to thank you for everything. Above and beyond the call. You have been… kind." She raised her glass.

Viv had always been one to cope on her own, it was her badge of pride, but today she stayed talking to Arun.

"It was nothing, it is my job. But if I may say, it was a miscarriage of justice in my eyes, you were the victim and did not deserve punishment."

Viv considered this for a while. Was now the time?

"If anything, V. J., I feel I let you down."

Viv placed her hand on his. "No, you must never say that, never. You did everything you could and but for you, my sentence would have been longer."

"It has played on my mind, V. J., and now that it is over I can discuss it with you?"

Viv nodded.

"Was there anything more that I could have done? I believed – believe – in you, and you of all people could never kill someone, except in self-defence. And yet, and yet, the jury thought otherwise. It made me question my calling."

At this last statement, he looked up at Viv. If she admitted that she knew herself capable of this murder, then his faith in justice but not his abilities would be restored. If she said nothing, he would be left without self-castigation. She studied his face; a few lines where there had been none before.

"Arun, we are both getting older. I want you to know that you have been my only constant friend throughout this ordeal and have never judged me. Around here," she cast a look around the club, "around here there is plenty of judgment."

"I am your friend, V. J. Indeed." He drank long and slow. "And I would like this to continue."

This was said with a hint of a question, a need to reply. Where was this going?

"I would like that more than I can say. As well, though, I would like to share what I have learnt, and that is that anyone is capable of anything. And before they are faced with the circumstances, they can never know themselves."

She studied his face as he took this in, but he did not flinch. As he chose to ignore the implications of this statement, Viv wished, not for the first time, that she was straight.

"And I need you, me, everyone, to know that I am not a victim." That was as far as she could go.

"So, what plans do you have now for your immediate future?"

Viv considered. "You know I had a book published while I was inside?"

"Indeed."

"Did you read it?"

A pause before Arun answered. "I counsel against retribution, if I may say."

"I have thought of little else."

Amanda's words came back to her: "Don't mess around in the shallows, it isn't you."

"You may have bridges to build also with your family?"

She studied his face, saw the kindness in his soft brown eyes.

"I have seen my mother."

"And how is your mother?"

"Well, I think, of course things have changed. She went back to her maiden name. Lives in Brighton."

"Ah. And your father?"

Viv laid both her hands face down on the small table between them and paused before answering.

"I have his phone number and his email; my mother gave them to me. Should I see him, do you think?"

"Well, you must know why if you do. As I say, I counsel against retribution."

"But, Arun, he has been the cause of everything. I'm still angry, there are still scores to settle. I have to be honest."

"Well, take time to consider well before you meet him, please. And now..." He glanced at his watch. "I have to be in court."

"Of course."

She watched him leave, his every step precise.

Just as Viv was resolving to listen to Arun's advice, if she could, a text pinged through from Amanda.

Linny has some information about the anonymous letters. It was the email that gave him the IP address. They came from your father.

No sign off, no fondness, but the text was gold and Viv's wavering resolution to be reasonable and peaceful dissolved in that instant. She jumped up and made her way to the exit with a return of her former strong stride. This was the call to arms she needed. She glanced over at Maurice, deep in the *Racing Post*.

"I don't bite, Maurice!"

Her mother had been a victim too, she had just taken a different path, perhaps, reflected Viv. It was her role just to make things conscious, perhaps it was that simple. And not just for her own family, but for all the women out there. Viv had to finish the job. With her father.

CHAPTER 8

Viv's thoughts were on her father and the past as she made her way to Reston. She thought too of Kelly, who had always had a secret serenity. She had tried to engage with her, see what made her tick. But it was when the summer had come and shirts were left unbuttoned at the neck that Viv had seen the elaborate crucifix around her neck. Her mother had slavishly parked her responsibilities onto a God she did not know existed, and Viv had felt only rage for that, but how to equate the two?

Over the next two weeks, she emailed and called Douglas, but there had been no reply, and the phone had gone to answerphone every time. At first she had left a message, but then she wrote:

Douglas,
I realise I have never had a proper conversation with you. I know you wrote the letters. Douglas, I need to talk to you – why have you wanted to hurt me so much? We need to meet. I need to understand.

But there was still no answer.

After having her beloved MG confiscated all those years ago, she had lost heart and connection with driving and nowadays took taxis, Ubers, trains. And so it was that she took the train and the same walk from Reston Station in reverse that she had taken on that dark and wet night. Now it felt like peeling back skin to revisit the place. They had put a guardrail up the station steps. The cars still came too close down the small side road that lacked a pavement. And along the main road, still ugly with the odd insurance shop, the quick food takeaway, the charity shop, she walked past the old church at the heart of the village. *At least that will stay the same*, thought Viv. Past the village pump and – here she gasped, she had forgotten – Dawson's garage, now with a new name and a tidy up, but it was still Dawson's garage. Looking away, she carried on up the road where her old house still was. It was only when she noticed that her old room still had the same faded-brown, faux-velvet curtains that it all felt real. She prayed her father would be home. That was why she had chosen to come early on a Sunday morning. He lived alone there now; she knew that from her mother. She tried to picture him but couldn't and decided to pause in the Pelican Café opposite and have a coffee to steady herself for this meeting. She chose a corner seat. There were only two other people there despite it being ten o'clock. The coffee hardly tasted of coffee, but at least it was warm. She tried to marshal her thoughts, but it was impossible.

"Everything alright?"

"Yes, yes. Thanks."

Ten minutes later, leaving the £2.50 on the table and making her way over the road, she forced herself not to pause but walked up to the front door. She knocked, then rang, and waited. For a second, she cursed herself for not making sure he would be home. Had it been a wasted journey? She stepped back and looked to the upstairs, then knocked again. She was about to leave, when she heard feet approaching and the door opened. And there he was. After all these years, king of an empty castle. A frown came over his face as he faltered, slightly closing the door, not asking her in.

She managed. "Hello."

"Oh. Now is not a good—"

"May I come in?"

"I don't think—"

But she had walked straight through the half-open door and into the hallway before Douglas realised what was happening. For a split second, Viv wondered whether he would take physical action to stop her; after all, it had been his way of doing things before. Her heart was beating. But no, here they were in the hall with Douglas slowly closing the door while gathering his thoughts. She could hear *The Archers* on somewhere.

"What do you want? Why have you come?" He was on the back foot.

"Why didn't you answer my calls? My emails?"

"I was busy."

"We are all busy, Douglas, but not that busy. Your daughter has been in prison, and she comes out, and you are too busy?"

As she spoke the words, she could feel the rage rise in her. She had meant to be adult, wise, over it, but here it was, the raw emotion.

Viv suggested they move into the sitting room, perhaps talk over a coffee? Keep it all on a level. As he was in the kitchen, Viv looked around the room, still tidy, but no warmth left in it from when it had at least attempted to be a family home. All the cushions had gone, and there was a desk in the corner she didn't recognise. And a framed photo of his mother that had never been there before.

He came back in with two coffees.

He began, "The past is the past, Evie, don't come here raking over old coals. It'll do no good."

She looked at him and could see that he too had aged. His shirt buttons were one out of synch. His aftershave was in the air – that was new, was he planning on going out? Old coals! Is that the name for memories of domestic violence now? Treating women like trash? Old coals?

"I'd just like to…" To what? She realised she had no idea how to begin. "I just need to know why…" Her voice softened. "Why…"

"Why what?"

"…I was never good enough. Why… you hit me… so often… and for no reason. Do you remember that night I came home? In the rain? That night? And what you did? Why? I used to think it was my fault, you made me feel it was my fault… I should never have been born. And… why you sent me those letters."

Hearing her own words out loud made Viv catch her breath. She had reverted to being a child and stood up as she finished the sentence.

"But I know now that it was nothing to do with me."

Colour had risen in his face. "You are being ridiculous. There is absolutely no point in this conversation. None at all. I think you should leave."

"No, Douglas, I need this conversation, I need it."

"I never hit you… at all."

"What?! Are you seriously saying that you never laid a hand on me?"

Douglas looked away. "You weren't the easiest child… and if you are coming at me with accusations, you can leave now!"

"I was a child, I left when I was sixteen. I was innocent."

Douglas turned away. Innocence and guilt he dealt with as a magistrate, but this was different.

"Innocent, Dad... Douglas. You can't just keep denying things."

The word 'innocent' brought tears to Viv's eyes. Now that she had said it, she knew that was it. It was in this house that her childhood had been stolen, her innocence smashed to pieces. Beyond retrieval.

They sat in silence in opposite chairs, drinking the coffee.

"You took that away from me, you took my innocence."

"Don't be ridiculous. You are being dramatic, you always were."

"No. No. No. You could say that before... I always believed it... but not now, you can't get away with that. You were the adult. I was a child. Innocent, caught in the crossfire of this hellhole. And why did you take the only friend that mattered to me? Paula was a child too. Paula, my friend that you slept with. Paula, my fifteen-year-old friend. You betrayed me even then. And her too, and how many others? She can't have been the only one."

He coughed and then choked for a second. His expression changed. He hadn't thought of Paula's name for a long, long time. Is that why she had come? He remembered the photo. He decided to alter his position, tried a smile.

"She told me she was sixteen," Douglas eventually managed.

"She was my friend. Why all of it, why? Did you hate me from the start?"

Douglas had the image of the photos that Viv had sent that night, of the hotel, him and Paula saying goodbye outside, kissing. Did she still have them?

"You come here making accusations."

Viv caught a fleeting expression cross Douglas's face.

"Ah... that was it, wasn't it? Why you wrote the letters. You were afraid of what I might do. She wasn't the only one either, was she, Douglas?"

"What do you want?"

"Answers. We both know what you did, there's no point denying it, none at all, it is why you did it?"

"You challenged me."

"I didn't mean to."

"All the same."

She remembered coming back from school that first Christmas and trying to warm herself in the cold duvet before he hit her for still wearing her shoes.

"What has happened to my room?"

"Still there."

"Can I have a look?"

The fifth stair still creaked. She tried the door, but it was locked. Why? Reaching up to the architrave, she found the key.

She opened the door gingerly, as though expecting to disturb someone. The air was stale, dust had settled on the dressing table, the window needed cleaning, but the curtains and bedspread took Viv back. She remembered that bed. It had a different duvet now. Closing the door behind her, she saw her eleven-year-old self, afraid, alone. She wanted to make her safe and now, closing her eyes, she buried her face in the pillow, traces of her long removed, but still it was her pillow. And then the tears came. How they came.

She hadn't heard her father coming up the stairs, standing by the now open door.

"There's no good coming out of this. You shouldn't be here."

She turned suddenly. "No, that's where you are wrong. I have to know why all this happened, I have to be here... and why is my room kept locked?" Tears were wet on her face. "It was... never my... fault." She said this last slowly and quietly, and asked, "Why? Why?"

"You keep asking that, as though there is an answer."

"What happened to you to make you hate me so much?"

"I don't hate you! You know we have never talked about personal things, I'm not about to start now."

"Perhaps that's exactly what we should do."

In silence, they both went back downstairs. This time Douglas poured two whiskies without asking her and handed one to Viv. She didn't know whether to be pleased he saw her as an adult or relieved that they were now about to enter new territory. It was an odd thing to do, and odder still that he said nothing more but drained his glass in one. Suddenly, he placed the glass down on the table.

"You should go."

And he was up and half pushing Viv to leave but Viv heard a movement upstairs. Was someone else in the house? Holding the front door open, he gestured for her to go.

"What was that?" She pointed upstairs.

"Nothing. It's an old house."

She was about to walk away without saying goodbye, but as she reached it, she turned. "No! No! No! You don't get off the hook that easily. No!" She was screaming now, hammering his chest in fury. "No, this is too easy for you, Douglas. You have got away with everything, everything! I've paid and now it's time you paid for what you've done. You are even still a magistrate. How dare you sit in judgment of others, how dare you? And do you let the pretty ones off?"

He wiped his brow with his hanky. "You can't prove anything. It's all too long ago. Just your word, that's all."

"Morning!"

His nosy neighbour walked by. Douglas did not respond but turned to face Viv.

"I wish none of this, Reg and you, had happened."

"That's so weak! After all this time, that's all you can say."

He didn't answer. Douglas was in turmoil, his thoughts disjointed; the morning had unsettled him.

He looked straight at Viv. "You're too emotional." Then, as an afterthought, almost inaudibly, he added, "My father used to say that women would destroy men with their emotion. And he was right."

Viv had a clear picture, just for a second, of a small boy caught in the crossfire of his own parents. Was it just as simple as patterns repeating themselves?

"Took advantage though, didn't you? Paula? Douglas. You need to pay. I need you to pay. I need you to stop. I need to know you have stopped!"

"Now you do have to leave."

And with no further words, he turned and walked back up the path, in through the open door, and slammed it shut.

She remembered what Amanda told her Linny had found, rang the doorbell again. Nothing. Then the knocker. The door was ripped open.

"No! No more!"

"Oh that's where you're wrong."

She could hear her voice rising. She had to keep control. And she held up the letter that Maurice had given her all those years ago, and the email she had printed out.

"See?"

Douglas looked away. "It's nothing to do with me."

"Oh no, you don't get away with that again. It is everything to do with you! What were you thinking? It terrified me to get anonymous letters. I thought I was being stalked, watched everywhere I went. What were you thinking? To your own daughter?"

"Come inside."

They stood there in the hall. This time, no noise except for the grandfather clock ticking. Viv walked over to the photo of his mother.

"What would she say about you now? Just think for a moment before you answer."

Viv had her eyes closed; this was the moment. He could turn back now. She willed him to look her in the eyes and say how sorry he was.

"I needed to control you… You were out of control… who knows how much vicious talk you would say about me. You would destroy me. That's why I sent it."

"Don't you see, you have never been sorry for treating women with such utter contempt – me, my mother, Paula, and God knows who else."

In the corner of the hall, she caught sight of a rucksack, a girl's rucksack. She pointed to it. He shrugged.

And this time, with that, she chose to leave. As she walked down the path, she could hear that Douglas had not closed the door. He was watching. She knew the power was back with her.

CHAPTER 9

So, was Linny right? Amanda's curiosity had got the better of her and she texted Viv.

She thought of their time in New York, the promises they had made, and the long time apart.

What action will you take now? You have to do something once and for all.

How like Amanda. Viv smiled. *Always direct and focussed.*

Knowing it was not what Amanda had meant, she texted back: *The action I'd like to take is to have dinner with you tomorrow. Come to the flat at seven. I have a signed copy of my new book I'd like you to have. We need to talk.*

Once sent, Viv was glad she had not reconsidered or overthought it; she needed to know if there was anything left between them. That, too, was another loose end, unfinished business.

This time, Viv had taken a more relaxed approach and kept supper at a kitchen-table level – pasta and salad, but a good wine. It was summer now and the evening was beautiful. She pulled open the glass balcony doors to their full extent. It seemed that the river was part of her home as she saw the evening sun glinting on the water where a boat had disturbed its surface. Amanda arrived shortly after seven.

"Come in, come in."

"How lovely that looks." Amanda gestured towards the river.

"Of course, you didn't see it before, did you? It was dark, winter."

Viv poured the wine and walked out to the balcony. Amanda followed.

"I don't know how you could ever leave such a lovely place."

"I didn't have a choice, remember?"

It broke the ice. They toasted without naming the toast.

"How's the film going?"

"Almost out, you must see it first."

"Yes, that would be good."

"So, what is this latest book of yours? I don't know anything about it."

Viv reached for a copy on the table inside the glass door.

"Here. Even signed."

Amanda opened the flyleaf, saw the handwritten message for her. *To inspiration.* She studied the biog and the blurb.

"So, what is your final sentence?"

"God, so direct!"

"But the dedication? To your father?"

"Yes, it's the 'without whom' dedication. I had a plan even then." And Viv talked at length about the past, this time remembering well.

"In New York, could you really not remember all that? Or did you just not want to?"

"Both. There were parts that would not come back to me then. But three years in prison is a long time."

Amanda reached for Viv's hand.

"I went to see him."

"And…?"

Amanda could still picture the house she had gone to all those years before. She shuddered at the memory. Cold and echoey came to mind.

"And I did not hold back. It was all there. I saw my bedroom. But it was like... he was beyond reach. It was one thing not to admit what he had done to me, apologise, but, you know, he hasn't changed, he is still abusing women, girls, us. There was a rucksack in the hall."

"So, what will you do? You do know it's no longer just about you. You do know you have to stop him, don't you? You have at last, at long last, to stop being so secretive! Brave victim!"

Viv slumped over the balcony, Amanda's hand gently on her back.

"Yes. I know that – but what do I do?"

Amanda walked back inside, pulling her jacket closer. The air had gone chilly, the sun behind the clouds.

"Well, you have at least tried to stop him, you have tried to repair the past, but you have got nowhere, have you?"

"I know, I know."

"Well, what would you do if it was anyone else, not your father?"

Viv slumped onto the long sofa. She knew.

"You have to go public. It's the only way. Look at me. Promise. You are doing this for all the girls, the women. And for you. I will support you."

*

Late into the night, after Amanda had left, Viv ignored the dirty plates; she'd deal with them tomorrow. She just ran a tap and left them to soak. She remembered the talk with Hugo. She had then been reluctant to have to host her own publicity for the book, but now all resistance went with the thought that this was perfect. Absolutely perfect. And in the half light of early evening, Viv started to make a list of guests for launching *The Final Sentence*. Central would be her father. He would come; he was flattered by the dedication and would see no irony, even after their last meeting, of Without Whom this book would not even have begun. His colleagues on the bench were also on the list. They wouldn't come, of course not. They didn't even know her, why would they? But she would ask them all the same. It would be the ultimate shaming, the ultimate calling to a halt that her father needed. How could he sit there, day after day, judging people when the trail of damage and abuse, going back years but still happening, was so clear. She remembered again the rucksack in the hall.

Then there were the loose ends of her own story. Amanda had told her about Geoff and how he felt he had let Viv down. So Geoff was on the list, as was his wife, as was Kate from the *Big Issue*; they would see she had made something of her life. She thought of Paula's lovely dad. No, she couldn't do this to them; they were nice people, that was clear. She would invite her mother; she should witness this night. Remembering that receding figure in Brighton, with the high heels, she realised with the slightest of smiles she was so very proud of her mother. Out from under. And Arun, but she would warn him he might not like what he hears.

Of course, she would ask Nancy. She would have to ask Hugo and the publishers. She needed Tom Adams, the *Mail* journalist she had cultivated, and would brief him beforehand. She would see whether with a launch party they would consider serialisation; they might. Mischief crept in as she thought of asking Evans the screw and Kelly – why not? And Amanda, yes, Amanda.

Of course, Amanda.

Hugo would supply the necessary additional people to invite, and she'd ask him to film her speech.

But where should she hold it? Courts of Justice – where else?

CHAPTER 10

Viv felt powerful and penitent at the same time knowing that her guests had no idea what was planned for this evening. She watched as the waitresses moved around with the drinks and canapés. They were probably temps – the uniform was put together – but they were so intent on their tasks they did not notice Viv standing in the corner of the room. She noticed one in particular; she was skinny still, not filled out, yet wearing false eyelashes.

"Hi."

Viv felt someone touch her arm. She turned to see Tom Adams and welcomed him; he was going to be important to tonight.

"Oh hi. I didn't think journalists were ever early?"

"Like your style… Where can I get a drink?"

"Come over here."

Viv led Tom over to the table.

"Red or white?"

"At this end of the day, all is welcome," said Tom, reaching for a white. "It's been a long day."

"Really happy you are here."

"Nervous?"

She was about to say no. "A bit."

"Greet the others, I'll watch – it's what I'm here for!"

He had a bag over his shoulder, and she invited him to leave it in the hall.

"No, no, never do that, precious material." He patted the sides.

Viv got him another drink and explained what she had in mind for the party.

"You can stay till the end, can't you?"

He checked his watch. "Till seven forty-five. That OK?"

"You've got my article though?"

"Won't be word for word, I'll go through it."

Viv looked at him for a moment and saw his untrustworthiness. She, too, had that in her; they were in a dance.

"Great."

Viv moved around saying hello here and there until the room felt quite full. *A bit like watching a bath fill up*, she thought. There was only one person her eyes watched for. Douglas. Tonight was for him. She knew what she and Amanda had planned, and all her senses were on alert ready to deliver and yet, she noticed, with each passing moment she was willing to reconsider her choice. Even now, with her plan formed, the PowerPoint ready, even now she promised herself if Douglas turned up and was really going to change, really change, then she had a second speech ready. She would hold out for that. Even now. There was something in her that resisted his destruction. She still wanted to give him a second chance. She sickened herself. How craven.

Amanda arrived early on the arm of an equally blond man. Viv's question was on her face.

Amanda quickly countered, "This is Linny. Yes, Linny!

Linny helped me find…" She was going to say 'your parents'.
"You. A long time ago."
"Well, please take a drink. We will talk later."
She briefly hugged Amanda.
Viv was intent on being in the centre of this relaunch party. She checked her phone. No messages cancelling. That was good. It was important that they all turned up. Her extremely careful article of three thousand words she had given to Tom Adams. Viv had always noticed the type of pieces he wrote, mainly for *The Guardian*; a bit victimy but with an edge that rescued it from that category. He loved a cause he could get behind.

She caught sight of her mother. Her mother's hair was now softly styled. She stood tall and well dressed – and she had lipstick on. This was so good. Viv turned and took a glass of wine for her from the passing tray.

"Here, take one."

Viv wanted to scoop up the intervening years of hurt on all sides, and make it not hurt, for anyone, anymore, but it was an impossibility. What had taken place had scarred them all.

It was now seven o'clock, and Viv, scanning for her father's face and not finding it, checked with the doorman to tell her if he saw him come in. She checked the time. How long could she wait? Hugo moved over towards her.

"Well, Wheeler, how goes it? Still not let off the depth charge, I'm glad to see!"

"Wheeler sounds good."

"I expect so. I expect so."

He took a drink of white wine from the passing waiter. He kept her gaze. She knew the question that was coming.

"Well, what was it? Was it a memoir? Or was it fiction?"

"That's on a need-to-know basis, Hugo, you know that."

"Your father here?"

"I think I saw him just come in."

"Won't you have to start anyway?" Hugo indicated to the lectern.

"Five more minutes."

And then she saw him. A smile was already on Douglas's face; he was looking to see who he knew. He was good at letting the world see that smile. She tried to picture the man she had known at home, his face a rictus of rage, of intent. But the two wouldn't merge. Still the same easy hypocrite. The god Janus lived on. Briefly, she acknowledged her father and drew him into a side room.

"I need to talk to you."

"Let me at least get a drink."

"Come with me." She held up a hand to Hugo. "Five minutes, Hugo, that's all I need."

Hugo pointed to his watch.

For a second, neither spoke.

"Well?"

"Well indeed, Douglas. Before I make my speech, I need to talk to you. We don't have much time."

"Are you sure?" He gestured back to the larger party room. The back of his neck began to itch.

"Never surer. I've spoken to..."

She noticed his old habit, when nervous, of picking at his thumb with his forefinger.

"...And I know that you took it out on her after I left. Tell me, for the love of God, tell me you know you did wrong."

"Well, clearly we have to talk."

"We *are* talking. It's now, Douglas, now. Tell me you've changed. Just admit it. Just say you are sorry. It's that easy. I'm throwing you a lifeline you don't deserve. Tell me you want to put it right and I won't have to go through with this evening."

It was as though he made a minute decision in that moment to disengage from this onslaught. He could hear the buzz of the party; it gave him confidence. He straightened up and looked away.

"Look, you've just made all too much of this. You've done very well for yourself. Of course I've changed. Don't go dragging up the past like this. I'm glad you have your book coming out."

The words hung in between them.

He had to contain this; it was going in the wrong direction.

"You need to know, Douglas, I have this." Viv held up her short book speech. "And I have this." She pointed to her laptop.

He tried to make out what was written, but it was a closed folder.

"I've thought of little else these past four years. How to make you see what you did. How to make you feel what I did. How to humiliate you the way you humiliated me. How to make you *accountable*. How to take away your ability ever to do that again... to anyone. I can't forgive you, I'm not that good a person. I will never forget; it has made my life what it is. That's all. Even now I could give you a second chance. Your choice."

To his credit, Douglas looked disconcerted; this was not what he had expected.

"This laptop has photos, Douglas, of bruises, of Paula, of... and this." Viv drew out her phone, pressed the button, and the photo of the Trafalgar that she had kept safely all these years lit up. And then the photo of fifteen-year-old Paula, all smiles. It was a second photo that Viv had taken, at a party, with her father's arm around her, and at the time she had not seen the relevance. She held up the phone to her father's face.

"Recall anything?"

"I... I..."

"And this!" She held up the anonymous note received all those years ago.

He at least didn't try to deny it this time.

She read it out. "*I know who you are, and I know exactly what you did.*"

"You've got to understand—"

"I don't have to understand anything from you. What I need is a promise. Contrition. You wrote the letter of a coward and never signed it. What a massive coward."

Even in the dim light of this side room, Viv could see that he paled. She laid an arm on his forearm.

"Please, Douglas, tell me I don't need to go through with this."

"Of course you don't. Of course you don't."

And then he made the fateful choice of trying to laugh it all off. He scratched the back of his hand, above the wrist, his eczema irritating. If a second could feel like a minute, it was now. She had done her best.

"Thing is, Douglas, I've paid my dues, you have nothing on me anymore, but I have power over you, and if you had admitted it, felt really bad about it, even tried to apologise, any of those options, I would not be doing what I'm about to do. I have also written an article. I only have to press send to my tame journo and you will be publicly shamed in a way you can't escape – any more than I could. You, a fine upstanding person, will be shown to be a vile abuser, a dishonest man – not exactly the image you've cultivated, is it?"

"Alright, alright. I see what you are saying. Of course I'm sorry for the past. But it can't be undone. I only wish it could."

He shot a glance at her.

"I... am... sorry. Shall we draw a line now under the past?"

Viv slumped. Was this enough? Was this it? She saw Amanda. At that moment, the young part-time waitress with her false eyelashes, blonde, pretty, a slightly expectant smile on her face, put her head round the door.

"Is everything alright?"

Viv held up her hand but in that second she saw the way her father looked at this extremely young girl, his eyes focussed on her. Before she left, he couldn't help himself despite what had just been said. He put his hand on her arm, then low down on her back.

"We'll come and find you. What is your name?"

As the girl shut the door behind her, Viv said quietly, "People like you don't change until they are made to change."

His voice was shrunken as he asked her, "You know people will believe prison has deranged you?"

Viv studied his face, heard his words. She was sixteen again, just for a second.

"Douglas, that is no longer the most important thing."

"And what is?" Again the mockery.

"What you need to know is that I have set up a website, composed six emails to the relevant authorities, with back-up proof, and the newspaper article. Convince me you have changed, or they will all go live."

He looked at her, a mixture of confusion and challenge in his face.

He made the wrong choice. "You are being totally ridiculous!"

"Your choice." Viv's voice was soft, even gentle, like a disappointed parent.

She walked out of the side room and crossed over to the dais and began her speech.

"Thank you for all celebrating my latest novel. Like all novels, it has its germ in reality. Somewhere."

She looked over at her mother and saw that her father was trying to leave but was trapped and the moment to leave had passed. The lights in the room were dimmed; there was a murmur and then silence. Viv had her finger on the button to start the PowerPoint display but a second after, there was a thud, a few "Ohs," and, "Lights up, please!"

A phone call was being made.

"Stand back, he needs air!"

Douglas had collapsed and his exit to hospital was being arranged. The presentation continued with no sound, but no-one was looking now. As the lights returned, Viv could see Tom Adams and made her way over to him. He patted his bag.

"I have to go. I'll call you tomorrow."

"Go ahead as planned."

Amanda was next to her as she turned.

"I'm proud of you. Let's just leave."

As the two of them walked down the Strand, holding each other tight, Viv broke in.

"I'll go and see him. I have to. Will you come?"

CHAPTER 11

Viv found the ward in the Chelsea hospital easily, but once there she had to search for Douglas's bed. She found it behind the drawn curtains. Before going further, she stopped the passing nurse and asked her how her father was.

"He's had a stroke. His speech isn't clear at the moment, but things might improve."

As she opened the curtain, he turned his head, but seeing Viv, he looked away. Viv drew up one chair, and Amanda sat on the other side, taking it all in. What they talked about, Viv could not later recall.

"I thought I would know what to say but…"

Even with his stricken face, he tried to say something. Viv leant nearer and she heard him say, after what seemed an eternity, "You weren't…"

He had a pleading look on his face. Viv looked over to Amanda, whose face had not registered any emotion so far.

"Yes?"

"…Any good."

Viv stared back at him, feeling the power of the moment. She remembered that violence on his face, that night she had come home after the rape when he had assaulted her for no good reason, she remembered that violation of Paula.

She looked at Amanda, who gave the merest of nods. Viv, never averting her gaze on her father, felt for the oxygen tube, felt the warm plastic, and gently squeezed. He was looking straight at her. She didn't blink. Suddenly, alarm flicked across his face, and then, looking full at Viv's face, he seemed to be pleading. Panic. Viv held it for just long enough for it to look like a blip in the charts, only releasing it when the job was done.

It was late afternoon as Amanda and Viv walked out of the hotel-like entrance of the hospital and made their way through the crowds and walked up the Fulham Road in the direction of Sloane Square.

"You OK?"

Viv shook her head.

"Let's find somewhere to eat."

It was one of those anywhere anytime restaurants that served anything at any hour, and they shared spaghetti and talked in a way they had not talked before, not even in New York. They were older, wiser, knew each other better and certainly had the battle scars.

"I'm sorry I couldn't come to the prison."

"Me too." Viv reached over the table and left her hand there. "But it has lasted all the same, hasn't it?"

"It has, Viv, it has."

As they left, the light was coming up. The next day's newspapers were reaching the shops, and Amanda asked her, "Are you glad you did all this? Are you alright?"

"I thought I would be, but I'm not. I know it had to be done, but I didn't want to be the one to do it. I thought it would feel satisfying, give me an end point to all of it."

"But it hasn't?"

Viv shook her head. "Just sad."

Amanda put her arm around Viv, removing Viv's fedora as she did so.

"But we must look to the future – our future – and not let that past frame it for us."

ACKNOWLEDGEMENTS

I'd like to say thank you to a few people who've provided enormous encouragement and help. I couldn't have completed *The Final Sentence* without you: Angela Burdick, Denise Cullington, Sally Dunn, Holly Porter, Linda Proud, Jimmy Ogen, Susan Walsh and my family.